CHILDREN OF WRATH

T.A. Ward

T.A. Ward
ISBN: 9781973441175
ChildrenOfWrathTrilogy@Gmail.com
Tawardbooks.com

"Like the rest, we were by nature children of wrath"

A book for those who ask difficult questions and accept difficult answers. In dedication to those who taught me to do the same.

CHAPTER 1

April 9th, 2041 4:22pm – Five Years Prior

I have no obligation to be in the laboratory. There are technicians for this type of work, yet the hospital laboratory is my place of reprieve; it is quiet and logical there. As always, the vent above the specimen microscopes is jarringly cool, a welcome change for my large body which produces heat as effectively as a radiator. The only sounds in the room are those of centrifuging blood samples and the grazing of my fingers against the keyboard as I confirm the results of one of my patients. The sample tested positive for *C-diff* as I suspected. That's the inevitable risk you run when hospitals and antibiotics become a staple in your routine.

My focus is suddenly jolted by exclamations of horror just outside of the laboratory. "Ethan, come quick!" someone yells at me while tapping frantically on the door. I move to my feet, hearing the squeaks of my shiny brown Derbies as they step across the linoleum floor. By reflex I peel off my gloves while exiting the bright, sterile room. I expect to find myself embroiled in a scene of carnage, or at minimum find an antagonistic patient threatening staff with a chair above his head, but I see neither. Instead, in the hallway to my right, six nurses gasp and cry as they huddle around the television screen hanging from the wall. As I approach, one of them anxiously increases its volume. On the television a brunette news anchor sits with a finger seamlessly pressing her sound piece into her ear.

"If you are just tuning in we are receiving breaking news that there has been a nuclear attack on Washington, D.C. I repeat, we at Action News 13 are able to confirm the detonation of a nuclear weapon in the Washington, D.C area. We are receiving our first images of the event now." I watch with dawning horror as the footage (which appears to be taken from miles away) focuses shakily on a mushroom cloud curling above the remains of Washington. Panic erupts. Some nurses begin to weep, others rush to their phones to call loved ones, a few grab their belongings and rush out of the hospital with impressive speed. A voice begins speaking through the intercom system:

"All medical personnel please be advised that we are under Emergency Operations Code C44. All medical personnel, please assume your EOC44 positions immediately." The voice repeats the message at least twenty times in a row, and then switches to repeating once every five minutes after that. I work at Philadelphia East Hospital, which is 152.7 miles away from Washington D.C.

Why could I not feel the explosion? Why could I not see smoke from the southwest windows? I am on the sixth floor, after all. Questions race through my mind while I instinctually follow protocol. EOC44 means that any medical doctor has to check out of all non-life-threatening patient cases and meet in one of two organizational rooms on the first and second floor to receive and triage emergency cases. If the bomb had exploded in any other city of equal distance our hospital would not be in EOC44. The Capital city is a different story, because in cases of attack and evacuation, all hospitals within a two-hundred mile radius are required by law to be on immediate standby. Three years ago I had been an adamant dissenter of this statute, because at the time it seemed to be an act of class concern. For the minuscule chance that a political elite might on his evacuation route find himself one hundred and fifty miles away and suddenly in need of medical care, all of our existing patients' care and our entire order of operations would be relegated to a secondary concern.

Today, my opinion changes.

I walk down the yellow painted hallway to the nurses' station, where Maureen, without saying a word, hands me a stack of files. She's one of the good nurses, unlike her usual shift partner Becca.

Becca is the type of person whose voice is so grating that it makes you conceive of doing things you've never considered before, like stabbing them in the eye with a juice box straw.

I carefully adjust my non-life-threatening case files which I need to sign out from. I open them one at a time, swiftly scanning the sheets to ensure that I have not missed something critical, and sign at the bottom of the first page. I come across my patient with *C-diff,* and write in large print on the outside of the file that this patient is in need of immediate treatment with microbiota transplant –not antibiotics– and then I sign the form. When I hand the stack of files back to Maureen I place that file on the top, and tap it with my index finger a couple of times.

"This is important," I say, and she nods. Already acclimated to the sound of the intercom system, I walk back through the hallway. I come to the elevator, press the glinting button to descend, and enter the rectangular box that smells like stale musk –something I noticed a few days ago but cannot account for. I press for the second floor and instinctually lift my pager and scroll through its messages. An earlier and non-urgent page for room 621, three resounding messages reiterating the intercoms message: EOC44. Lastly, and most importantly to me, a page from my wife, Liz: "I'm safe. I know you are too. Call when you can."

I look up and see a mildly distorted reflection of my unkempt face in the doors. My chestnut brown hair is outgrowing its crew cut, a five o'clock shadow is beginning to pierce through under my nose and down my jawline, and my almond-shaped eyes look reticent, though that's typical. Their green-brown color is just like my mother's, but today bags of exhaustion set in below making them look darker than they truly are. My frame looks strong, but I feel so weak. The day has been long enough and it's only just beginning.

The elevator doors open, and the swarm of nurses and doctors meshing one through another looks more like the forming of a bacterial biofilm than the workings of independent human agents. I join the mass, moving directly to my organizational room. I recognize faces that pass beside me, but in some hazy depersonalized way where each face vanishes as quickly as it came. What I notice more distinctly than ever is the silence of chaos. Shoes and stretchers create friction along the flat tile floor, voices are sounding in every direction, the intruding intercom message broadcasts indifferently above it all, but I hear nothing. My mind is nestled somewhere beyond where ears can reach, a place protected from the loud squeaks and shouts that I typically find so grating.

I turn to my right, and push through the glass-plated door separating chaos from my organizational room. In the small square room are six doctors and our Associate Chief of Staff, Dr. Singh, standing rigidly around the center-table intended for board meetings. On the table sits a clipboard, and a phone broadcasting the coverage of the incident.

"What we know so far is that a WMD has exploded within the nation's capital, and that fires are expected to spread as far as twenty miles outward in every direction from the point of impact. As far as we know, the bomb was not dropped from an airplane, but set off from within the city limits. We do not have confirmation of the location of POTUS, or other public officials beside Secretary of State Bryan Powell who is confirmed to be alive though his location has not been released."

Three more doctors enter the room in a jolted manner.

"Our estimates are that up to 1.5 million individuals will be killed as a result of this attack, and that another 3 million could be among the injured. These are, of course, worst case scenarios. There is no official word on who is behind this attack, though the Mujahideen are fairly suspected. We are awaiting further update, however our communication is limited due to the catastrophe that is facing the Northeast at this present moment."

I hear the words, but I do not feel disbelief or fear. I'm not sure if I'm feeling at all. Reality seems distorted, like when you have a high fever and cannot be sure whether you are dreaming or truly eating a bowl of tasteless tomato soup. Dr. Singh grabs the phone and turns off the broadcast. I briefly catch his eyes which lack their typical light-hearted gleam. He and I have a good rapport, though he often subversively attempts to convert me to a belief in some fatalistic force that orchestrates our lives and choices for a greater purpose. Several more doctors push through the glass door. The room is now a woven mesh of white coats, blue scrubs, and lifeless faces reflecting the solemn weight oppressing the room.

"Alright, everyone," Dr. Singh begins, his trepidation not hidden by his thick Indian accent. "In a situation like this, I am aware of the emotional burden and family instincts you are sensing. Like you, I have friends who live in D.C. However, as the situation would have it, you have been chosen to be in a position of leadership and I will expect you to maintain the dignity of that position. Now. All of my surgical doctors and residents raise your hands."

Less than half of the doctors in the room raise their hands. I am not one of them. The two organizational rooms are supposed to hold the same number of emergency specialists, general surgeons, and other doctors on duty by specialty. It is common practice to look down on my specialty, Infectious Disease. The point of ridicule consists in our constant need to innovate in order to treat complex infections. This means testing unprovable theories via treatment therapies on our patients, which is unsurprisingly contra standard medical practice. We are like the conspiracy theorists of the medical world – attributing every major illness to the ever-elusive infection or parasite, all the while accrediting the detriment of our patients to their preceding doctors for not knowing better. Today, these caricatures do not matter. In this room we stand as unified doctors, bonded together by a fear that makes us feel like children and by a task that thrashes us into adulthood.

"Okay. What we are going to do is serve as a second emergency floor, receiving what cannot be treated from floor one. We cannot know what we will be facing in the following moments or hours. So, take a few breaths while you can. What I can tell you is that we *will* be receiving injuries and we are working in harmony with Presbyterian, Pennsylvania, and University hospitals. Victims of the attack are already being airlifted to surrounding hospitals, and it is only a matter of time before the surrounding hospitals are full. As you are aware we have a limited ability to care for burn victims, but we have made an agreement to receive up to six severe, and four minor burn victims. All burn victims will be received on the first floor, and the second floor will serve to treat other emergency cases as they arrive, if they cannot be treated by the first floor ER. I expect you to triage as you have been trained, and to perform examinations by following your standard emergency check-sheets." His voice begins to sound more confident.

"Every two stations will be directed by one of our ER natives. I will be consulted directly for surgical operations, and our CNO Kathy is on her way in with a number of other staff to better prepare for the incoming cases. You will be updated on your existing urgent cases by page, and all of your other cases are currently being handled by our highly capable PA's and RN's. Now, please listen for your station..." he lifts a tan clipboard from the table and smooths the paper down with his thumbs, squinting fixedly at it for some time before speaking again.

"Station 1 and 2 will be overseen by Dr. Garcia." A short Hispanic man wearing grey-blue scrubs to my right raises his hand to identify himself.

"Kennedy and Wei are in station 1, Dawson and Garcia are in station 2. Station 3 and 4 will be overseen by Dr. Wilson." Dr. Wilson, a lanky pale-faced man raises his hand just behind Dr. Singh. "King and Wilson are in station 3, and Station 4 has ..." I stiffen at the sound of my name, King. Before our wedding day,

Liz used to cheerfully sing over and over "I just can't wait to be King." I hate hearing my name now. I am ripped from the safety of observance and plummeted into the pain of participation.

The separation we feel in emergency situations protects us. When something traumatic happens, the amygdala causes a chain reaction of secretions: adrenaline, and epinephrine, then testosterone, and cortisol, then dopamine and serotonin. The mind-altering concoction creates a sense of derealization so that we can kill enemies without moral qualms, engage in fighting without pain, lift cars without consideration to physical capacities, and most importantly, feel afterward as though it was all a dream or that it was someone else acting.

But I am no longer allowed to feel separated. I must pull myself as completely into reality as I can, because today I will be evaluating a set of patients that I am unfamiliar with, I will be performing examinations which I do not regularly perform, in a room that I rarely step into, with a partner I have only met once. I will be treating emergency cases and likely some of the three million men women and children injured by an atomic weapon detonated one hundred and fifty miles from where I stand. I am an ID doctor. I can help in cases of parasites, HIV, Meningitis, Malaria, TB, Lyme, even the bubonic plague – but what use am I for the random emergency cases about to flood our hospital?

Our annual training seminars and workshops are designed to prepare us for days such as this. During the workshops we are continually told that "You are doctors," and "Lives depend on you," which is supposed to make us feel a sense of obligation and high calling to our fellow man. But right now, in this moment, I do not want to be a doctor. I want to be an ordinary man, at home holding my wife, watching the television attentively for every new update; able to cry, and able to process the weight of what just happened. I shake the thought away, knowing it isn't an option. The task at hand requires focus, strength, and skills that I don't possess. I was thirty minutes from clocking out of the hospital, and now I have an indefinite stay in ER torment.

When Dr. Singh finishes reading the list he dismisses us to our stations. I make eye-contact with Dr. Wilson before we all funnel slowly out of the tiny meeting room. He has ash-blonde hair and bright blue eyes. The hallway which had moments earlier been swarming with staff now only echoes our footsteps as we walk toward the second floor emergency without a word. My heart begins to pound, making me feel out of breath. My mouth is dry, and my hands are cold and clammy.

Our group makes a sharp right turn through a hallway, allowing us to bypass the emergency patient-waiting area, and proceed directly to the ER nurses' station. It is a large semi-circle in the center of an enormous open-spaced room. I am facing the center head-on and two hundred feet behind it on the right I see the ambulance entrance. Daylight pierces through its automatic glass doors, sucking stagnant air into the street with each opening.

Just then Dr. Garcia stops the group, and begins shouting to my right.

"Those of you not familiar with the ER, please pay attention. Nurses and staff are currently arranging our stations, which are numbered on the floor by tape for your convenience. These elevators," he gestures with his hands to the far wall across from the nurses' station, "lead to patient rooms for every level." I am familiar with those elevators.

"These elevators lead to floor one emergency," he points behind my back and to the right, on the same wall which had the hallway we walked through.

"Finally, these doors lead to operating rooms." He points with his thumbs at two white and silver swinging doors behind him. On the nurses' station sits a radio turned on low, which two nurses are leaning toward to hear over Dr. Garcia. I catch fragments of it.

"Get familiar with your station, and be on alert! For any other questions speak with your station lead. Thank you." Finishing, Dr. Garcia swiftly moves to his station with four doctors trailing in tow.

I try to survey the large floor for my station number, but conclude that it is wiser to look for my station lead, Dr. Wilson. I browse the dissolving crowd and sight him. I am typically the tallest person in a room, but Dr. Wilson might surpass me. I spot his face unmistakably overhead the rest of the crowd. He walks toward the ambulance entrance and behind the nurse's station. Once there I am able to see the numbers written in white medical tape on the floor. Dr. Wilson moves toward the number 3, and I follow. In a few moments I am able to survey our station.

There are seven stretchers in a single-file row, their heads leaning against the grey stone wall. There is no warmth in this room; no color upon the walls, no carpet on the floor, just stone and tile and draft-frigid air which smells like a mix of rubbing alcohol and plastic. The stretchers have no privacy between them, but on the left side a curtain separates our section from section two, and on the far right a curtain marks the only divide between us and the backside of the nurses' station. To the right of the seventh bed there is a standing desk made of plastic-laminate, no wider in diameter than the top of a music stand. Sitting on it is a silver outdated laptop, which a nurse is plugging into the wall behind it.

"Dr. King, my name is Jim Wilson," Dr. Wilson says abruptly with a pronounced southern twang. He holds out his gangly hand, and I follow suit with one strong shake.

"Call me Ethan."

"Alright Ethan, you look a tad nervous. Do you have family in D.C?" he says, and cringes as if he instantly regretted asking.

"Oh." it's true that I am nervous, but not about family. I am nervous about the job I am about to perform. "No, I don't have family there. A few friends from medical school, not any that I

9

keep in touch with. What about you?" The dryness of my throat feels like a lump while I speak. I gaze around our station for a bottle of water, but I find none. I return my sight to Dr. Wilson, whose eyes are glossy now.

"My parents live there," his voice shakes. My thumb and forefinger instinctually press against my chin while I shake my head in concern.

"Damn. I'm sorry."

"I'm sure I'm not the only one." He shrugs and tries to blink back his emotion. In a moment his face returns to normal, but I find myself still staring at him. How do you stay at work if both of your parents were just murdered? An ache of emotion begins folding my heart and lungs together in a pretzel. I swallow it back and try to salvage my concentration.

"So what's your specialty?" he forces a smile at me.

"Infectious Disease."

"Out of your element, then?"

"You could say that," I half laugh out the words.

CHAPTER 2

5:07pm

While Dr. Wilson calls his wife before briefing me on procedure, I take the same opportunity to call Liz. I pull my phone from my back pocket, and walk toward the ambulance entrance. The glass doors slide open smoothly, letting in a warm rush of air, and I step outside into the sunlight. It reminds me of the state parks Liz and I frequent for summer picnics. I love everything about Pennsylvania in the summer. Outside the city the grass is indulgently soft and bright green, the rolling hills are covered with life, gardens are full of flowers and fruit, fresh streaming brooks accompany every hike, and bright pink sunsets adorn evening after evening.

For a second I let the warmth pierce through my laboratory coat and into my skin, revitalizing me. The glass doors slide shut behind me, and my eyes begin adjusting to the brightness. A light breeze sweeps in accompanied by the faint smell of exhaust from the city buses. I turn away from the view of the parking garage to my right, which is connected by a ramp and shades part of the hospital. On my phone I swipe away a dozen messages and dial Liz. Before I can hear the first ring of the phone, a sound catches my attention. Behind me, far off in the distance, there is a soft rumbling in the air.

The phone rings once. The rumbling increases, growing closer and more familiar, like thunder or a stampede. The phone rings twice. The sound becomes clear; that of a jet fast approaching and too close to the ground. I step out from the awning and look into the sky. My wife's voice pours out of the phone "Baby, thank goodness! I'm so scared." A military jet soars just above the hospital, accompanied by a sonic boom which penetrates every bone in my body and causes me to crouch toward the ground and

11

clasp my hands over my ears. Glass shatters and falls from above. Then I see it. Falling from the jet about one mile in front of me is a bomb. Time slows down as I watch it descend into Center City.

Without warning, more bombs begin to fall from the jet across the city. In-between old and crumbling city buildings eight bombs plunge to the earth, unyielding to gravity, hitting against concrete and cars, signs and street vendor carts. I wait for the vibrations and bangs from the explosions, but there are none. I feel a rumble under my shoes as the city's tornado siren begins ringing. I rise up and stare closely into the city. Between buildings I can see the rising of smoke, but I am unable to reconcile that with the lack of explosion. My pupils dilate, my breathing for the moment slows, and I stare deep into the city. The smoke rises just high enough between the buildings to catch on a beam of sunlight and I can see that it is not the color of smoke from a fire; it is too light in shade for that and possesses a yellowed hue. If there was no explosion and no smoke, then they are not bombs. But if not smoke, then what? My next breath trembles out of me as I realize what I am looking at. The substance rising up from between the buildings is not smoke, but gas. It's a chemical weapon.

I raise the phone to my ear, still focused intently on what I am seeing within the city.

"What was that? Ethan! What was that!?" Liz's voice sounds shrill and panicked. I respond so quickly that I almost skip over my words.

"Liz, I think the city was just attacked. Go into the basement and stay there! I love you, and I cannot explain, but I have to go." I hang up the phone before she can protest.

I turn around and rush into the ER, my heart racing in my chest. Inside I enter a cloud of indiscernible noise; screams and shouts escaping from a horde of people anxiously peering through the windows to view the city.

"It's gas! From a chemical weapon! Gas, not smoke!" I shout above the clamor, my voice deep and commanding. A dozen nurses and doctors begin to surround me. There is a heat in my chest like after running a marathon, and I can hardly swallow or breathe.

"Chemical weapons – they are chemical weapons!" I exclaim again.

"Are you sure?" I hear Dr. Wilson's drawl.

"Yes."

"How can you be sure?" His stance is strong, but his tone is not antagonistic. While others around me are panicking, I can see that his face, a head-level above the others, is calm. I still pause to reassess the details in my mind. An impulsive surge of skepticism barrels through me. Maybe I am wrong. Maybe it's not at all what I think, maybe it's some inoculation from the government for something more serious that was released in the attack on Washington, or maybe my eyes are missing important details.

"There was no explosion and no smoke. Gas doesn't explode. Smoke is dark, gas is light--" He interrupts my thought.

"Then we need to know what kind." He rushes away from me back to the window to look outside. Suddenly Dr. Singh's voice crackles over the intercom system, shaky and fast.

"This is an urgent message – We are currently in EOC39, in preparation to receive victims of a biological weapon. All staff please be advised that we have suspended EOC44. Emergency specialists please instruct the staff in your care on EOC39 protocols, and begin preparing your established decontamination units in the parking garage. Our Chief Safety Officer Dr. Hart will be making an announcement shortly."

I can't believe this is happening.

I push past several nurses who stand between me and Dr. Wilson as he peers out one of the windows. The ringing of my heartbeat in my eardrums is making it difficult to think, so I try to slow my breathing. In a moment enough adrenaline is circulating my body to give me resurrected focus.

"Jim, I need to deconstruct my infection contamination rooms and bring the materials to the decontamination units outside. This room needs to be converted to receive a lot more individuals – and you need to set up a filtration system for all those entering the hospital!" I say before rushing to the center elevators. When they open I press the unworn button that orders the back doors to sweep open, leading to the two infection contamination rooms. These rooms, and the decontamination process, were well used only three months ago during a severe anthrax outbreak where I was one of two chief doctors assigned to the cases. At the time, I was the most familiar with contaminant control, which I am worried may be the same case today. As I step forward and scan the two rooms, one on either side of me, I am reminded that our nation has not been at peace for a long time, and that today's attack is simply one of the many American massacres.

They began in 2037 by Mujahideen, a radicalized Iranian caliphate that gained power over Iraq, Syria, Turkey, and Georgia. Internal rebel factions in these countries pledged allegiance to Mujahideen, and performed the most successful, albeit the most despicable, insurrections in recent history. When forty-five thousand American troops were sent into Turkey to push back the conquest, cells of Mujahideen began to appear in the United States. Suicide bombings, water poisonings, train derailments, arson, and workplace beheadings became a staple of American news. Though everyone could sense that it was growing, I could not have predicted this.

I swipe my hospital ID and the first of two doors slides open to the contamination room on my right. I take a breath of quintessentially stale air, and the first door closes behind me. The space between the two doors could rightly be described as claustrophobic, but in only a few moments the second door opens, allowing me entrance into the painfully bright and overly sterile room. A single bed sits in the center of the room pressed against the back wall with pristine sheets tucked into its edges. The constant sound of pulsating air echoes in the room from the HEPA system which ensures that air flows in only one direction: outside in.

I walk to the back right corner of the room which is temporarily home to a large, pale metal cabinet. It is kept in the room when there are no active patients in order to provide an extra measure of security. Thankfully it has wheels for easy transport. The cabinet contains a legally required stockpile of decontamination foam, which is essentially glorified hand soap in a spray-container, and one heavy and expensive ultrasonic water purification system used in every type of decontamination.

I clasp onto the pointed corners of the cabinet with my hands and bend my knees before jerking backward to get the cabinet to roll. I swipe my hospital ID again and have to contort my body to fit into the filtration subsection with the cabinet. Leaving the room I rush to the left of the elevator doors where a transparent cabinet reveals four offensively orange biohazard suits, complete with independent oxygen systems. I carefully pull them out, one at a time, and stuff them awkwardly into my rolling cabinet. When I am done I move to the right of the elevator doors and into a storage closet. Inside is an unopened box with stark black lettering which reads "DECONTAMINATION TENT. LIFT WITH A FRIEND."

Lift with a friend? Is this Disney?

I lean down and carefully lift one side of it, which causes sharp splicing pain to begin pulsating through my back and triceps. "Lift with a friend" repeats in my mind. If Liz were here she would be nagging me in her uptight voice for "being stubborn" and "not knowing my limits." The thought of her makes my chest throb with fear. I shake the thought away as I wrap both of my arms around the box and begin dragging it awkwardly out of the closet until I am in front of the elevator. I stretch out my right arm to press the elevator button, and nearly crumple under the weight of the box. The doors open and I slug myself backwards, dragging the box in front of me. I can hear the chaos from the ER just one set of doors away. They open without me hitting a button, and a recognizable accent rings from behind me.

"Ethan? You need help!" It's Dr. Singh.

"Yeah..." I reluctantly admit. I step backwards, pulling the tent out of the elevator, and he helps me to lean it against the ER wall. Without thanking him, I re-enter the elevator, and roll the cabinet into the ER.

"You will be a decontaminator, yes?" he asks, and nervously searches through papers on a clipboard in his hand to ensure that this has been the prearranged agreement.

"Yes. I need help bringing these things to the garage."

"Okay, yes well, first..." he pulls a sheet out of his clipboard and hands it to me.

"Familiarize yourself with these procedures, and did you hear Dr. Hart's talk about safety procedure?"

"What?" I stare confusedly at him.

"Dr. Hart's briefing on hospital staff safety. It was over intercom about a minute ago. Well, you are already familiar with some infectious decontamination, I know I know, but, I have to tell you that the symptoms already reported to us from the few cases in ER 1 are SLUDGE." He says it with a terrified look in his eyes. I try not to match his expression but fear instantly simmers in my chest. SLUDGE is the unaffectionate acronym for the symptoms of nerve gas exposure. Nerve gas causes individuals to lose their ability to control bodily excretions: saliva, urine, feces, tears, and all others. But with severe exposure they also experience seizures and lose their ability to breathe, which rapidly leads to death.

"I have to tell you that risk of exposure is very serious, and even if you are not exposed, you could die of heat stroke being in a hazmat suit out there. I have put a limit of two hours on our decontamination staff, and have been assured that federal

HAZMAT workers will be prepared to replace you by then. Destiny would have you do this today, yes, but your safety is the most important thing. What I am saying is a hero knows when not to be one." He looks seriously at me, his large eyes opening even wider, before he pats my right shoulder with his hand. It is slightly comforting to know that he makes just as little cogent sense in an emergency situation as he does in daily life.

He leaves to join the rambling noise of the ER, instructing individuals here and there as to their responsibilities. I take a brief stare at the procedural sheet, and someone, though I am unsure who, stuffs an unopened water-bottle into my hand. I pull one of the hazmat suits from the cabinet and push through the door of a single occupant bathroom. I twist its metal lock, before falling to my knees and vomiting up both my lunch and emotions. Painfully hard tile grates along my knees, and cold air prickles against my clammy neck.

I can remember vomiting up stress from the time when I was a child. Before any big event in my life, whether a soccer game, the first day at a new school, or a big test, I would stay up the night before ravaged with anxiety and nausea. Around midnight I would inevitably vomit once and feel immediately relieved of my distress. Today, however, no such relief comes. With trembling hands I rinse out my mouth in the cold ceramic sink, patting some cold water onto my forehead. The mirror does no service to me. I am thirty-eight going on sixty-five, six feet and two inches of cowering incompetence. Thankfully, I think I'm the only person who can see that.

I stare steadily at my own reflection, harshly blinking to regain focus in my blurry eyes. After a few deep breaths, I drink water from the bottle, and ignore my quivering hands while I dress myself in the hazmat suit. It fits too tightly in all of the wrong places, and too loosely everywhere else. I turn on the proper oxygen settings, and walk once more through the ER, exiting through the ambulance entrance which already has a filtration tent set up on the outside. I walk up the right side ramp entrance to the parking garage and see that the decontamination tent is almost entirely blown up. Three other individuals are preparing the station in hazmat suits. How long was I in the bathroom for?

I hear and see crowds of people congregating on the first floor of the garage while two men in hazmat suits guard the elevator and staircase. As I approach my team I already feel my suit being converted into a sauna by the summer heat. The tent is set up one hundred feet from the second floor elevators, with traffic barrels functioning as barricades to keep individuals from crossing an arbitrary, yet important, dividing line between unclean and clean. The center of the barricades has an opening to an aisle which patients will walk through, or be wheeled through, three at a time. They will then enter the decontamination tents with our assistance, where they will be stripped, sprayed with decontamination foam, showered, clothed in a hospital gown, and triaged according to the severity of their symptoms. The distance between the tent and myself closes, and though I expected to be put to work connecting the water and air plumbing, it has already been done.

"Ethan, great. I'm glad you're here," a muffled voice says to my right. I turn and see a small portion of Jim Wilson's face through the divide of his mask. His suit appears even tighter than mine. The other two suited workers join us.

"Dr. Amanda Jones this is Dr. Ethan King, he's our ID doctor. Amanda is an ER native like me." Jim makes my introduction to a thin, or at least I think she is thin, woman with blue eyes and a faint smile. She is swimming in her hazmat suit – proof that one size fits none.

"And Ethan, this is James Dickerson. He is actually on our lift-team –and will be assisting us with incapacitated patients." He gestures to the last suited man, whose skin is so dark that his eyes seem to be glowing white in contrast.

"It is nice to meet you both." The sound of my voice echoes within my suit, hot breath bouncing back into my face.

"Alright, let's grab our triaging stickers and get ready to roll." Jim picks up a stack of sticker sheets from the ground, and hands us each several pieces. On each sheet are four rows of large circular stickers. A red colored sticker which reads "Immediate," an orange one to its right which reads "Delayed," a yellow one which reads "Expectant," and finally a green one farthest to the right which reads "Minor." Their meaning was on the procedural handout Dr. Singh handed me, and I am almost certain that I remember what each one designates. Immediate requires immediate attention or the patient will die, delayed means that the patient needs treatment but can be delayed without causing further harm, expectant means that the patient is expected to die without the use of extensive time and resources – which are not available in a mass-casualty situation. Finally, the highly desired "minor" means that their sustained injuries are minor enough that they do not warrant emergency medical treatment. Immediately, Jim speaks through a radio that we are ready to receive patients. James picks up a megaphone from behind the tent and moves to the front of the aisle in preparation to vet patients through three at a time. Amanda, Jim, and I stand cohesively in front of the decontamination tent, which has three doors so that three individuals can be decontaminated at one time. Jim leans over to me and attempts to whisper through a stifled suit.

"So do you know anything about triage?"

"Intellectually." I attempt to give him a cynical expression, but it's lost through the mask.

"Do you know anything about decontamination?" I ask in return. He pauses for a moment.

"Intellectually. So... this should be interesting." He laughs, while still facing forward. I nod in agreement.

A small rumble with no other notice marks the entrance of several dozen people into the garage. Some push through the staircase door, while the severely injured come up two at a time on wheelchairs from the elevator, healthier individuals pushing them forward. James seamlessly organizes them, serving as a human shield to block the aisle and yelling directions into the megaphone. Behind the tent a line of nurses has formed to take patients into the ER as we finish with them. I take two prolonged inhales of my circulated air, and by that time James has sent the first three people toward us through the designated aisle.

A tall African American man with noble eyes supports his stumbling wife as they approach us, next to them is a young girl no older than ten, with olive-toned skin. She is alone. As they approach, Amanda innately grabs the hand of the young girl, and takes her into the farthest left room of the tent. I hear the sound of Velcro as she seals the opaque nylon door shut.

"Here sir, I can take her." I gesture to the man's wife. The tall man carefully transfers his wife's arm to my shoulder for support.

"Her name is Aliyah," he says with a crack in his voice and tears in his eyes. The woman has short wavy black hair with bangs clinging to her forehead from sweat. Black makeup descends from her eyes, which are seeping tears as part of the body's natural defense.

"She is going to be okay. We are going to do our best," I assure him quickly. I take intentional strides into my room, leaning to offset her weight. Once inside I lift the woman onto a thick plastic patient table on wheels. It hardly fits inside the narrow, inflated room. I am thankful that she is thin, but a sharp pain stings my injured back regardless. The table has slots to allow water to run through so that we can shower patients who are unable to stand. I lay her down, seal the tent door, and do an initial examination which lasts no more than a few seconds. Her right arm is shaking uncontrollably, and she lets out a cracked groan of pain. I can see that her pants are soiled from urine.

"Aliyah, in order to help you I need to undress you and bathe you. Do you understand?"

Her head begins to jerk involuntarily left and right in short sudden bursts. She is having a myoclonic seizure, her condition is worsening. I move quickly, standing at the bottom of the patient table and quickly remove her shoes, throwing them to the entrance of the tent. I grab cloth cutters and cut upward along her blue jeans, through her underwear, and continue moving up her shirt on the right side of her body. The scissors feel unnatural in my double-latex gloved hands. I do the same quickly for the left side, and in a single movement I toss all of her clothes to the front of the decontamination tent. I grab the decontamination foam, and tell her as clearly as I can through the suit, "This might be cold." I then spray, covering her entire body evenly, moving limbs to apply it as needed. I notice how her warm, brown skin contrasts with my bright blue gloves, until it's no longer visible under the layer of foam.

I push her body, leaning it on one side, so that I can coat her back. I lay her down, and spray the foam into her hair, roughly massaging it in, and then carefully scrub her face. I reach upward, grasping the moveable showerhead which feels like a cold alloy baseball bat in my hand. Ignoring her jerking movements, I rinse the solvent from toe to hair, leaving her face for last, which I carefully wash to ensure that she does not choke on any water.

It is an unnatural thing to watch ordinary and healthy people lose all control of their bodies. This woman, who may on an ordinary day be striking, looks as little more than a frail and shattering shell of a person. Now the uncomfortable part. I grab a tiny water instrument from above the table, similar to what dentists use to rinse mouths, and bring it close to her face.

"Ma'am, I have to flush your eyes. It isn't pleasant, but it is fast," I say, her head still jerking left and right. More groans of pain escape from her mouth. I pry open her right eye and begin to flow the purified water directly onto her eyeball for fifteen seconds, and repeat with the left eye.

"My patient is going to need a wheelchair!" I yell through the sealed nylon back door.

Along the backside of the tented room I dry my hands with a towel, and grab one of fifty hospital gowns protected from water by a plastic transparent sheet. I drape it over the woman, without drying her, and lift her body upward so that I can tie it around her. The robe ties on the side for better modesty. I then move my right arm under her torso, my left arm under her knees, and lift her from the table. Holding her tightly against me to restrain her jerking, I pull open the Velcro back door. There a nurse waits for me with a wheelchair. Her husband is already standing beside it, and I carefully seat her in it.

"Thank you," I say to the blonde-haired nurse standing behind the wheelchair.

"Wait... Where is her triage marker?" she comments. Right. I did not even perform a true exam on the patient. I pull one of the sheets from a back pocket in the suit, and fumble with gloved fingers to pull off a red "immediate" sticker and push it against her robe in the center of her chest. I see that Amanda's patient, the little girl, is being carried by another female nurse and is almost at the ER entrance already. I re-enter through the tent exit, seal it, pick up the contaminated clothing and shoes at the front of the room and toss them in a hazard bin set in front of the tent. I re-enter my room, seal the front door, and press the "Reset" button. A steam fills the room with water that is a sterilizing pH, and then all of the water in the plastic room drains through a suction system. I feel thirsty, and begin to drip sweat within my suit. I take one deep breath and begin again.

My next patient is a cogent elderly man, with good verbal and physical responses. He has sparse wild white hair on the top of his head, and bright blue eyes which are watering uncontrollably. While in my decontamination room, he vomits twice – once on my arm, and once on my feet. Both times he apologizes but appears in good spirits all things considered. While spraying him with the decontamination foam, he explains to me that his penis was on a normal day four times as large as I was seeing it, and this could be accounted for by the fact that it was "cold in this room." I can't help but laugh, and once he dresses I give him an orange "Delayed" sticker, based on his vomiting.

The next patient is wheel-chaired in, and I need James help to lift him onto the table. He is a stocky, middle-aged man with greyish brown hair and a beard. He is unconscious, and is unable to control his bowels, saliva, tear ducts, or virtually any other autonomic bodily function. While I am attempting to wash him he begins to choke for air. Gasping and gurgling sounds echo in the room as his lungs begin to lose function. I wash and rinse him as quickly as possible, wrap a robe around him loosely, and wait for a nurse to roll in a clean wheelchair from the back door. She's not able to help me set the man into it, so I place the wheelchair against the table and struggle with all of my might to pull the man off the table and into the chair. He falls into it with a thud and pain penetrates my back like my spine was just threaded with a meat hook. I attempt to pluck off an "expectant" sticker, which I know is this man's death sentence.

I want to stare at it for longer, to come to peace with its implications, but these luxuries are robbed of me. The label sticks to my glove, and I yell profanities while trying to get it to transfer to the man's robe. It finally sticks. "Go!" I tell the hospital worker in front of me, who rushes off. I hear panicked mumblings arising from the swarm of people huddled inhumanely close to each other on the far garage wall, still waiting to be treated. I keel over and choke on my breath, on this recirculated air, on the scent of my sweat, on the life about to end, and suddenly my suit becomes a claustrophobic cage that I am trapped in – a prison that I need to escape from. I need fresh air, I need to breathe! Hot tears fill my eyes, and then they pour over, and now I can't see because I can't wipe my eyes, because I am trapped in this harrowing suit that is going to steam me alive!

Pull it together, count and breathe. One. Two. Three. Four. Four. Three. Two. One. Breathe.

I re-enter my tent, and perform the same routine of removing contaminated clothes, sterilizing and draining the room. I repeat the process several more times, some patients healthier, some patients sicker. The noises of the crowds from outside the tent, the noises of Jim, Amanda, and I all repeatedly explaining the process to our patients, the sound of plastic rubbing against plastic both inside and outside of my suit wears on me. It has only been thirty minutes, and we have decontaminated a total of twenty patients. There are at least one hundred people waiting in the crowd on the second floor alone. Jim and I meet in the front of the tent for a moment. I suggest that we decontaminate the most severe patients on the second floor first, streamline the process for the remaining patients, and only then allow for another group to enter the second floor. Jim agrees. James makes the announcement through his megaphone, and a roar of noise amounting to desperation bellows from the already impatient mob. Soon only wheel-chaired and incapacitated patients approach us.

My next patient is a twelve year old African-American boy who is having grand-mal seizures. He is wearing a faint yellow graphic t-shirt which says "Play ball," and light blue jean shorts. I can lift him easily, but I cannot control his seizures while washing him at the same time. I desperately wish that we had benzodiazepine injections in here, but decontamination exists for only one purpose – getting rid of contaminants. Other doctors will treat the patients once they are inside of the hospital. The boy begins to make weak wheezing sounds, muffled with gurgles as saliva slides uninhibitedly down his throat and into his lungs. A few strained gasps for air and then he stops breathing altogether. My heart begins pounding, and panic rushes through my bones. I want to perform mouth to mouth, but I can't. His tiny chest lies flat, still, unresponsive, like it will forever without immediate intervention. I can hear Jim yelling something out of his door, and I yell as loudly as I can over him.

"This patient needs intubation! This patient needs immediate intubation!"

I rinse him off faster than the other patients, throw the gown over him, and push him through the nylon door. I place him in a wheelchair and a nurse swiftly places an Ambu-bagged oxygen mask over him, squeezing the pump consistently. I, with some difficulty, pull an "immediate" sticker off and place it on the boy. It is the only dishonest sticker I've placed today. Had I given him the proper "expectant" label, he would likely be left without treatment to die. Today his blood will not be on my hands, and if that meant I have to lie, so be it. His shirt "Play ball" circulates my mind. "Play ball," he has a father and mother. "Play ball," he lost them somewhere in the attack. "Play ball," he's going to die alone. "Play ball," it says, but he never will again. Anger breeds in me against those who caused this, against the paramours of violence, and of suffering, and of death. Just then Jim exits his room with one of his patients.

"Stickers? What the hell is this? Who thought to do stickers?" his fingers, thick with latex pull agitatedly against the paper unable to grab the "expectant" sticker. "Get me something other than stickers! Seriously! Get someone to put the damn stickers on hospital bracelets or something – this is NOT working!" he almost screams out the words, and then re-enters his tent.

We work through six more rounds each of severely debilitated victims. Sweat is dripping down my entire body, and my skin is raw from chaffing against the plastic suit. I can strongly smell my own body-odor, which is still a better smell than the decontamination room. The heat of my suit is beginning to fog the clear portion of the mask, obscuring my vision. My back hurts, my shoulders ache, I desperately crave water and sleep, and to be anywhere, truly anywhere but here.

CHAPTER 3

The three of us step out of our rooms to begin to receive healthier patients. The sun is beginning to set, bright beams of golden light piercing through the open panels of the garage, giving us a better view of the number of victims ahead. James sends three more through, all healthy enough to walk, which is no small cause for excitement. Just then the elevator doors open, revealing a short Hispanic woman holding a child in her arms.

"My son needs hepp! My son needs hepp!" she cries with a thick Cuban accent, pushing through the crowd. As she approaches the front, I see that she is covered in dirt and bodily fluids —but not her own.

In her arms lies a limp boy with short black hair and big cheeks. His eyes are open but unresponsive and rolled to the side in an unnatural way. I run from the tent to the front of the aisle and grab the child's wrist with one hand, pressing two fingers of my other hand against his neck. Ten seconds pass. No heartbeat.

"What you doing??" she asks impulsively.

"Shhh!" I quiet her, but it's of no use with the murmuring of the crowd surrounding them. I feel closely, still counting the seconds in my head. Ninety seconds pass. No heartbeat. I look down at the woman with remorse.

"Ma'am, I am so sorry. There is nothing we can do for your son."

She makes eye-contact with me but she does not cry or scream. She just stands there staring at me. I'm not sure she understands.

"I am sorry. Your son has died," I say calmly and slowly, never breaking eye-contact. I mentally review the pithy expressions I have been taught to deliver to loved ones when a patient dies: "he fought valiantly," "his little body wasn't strong enough," "we did everything we could," "is there someone I can call?" and nothing fits for this scene, for the inhumanity of this limp boy hanging in his mother's arms. I can't give her a cup of coffee, I can't clean her child's face, I can't wrap her in a blanket, or sit with her until someone arrives. Instead I have to return to my post, leaving her to stand alone with the body. It's so wrong that I begin to shake in fury.

When you are first shown a cadaver in medical school, they initially cover the body's face and hands to help promote depersonalization. You receive half a dozen lectures on compartmentalization, and are told repeatedly that in the company of the dead you are a scientist, not a father, husband, or son. I understood that I was dissecting, examining, and performing small procedures on a human body – and I was certain that seeing the face and hands of that human body would change very little in my performance.

However, on the first day that the sheets were removed and I could see a cadaver fully uncovered, I could not even touch my instruments. The woman who we were to work on was twenty-five years old, with soft delicate facial features and long ebony hair which flowed backward off the table. Though stiff and pale as death, this woman's life weighed in my stomach like an anchor in port. What seared my mind was that she was permanently bruised across her body from being beaten. For the living, bruises heal, but for the dead every injury tattoos them until decomposition. This young woman had a silent story with her that her voice could never tell. It didn't seem right that young life could end in such brutality, and I wasn't even sure what it meant that life could end at all. It felt like humanity demanded more dignity than death, or at least, more dignity than a lifeless figure lying on a table to be operated on by inexperienced first years, or being held limp in a mother's arms covered in bodily fluids.

"Should we decontaminate him, and then send him into the hospital dead?" Amanda asks me as I approach. James follows behind me, pretending that he can't see the dead child, or his mother's begging eyes.

"No. There are not supposed to be any casualties here. Decontamination is a warm zone, casualties are supposed to be filtered out in the hot zone to prevent further contamination – and to conserve decontamination foam."

She nods, acknowledging that we are already low on supply.

"What do we do?" Four desperately worn out eyes stare at me.

"The only thing we *can* do is get the body as far away from us as we can. At least to the farthest west-side corner of the garage, but the first floor would be better."

Their glaring eyes turn dismal. My internal alarm warns me that I'm close to my breaking point, and I see that shared in their faces.

"Then what do you expect her to do?" Amanda snaps at me, some of her red hair sticking to the inside of her mask while tears fill her eyes. "Carry her dead child to the corner of the garage and just drop him there?"

"Yes. Unfortunately." I respond as even-handedly as I can bear to. Mind over matter is a real phenomenon but it has its limitations. If you find yourself pinned under a 3,000 pound rock, your mind cannot save you; matter has conquered, and the mind is useless. Telling a woman to throw her dead child in a parking garage corner and leave him there feels heavier.

I hear new noises coming from behind us, and walk around the tent to see eight federal HAZMAT workers approaching from the hospital ramp, carrying a second decontamination tent. I catch eyes with Jim, James, and Amanda, all who have the same sense of relief. Amanda even does a joyful skip in place. We naturally regroup, agreeing to leave the woman and child to those better trained for this situation. James sends us our final patients. I receive a stout middle-aged woman, who, apart from not wanting to undress in front of me, is fairly healthy and cooperative. She has stinging in her eyes and lungs, but no noticeable neurological damage which is significant given the amount of time which has passed since the initial attack. She stands for the foam and the shower, and once dressed I joyfully deliver to her the very last sticker of the day: Minor.

The rest of the evening fades into blurring flashes. Being washed in my hazmat suit by another hazmat worker. Being undressed by hospital staff in a break room. Someone handing me my clothes and water. Vomiting again, and calling my wife to tell her I'm coming home. The drive is undoubtedly the most miserable of my life; three hours for an ordinarily twenty minute commute out of the city. Even using the back roads to avoid National Guard barricades does nothing to diminish the time. My depleted adrenaline reserves make every touch, every sound, and every sight feel like another chisel into a nearly shattered pane of glass. The choking and gurgling sounds of my sickest patients play uncontrollably on repeat in my mind, and the memory of the "Play Ball" shirt makes me want to weep or puke. I try to distract myself by systematically replaying Lennon lyrics in my mind.

Everyday we used to make it love, why can't we be making love nice and easy... It'll be just like starting over.

I wish I could start over. I wish that I would wake up and discover that today was only a nightmare, a blurry falsehood that will fade as I settle into reality. But the painful overload of my senses testifies that though this is a nightmare, it is no dream. When I finally enter through our large oak door, Liz is sitting on the stairs. She looks at me with eyes full of tears, rushes to wrap her arms around me, and infuses me with the first bit of comfort I have felt in half a day. I shut the door, and slowly slide down it until I am sitting on the floor. I made it home.

"I love you," she says softly, pushing my hair from my forehead. She joins me on the floor, examining me head to toe for injuries with her anxious brown eyes.

"I'm fine," I urge.

"But are you?" She stares solemnly at me now, her thin jawline trembling. I am not okay. She knows it and I know it. I lean sideways to embrace her, letting her hold me tightly to restrain jerking inhales as I begin to weep. Hot tears wet her midnight hair, and in the background a voice reels from the television.

[Associated Press Transcript – President Bryan Powell National Address 12:00am, 04-10-41]

My fellow Americans,

Today our nation was shaken by an evil greater than the world has ever seen. At 4:21pm, a nuclear weapon which had been smuggled into the city of Washington D.C. was detonated. Our capital city was destroyed within seconds. Many of our political leaders, friends, and family were lost in an instant. Between 5:05 and 5:15pm, chemical weapons containing nerve gas were released in eighteen major U.S. cities, while government officials were able to circumvent seventeen additional attacks. It is with grave solemnity and sorrow that I relay to you, that The President of the United States David Martinez, The Vice President of The United States Sophia Wolfe, The Speaker of the House Mark Wells, and The President pro tempore of the Senate Noah Nottelling have all been lost in today's attacks. I, Bryan Powell, have taken the oath of office of the President of the United States and have sworn to uphold and defend the Constitution of the United States of America.

Within minutes of today's attacks, I implemented our government's emergency response plans. Our government continued to operate under a state of emergency, and martial law was declared. Federal teams were deployed immediately to help with rescue efforts in Washington, New York, Jersey City, Boston, Philadelphia, Chicago, Detroit, Portland, Indianapolis, Atlanta,

Orlando, Miami, New Orleans, Charlotte, Memphis, Houston, San Diego, Sacramento, and Seattle. Our hospitals have been dispensed all the supplies that they are in need of, and our banks and economic functions have been suspended until further notice. Our allies have offered their support, both tangible and intangible, to help recovery efforts, and they stand with us against the wicked power which is behind today's attacks.

My friends, one hundred years ago our nation was violently attacked by men who had succumbed to despicable evil. December 7th, 1941, a date which will live in infamy, threatened to shake the fabric of our faith, the security of our freedom, and the resilience of our resolve. That date marked a moment in our history where we were forced to be brave as we simultaneously cared for our injured, and rose to fight the forces of evil in the world. In that day, we were mothers and medics, sons and soldiers, husbands and heroes.

Forty years ago, in 2001, we had learned strength and bravery from our predecessors, and were better equipped to face a new evil which endangered our way of life. Some of you may be old enough to remember the solemn day on which the icons of our nation, brilliant and strong, fell to the ground. On that day, we rose with tears in our eyes and took to the streets to search out our loved ones, to rebuild our cities, and to bring an end to the forces which could cause such horror. We faced murderous attack with such dignity and power that the world stood in awe. Today, we have been called to join a long tradition of bravery. In 1941 evil used bombs to shake our faith, in 2001 evil used airplanes to crumble our icons of hope, and today evil used weapons of mass destruction to displace our courage, but they have failed. Though quiet anger boils within us against those who have committed this great crime, today we have proven once again that Americans were made strong for the day of destruction.

Our military men and women, our police forces, our medical professionals, and our first responders worked with diligence and distinction to care for our injured and to capture the perpetrators. In times past our nation has called on tens of thousands of Americans to be brave during times of calamity, and to sacrifice as they serve their neighbors in an attempt to rebuild our peaceful existence. But today our nation calls on tens of millions of Americans to be brave and to do whatever they can to help their neighbors in this time of affliction. Does your neighbor need rest? Provide it for them. Does your neighbor need food? Give some to them. Does your neighbor need love? Give all that remains in your heart.

On a day when much has been taken from you, I ask you to give more. I ask you because you are strong, and your resilience is palpable. Evil believes that it has robbed you this day of peace, but I am well aware that the American people will reestablish the peace due within our borders by morning. We may anguish in emotion, but we will prevail in strength. We may weep this very night, but our fortitude will be shown to the world in the morning. Our enemy, Iran, will be proven powerless – and its evil regime will be utterly destroyed. We felt the pain of injustice for one night, but they will feel the pain of justice for ages – we lost our peace for one day, but they will lose peace forever.

Our nation will rise up from ashes and the healing of our cities will be a light of hope to all mankind that the destruction of terror will never prevail. We shall prove once again to the world that we are a nation who seeks to preserve justice, freedom, and peace for all mankind.

Thank you, goodnight, and may America be blessed.

CHAPTER 4

November 1st, 2046 – Present Day

The snowy air is oppressive tonight, like each stray snowflake floating through the parking garage is a living spur burrowing into my face. Liz was right, of course, I should have worn gloves. The light above the cars every few meters is a dim grey, unable to overpower the blackness peering through quartered blocks of cement. The whistling wind drowns out the usual tapping sound of my dress shoes marching across the garage to the shiny black sedan Liz picked out.

All I can think about is the Dopimazipal injections, "D-MAZ" as it's now called. I cannot explain my fascination with them but I just have an unsettling sense that something is missing. I've chewed on the clinical studies so frequently that my dreams are pitiful regurgitations of the same information: Liz, while preparing one of the three recipes she knows how to cook, will begin quoting to me sections from the studies verbatim, or a patient will enter the hospital complaining of "biosynthetic absorption of the ribosomally synthetized constituents with the exclusion of LRRK2." You would think that a drug used daily by twenty-seven percent of the population would have updated studies, but no. Just three. The same three since it was first formulated, which all corroborate the injection's success in treating the long term effects of Obcasus, the name of the chemical gas used in the attacks.

I've seen the success myself, we all have, but that nagging suspicion that something is off never leaves me alone. Never in our nation's history has a drug been more easily accessible or widely used. There are automated dispensaries on every street corner of center city. Just swipe your ID and receive either a daily dose or a week's supply. If you're poor, the government pays the tab, if you're wealthy it's forty dollars a unit. The fraud surrounding the automated dispensaries is as extensive as it is heartbreaking. Every few days a teenager comes into the hospital sick as their first exposure to Obcasus. They suffer from seizures, tremors, memory loss, and oxygen depletion, all on account of some drug-addicted parent selling their kid's injections for fast cash.

As I walk between a dull red SUV and my driver's side, a sudden movement between the front of my car and the garage wall catches my eye. I thought it looked like ... No, it couldn't be, not in this weather. I force my eyes tightly shut and open again, narrowing them as I slowly approach the garage wall. With each cautious step I see more of the impossible. An elbow, a thin pointy shoulder, a shirtless bony torso which is pale white, and young, and dead. Only not dead, but shaking uncontrollably, quite more alive than it ought to be.

My next inhale feels difficult, my heart constricting and expanding faster and faster to pump adrenaline through my veins. It's one of them. An Inexorable, I'm sure of it, curled up and half-clothed trying to hide itself between the front of my car and the grey cement wall. I can't remember the last time I saw one in person, and I haven't seen one this close since the Assistance Centers opened. It's small, so much smaller than I would have expected, probably starving to death. It doesn't look dangerous: tiny hands, minuscule fingers, and a child-like freezing red nose extending out from under dark, wet curls. The best predators never look dangerous, I remind myself.

I know what I'm supposed to do, I'm supposed to call the Assistance Center. They will take it and euthanize it, or as they say, 'resolve' it, in a more or less humane fashion. It's the responsible thing to do, the right thing to do, but the thought makes my throat tighten. They're not human, I know that. Hell, I even *feel* that. They're deformities of nature, murderous, brutal creatures, children of wrath, Inexorables as good as their name.

But they are human too. Their DNA always says it: Human. I am a doctor, and I took vows, and my vows included for better or worse protecting human life without qualification or discrimination. I have treated death row inmates before, why is this different? But I know the reason. Inexorables are unalterable, incurable, a claim I'm not sure could be univocally made for death row inmates. These are creatures so degenerate that they'll bite off their mother's nipple during breastfeeding, and giggle while she bleeds and cries. An evil that innate cannot be cured, and should not be trifled with.

In between shreds of worn out grey sweat pants I can see pale skin already turning a bluish hue, the beginnings of hypothermia. It reminds me how pained my own bare hands are. I picture myself grasping the silver handle of my car, sitting down in its leather seat, turning the heat on high and driving home through snowy darkness to an ordinary evening of medical journals and frozen pizza while forgetting about the Inex entirely. It is only in seeing this picture that I realize I can't go through with it. It doesn't seem right to see a living creature, even a monster, and to let it die when it is in my power to save it. A heat begins to grow in my chest, strong, impulsive, but right. I peer over my shoulder, examining the garage for people who might see me, but it's empty. I take a deep breath, let go of my thoughts, and act.

I bend down, ignoring my fear of retaliation, and lift the Inex into my arms. It's heavier than I expected, maybe forty pounds, and has dirt all over its bare pale chest and face. The impressions of its rib cage frame its undernourished torso. Wet mud drips from its dark curly hair onto my coat. I unlock the car door and carefully place the Inex in the back seat, pulling a seat belt over its frail trembling body... I think it's a boy.

I get in, turn the heat on as high as I can, and begin my commute home. Out of the parking garage, out of downtown, onto the highway, past the city's edge, and no one seems to notice. There are no flashing red and blue lights, no people peering into my windows with suspicion; it's as though nothing really happened. Once the initial rush of adrenaline runs clean, it almost feels like an ordinary Friday. I've just finished a ten hour shift, I wrote a dozen or so prescriptions for antibiotics, reprimanded a menace of an intern who refused to inject a patient with the proper dosage. The only thing reminding me of how unordinary the day is, is the chipping sound of tiny shivering teeth behind me.

He's strange, dirty, and heavy. Even if he wasn't an Inex, he is by definition someone my wife would never want in her house. Of course, it is our house. A mutual house. A house, even, primarily afforded by me, not that I would dare raise that in an argument. Liz would be livid, and how could I blame her? Part of me feels without defense, because I sense the danger that I am exposing us to by bringing him in. But another part of me feels I have the best defense, the defense of saving a life. Well, a half-life.

The sight of our driveway is accompanied with the familiar sound of tires against stone, the slow rolling friction that is typically so comforting to hear. Today it makes me anxious. I exit the car, once again lifting the tiny creature in my arms. His shivering has already reduced, which is a good sign. I walk left toward the dark wooden door and I can tell that Liz recently salted the pathway, likely just for me. It is watery compared with the snowy mush that surrounds it, but I'm pretty sure she missed a step. The lantern fixtures on either side of the door toss golden light across the damp slushy ground. The oak door in front of my eyes stands for everything I am about to have to own: the fact that I just took in Inexorable, the fact that I'm willfully choosing to disobey government protocols, and most importantly, the fact that I am about to subject Liz and I to terrible danger. I take a few extended breaths of chilly air, and stare forward with resolve. It's just three bold steps, one turn of the key, and the feeling of hot air rushing over my hands and face greets me.

Directly in front of the door are the stairs, and to the left of the stairs is our living room, full of warmth. The fire place is burning inside the left wall, the large area rug is full of deep reds and browns. Our mahogany coffee table still has a cup of Liz's afternoon tea sitting on it, but the brown leather couch facing the window is where I am heading. I lay him down on the couch, feeling his bony spine along my fingers as I pull my arms away. I grab a quilted blanket from the basket beside the couch and wrap it over him.

"I'm going to make you some hot food, and grab you some water. Alright?" I say and move through the open archway into the kitchen.

"Ethan, are you talking to someone?" Liz's mild voice echoes smoothly from upstairs.

"Uhm. Yes," I yell rather tersely.

I open the freezer and pull out one of the cloth rice-bags kept there for when I inevitably injure myself on home projects. This one was handmade by my mother with cloth that looked like a prescription pad and doctors' scribbles. When she had given it to me for Christmas many years ago I laughed out loud, and she laughed too. I don't give even a smile at it now.

I walk across the kitchen, swerving around the marble-topped island, and place the rice-bag into the microwave on the far-back counter. While it heats up I lean back into the living room to watch the Inex. The boy. The Inex. Hell, I don't know what to think. But this is my first time really seeing his face. He has a medium-framed nose and strong cheek bones. Though he still looks bluer than I am comfortable with, I am beginning to see that his skin tone is olive, maybe Middle-Eastern. He won't look at me, so I cannot see his eyes. The microwave beeps. I replace the rice-bag with a microwave pouch of pasta and fill a glass with water. When I re-enter the room I am startled by a gasp. Liz.

"What is that?" Her tone is biting, and her expression condemnatory. Her long black hair frames her face, making it look thin and solemn.

"A ... child."

"A human child? Or one of *them*?" Her face is incredulous, and then she stares angrily at the boy.

"Liz, they are human children. They're just.... They have an illness," I say with less conviction than I would have liked. I don't make eye-contact with her but I can still feel her fury stabbing through me like needles. "Hold on, little one," I say, hoping it will humanize him. I place the warm rice-bag over his head, and help him to sip some water, which is rather difficult given his trembling. Out of the corner of my eye I can see Liz staring in disbelief, jaw-dropped and wide-eyed. I pretend not to notice.

"You shouldn't have brought that thing here. This could be illegal. That thing isn't human!" Her voice gets higher pitched with each word.

"He was going to die. He was left out for exposure in the parking garage. Would *you* want to die in a parking garage?" I look up, trying to show her my sincerity.

"He? No, Ethan. This isn't a 'he.' This is an Inex. I'm calling the center," her voice begins to sound shaky. "Why did you have to do this?" She begins to cry and walks into the kitchen. This child is my patient now, my responsibility, but she is my wife; who do I have the greater responsibility to?

"I am not going to let you die," I whisper to him.

The Inex glares up at me suddenly, giving me my first view of his eyes. I instinctually gasp at their deadness. They are a dark brown, sharp and foreboding. Large penetrating circles look over me, up and down, with a calculated pace as if he is examining me for weaknesses. There is a quality in them which is undoubtedly inhuman, dangerous, and void of emotion. An abnormal smile curls up on the corner of his left cheek, as if he is thrilled by my frightened reaction. My pulse surges, and I feel my blood pressure increase as a throbbing grows behind my eyes. It is a scary thing letting one of them into our home; it is a scary thing that they exist at all, but I'm not sure what choice I have. It--no, *he*--is a helpless being and would have died without me. I commit to ignoring his eyes, and go to intercept Liz.

It wasn't always the case that Inexes were left out for exposure or turned over to the Assistance Centers. After President Powell had the Dopimazipal injections formulated for the long term effects of Obcasus, it seemed like we had recovered. Even as those exposed to Obcasus began having children, things continued to seem fine. It was not until that first generation, following the Obcasus attacks, turned one or so that we began to notice such severe violent tendencies.

By the time those first children turned two, our hospital and all others were flooded with parents desperate to understand what was wrong with their children. What we discovered was life-shattering. Mothers who were first-exposure victims of Obcasus appeared to pass down some sort of genetic abnormality, still unidentified, that caused fetal development issues in several key areas of the brain controlling empathy, emotion, and pleasure. Malformations, which appeared like scar tissue, permanently injured the children's brains, turning them into something a degree worse than psychopaths. We tried every type of treatment: surgeries, stem cell therapies, antipsychotics, but nothing worked. For a year the news contained nothing but stories of whole families stabbed to death, or set on fire, or worse, by these 'children.' They would eat the faces of strangers, or cut up their baby siblings alive, piece by piece – and there were no exceptions. Any child born to a woman exposed to Obcasus exhibited the same violent behavior. Thus they were given the name "Inexorables" by the media, because they were unable to be changed.

A small percentage of women sterilized themselves as a response, but the majority of women continued to have children anyway, because they reported feeling healthier during pregnancy than they had since before the gas. We had a national crisis, and in short order President Powel invented a system to keep our society safe: The Assistance Centers. There was a lot of back lash when they first opened; however, as the stories of torture and murder continued, and particularly as the Inexorables grew older and more capable, their threat to society became irrefutable. "Wait until they are old enough to know how to make bombs," was the remark by a newscaster that put the final nail in the coffin. The Assistance Centers are almost universally accepted today.

The next morning Liz and I awake early, too nervous to sleep for long. At four-thirty, it's still dark and too cold to escape from the weighted blankets. I'm not sure if she slept at all. She heeded my pleas for a stay of execution last night, but I doubt she'll do the same for the Inexorable today. She faces me, intertwining warm long legs with mine. The longer you're alive and the longer you've been married the more you cherish the simple things; such as the fact that while at night your wife's legs are ice cubes, in the morning they are warm and inviting.

"It's not fair, because you're pushing all of my buttons at once, ya know?" she half-whispers to me. I take a louder breath so that she knows I am listening. "I could handle infertility, I think. Right? My body is broken and I understand it. I married a man who fixes broken bodies. I obviously can handle if my body is broken somehow. But when the bombs dropped, and when the babies stopped being normal, and when there was no more adopting because there were no more healthy babies... That. That broke me in a new way. A broken body I could handle, but that brokenness. God." Her voice cracks. "What I hate so much about what you've done here, is that you brought fake hope into my life. Fake. A lie. Because I know you, and I know exactly what you're thinking. You're thinking we can take him in, fix him, that you could heal him, that we'd be a family, that it'd be something beautiful out of so many broken things."

"You make me sound like an optimist," I say almost bitingly, but continue to listen to her.

"Well, in this case you are. He cannot be ours, he ... it, is a monster. He only looks like a boy." I begin to feel her hot tears rolling onto my arm, though she has been trying to keep them hidden. I sigh deeply.

Suddenly we both hear the sound of glass shattering downstairs. Or was it? Maybe it was something from outside. I find myself racing down the steps toward the kitchen. Once I'm in the archway I see broken glass all over the floor, and look up to find a sharp shard held in the hand of the boy. He is laughing manically.

"Hi little one. Please put down the glass," I try to reason, inching toward him slowly. He cocks his head at me, and giggles in delight – but not a happy giggle, it's something cruel, something dark. He squints at me, making direct eye contact, and then suddenly he charges, the glass shard pointed directly at my thigh. When he gets within contact-distance I defensively kick his entire body to the left with my right leg – not too hard, but enough to divert him. He crumples to the ground and begins to cry. I am unsure whether I should try to comfort him, or call the police. My heart is racing frantically, and I take a few deep breaths. Think... think!

I rush toward him and pull him from the floor before he can pick up another piece of glass. Liz enters behind me and surveys the ground which is covered in broken shards, then looks up at me with concern. The boy is only sniffling now as he nuzzles his head into my shoulder.

"Is he okay?" she asks. Is *he* okay? I think to myself. He just tried to stab me!

"He's fine. I don't think he cut himself," I respond calmly. Liz comes around behind him and surveys his skin skeptically, but does not touch the boy. He begins to wiggle and then writhe in my arms. I try to control him while Liz sweeps up the shards of glass, creating discordant scraping sounds along the tile. He is strong and loosens one of his arms and then the second. He uses them to push against my chest, trying to pry his way out from my grasp. I wrap my large arms around him again, and this time tighter. Suddenly a high-pitched voice shouts: "DOWN!" Liz and I both stare at the child.

He can talk.

CHAPTER 5

Our shower is a three-cornered stone chamber sectioned off by one frosted glass door with an acid-relief design of an oak tree. Each morning it grants me twenty minutes of unremitting silence to process the preceding day, a carking memory, or an abstruse diagnostic set. At the beginning of our marriage Liz incessantly requested that we shower together, which really meant melting my flesh off while she enjoyed a shower. We have not shared a shower in the last fourteen of fifteen years of marriage, which has permitted me a world for myself, a universe of naked, joyous solitude.

Today, warm water washes over my face, steam particles fill my lungs, the sound of splashing water clouds my ears, and wet smooth stone grounds my feet. I see, but attempt to ignore, much of my middle-aged body: the two inches of pudge which has fitted itself securely around my mid-section, the ever-migrating dark and grey chest hair working its way toward my neck, the increasing wrinkles and veins which distinguish my hands from that of a young man.

I try to understand why it is that I cannot let the child die. Isn't death preferable to an evil existence? Isn't it safer? Isn't it legal? The months immediately following the attacks were the most difficult of my life. The nerve gas which affected more than 80 million Americans was new and complex, essentially giving a quarter of the American population Parkinson's disease overnight. Unlike ordinary nerve gases which blocked acetylcholinesterase, this nerve gas metabolized dopamine in the brain and caused permanent damage to the dopamine producers. This effect was not immediately understood, but the biggest key to understanding that the damage was permanent is that the symptoms persisted indefinitely in those affected, according to how severe their exposure was. Many individuals only experienced moderate tremors, memory loss, and depression. Unfortunately, many also experienced continual symptoms as debilitating as seizures, inability to control motor skills, speech or excretion, and they had permanent memory loss. These symptoms when paired with the depression typical of dopamine depletion resulted in a high suicide rate for those exposed to the nerve gas.

The gas was named Obcasus, a Latin term for the setting of the sun; both because of its yellow-orange hue, and because it was a Latin euphemism for death; and in a real way it felt like the death of our society. Working at the hospital became the nightmare of all nightmares. Thousands of patients came in everyday looking for relief from their symptoms, and there was little that we could offer them. During this time doctors at the hospital still treated the patients in their own specialty, but in addition were required to work a minimum of two hours a day evaluating ER patients, who were made up almost entirely of individuals exposed to the gas. It was during this time that Jim Wilson and I truly became friends. We bemoaned every hour, every minute at times, but were sustained by his southern quips and my northeastern sarcasm. We were skeptical, unhappy people, but so was everyone in the medical field during those first months.

Salvation came from President Powell. Directly following the attack, he formed a commission to develop a "cure" for the long-term effects of Obcasus. Several months later he unveiled a treatment method that alleviated virtually all major long-term effects of Obcasus in three separate clinical trials. The Dopimazipal injections were formulated similarly to the dopamine injections used for Parkinson's treatment, however, they possessed a unique compound of enzymes and neurotransmitters that had far superior results. Life changed overnight. Though we never left martial law, our society began to reconstruct itself. When you treat a bacterial infection such as staph or salmonella with antibiotics, your goal is not to entirely eradicate the infection, your goal is to merely eradicate enough of the bacteria that the body's natural immune system can recover and fight off the remaining infection itself. If the immune system is not able to combat the infection on its own, then treatment will inevitably fail. What the President did was enable society to fight on its own. For a brief moment we all had an emerging sense of positivity, as though life would return to normal, and we would come out of this furnace dense and refined, strong and polished.

But then there's this.

I sit on the living room rug, still in my towel, but now covered in sticky blood and organ discharge. The rug is stained with gore and I look into impassive Inexorable eyes, dried red god-knows-what crusted on its tiny face. The only reason I was able to restrain him was because he refused to let go of the eyeballs, one in each hand that he was continually squeezing, each time allowing small soft pieces to drip out between his fingers. Even now, while tied to a chair, I can tell whenever he squeezes them because he grins in pleasure.

"How do I fix you?" I shake my head in defeat and shift my gaze to the rug. On it lies a stomach and heart crushed into slime, with only small intact pieces that allow me to identify them. When I came down the stairs after my shower he was jumping on top of them and laughing. My white under shirt which I had put on him is reflecting a dim reddish-brown because of the amount of wet blood it has absorbed. On the kitchen floor lay the neighbor's cat in a puddle of its own blood and fluids, its severed tongue stuffed in one of the empty eye sockets, and its gut emptied of its contents.

"Red," I hear his high-pitched voice, and look up. "Red and red." He looks at the rug with his big insidious brown eyes and smiles. The color of the organ slush is directly over one of the red blocks in the rug pattern. I wonder if that is what he means, red and red.

We've only had the child for the weekend, and Liz has just left for groceries. I wonder if I can clean everything before she gets home, but it's unlikely since she pre-ordered them and only needs to pick them up. There isn't time to consider any longer. I take another gaze at the boy, verifying that he is tied securely, and run up the dark wooden stairs to grab a pair of shorts – careful on my way up not to touch anything. When I come back down, I use the bloodied towel I was wearing and lay it flat on the wooden floor beside the rug. I dread my walk into the kitchen, where wood changes to cold white tile, coated in thick brownish blood, pouring out of the empty gut cavity of one heinously mutilated cat carcass. The smell wafts upward, entering my nose and seemingly depositing into my stomach. I fight the urge to gag. It is not the smell of blood that bothers me – it is the smell of bile. The kid had ripped open all the viscera, and what remained in the air was poignant putrid cat particles.

In medical school, you're trained to ignore smell, to fight your gag reflex, to remember that whatever it is that you are smelling is nothing that can in anyway harm you- it is only part of the body, and it is very natural. When you begin dealing with actual vomit, bile, pus, blood, and excrement, you force yourself to intellectualize the scent. You separate yourself from what you are smelling, and in a real sense, begin not to smell it anymore. But something about this dead cat, and the horrific condition in which I have found it, won't allow me to intellectualize it as if it were a patient. It was Landon and Halley's cat, whose fur was such a dark grey color that he almost possessed a bluish tint: like the sky when a commanding summer storm turns an afternoon dark.

I hold my breath and lift the carcass, tail in one hand, hollowed head in the other. Drops of blood fall upon my legs and smear across the floor with each step, before I set the carcass on the towel in the living room. I roll the cat in the towel, and throw the bundle onto the rug. Using scissors I cut my shirt off the Inex so that he can stay restrained while I continue to clean. It too gets thrown onto the rug. I wash my hands, scrubbing under my finger nails and up my forearms. Pink and tan colors rinse down the drain with intertwining bands of clear water and soap bubbles. I move everything off of the rug, the mahogany coffee table and the restrained Inex. He looks at me, long black lashes contrasting with his already pale olive skin, but he says nothing. I methodically roll the rug into a cylinder, afterward folding it in half so that nothing will spill from its openings. Even so, a round blood stain marks the left side of the floor where organ broth had already seeped through. I fold the rug a second time so that it can fit into the outdoor garbage can, and there I dispose of it.

The rest of the cleaning is somewhat easier, I only need to successfully sanitize everything else and shower with him. My heart begins to pound as I realize how quickly Liz could be home. I pull castile soap out from under the sink, primarily because I think that it smells like vomit, and vomit is my explanation for why the rug has disappeared. Everything gets wiped down in castile soap and water. The kitchen and living room floors, the chair, the table legs, the sink. Lastly, I untie him from the chair, lifting him in my arms, just like the first night. Tonight will be the third night, and things already feel so different.

While he's in my arms, staring at me with a piercing scowl, I ascend the stairs to shower us both. Once we enter the bathroom, I notice that his hands are still in fists and suddenly I remember the eyeballs. Just then I hear Liz enter through the front door. I repeat expletives under my breath. I can hardly breathe. I pry the Inex's tiny hands open, and it feels as though his finger bones could snap at my effort. He begins to scream, and he scrapes his long fingernails against my face in retribution. I ignore his unceasing screeches, and force the white sticky material out of his hands. I quickly throw the slob into the toilet and flush, pretending that it is mucus instead of what it actually is. I pick him up and carry him into the shower, stripping my shorts as I go, accidentally leaving eyeball residue on them. In between sobs he repeats "Red and red, red and red."

"Shhh. Be quiet!" I urge while starting the shower. Defiant screams echo around the stone. At last, with both of us wet, I rub the sclera off our hands, rinsing them under the water. Liz's shoes thump hastily up the staircase.

"Is everyone okay!???" She rushes in, panicked.

"Yeah!" I shout over the sound of his screams and running water. My voice sounding deep, even unfamiliar, probably from my panic. "He just doesn't want to shower," I explain, trying to return to my normal tone of voice.

"Why is he showering with you? It's weird!" She walks closer to the frosted glass.

"He threw up downstairs, all over the rug. I had to throw it out."

"What? Why? Why couldn't you clean it?" she asks. In the speed of the events, I hadn't even considered this question. It is a reasonable one; why throw out an inordinately expensive rug when I could clean it myself, or at the very least have it dry-cleaned? Think, think. I can't think with the sound of echoed screams railing around me.

"Hold on, baby."

I set the child down, rub some shampoo in his hair and let it run down his body. I quickly use my soapy hands to clear the remaining blood off of my shins. After rinsing, I shut the water off, open the shower door, and wrap a towel around the boy. When I pick him up again in my arms, he stops his insolent squealing. For a moment, he even leans into my embrace and looks up at me as if with affection. Around his lips grows a contented smile, and for the first time he doesn't look scary. He looks like a boy, a cute boy, and even familiar, like he belongs with me.

Looking down from the child I can see that Liz is treasuring the same moment even more than I am, with a warm dimpled smile and tears forming in her eyes. Her cheeks are glowing a warm pink, and a drop falls along one of them. She is looking at me as though I am holding our child for the first time, as though we have found our answer to prayer. My heart begins to throb with pain, because I love to see her like this, I would love for this to be the child to end all of her waiting. But this isn't the child. The white sclera that I can see stuck to my shorts from the cat's eyeball assures me of that much. But I force myself to ignore it. In this world of sickness, death, and suffering how wrong can one day of joy be, even if under false pretenses?

CHAPTER 6

She and I watch the Inex nap for over an hour in our king size bed. We sit together on the floor, leaning against each other. She occasionally kisses my cheek, and I occasionally stroke her shadowy hair.

"He looks so innocent," she whispers.

"He does *look* that way," I say through gritted teeth, unsure if I should divulge what happened this afternoon.

"Don't you think he could be trained? We're all a blend of nature and nurture, right?"

"I think it depends on what kind of nature you're dealing with," I suggest.

"He cuddled you after the shower, I think there's something human in there," she says optimistically, then nuzzles her head into my shoulder.

We first met in undergrad at Washington University in St. Louis. She lived with her family in Missouri while going to school, and I lived the disenchanting dorm life separated from my mother in Fairfax. I was properly a nerd, and she was entirely not. To this day I cannot understand why she took notice of me. We met in Intro to Anthropology in my first year, when I still laughably thought that I wanted to be an anthropologist. She walked over to me one day after class, in a tight fitting yellow dress that accentuated her natural curves and drew the eye with every movement. She said, verbatim, "Hi, Ethan. I am starting a study group for the next test, and, well, I'd like it if you could join us." Her voice was so soft and sweet. My nineteen year old bones craved to hear it again, needed to hear it speaking my name again.

Of course I joined, and quickly realized two things: first, that the study group met at her parents' house, where her father

watched us men assiduously, and second, that she was smart –
and not simply the good at academics smart, but that type of
socially smart full of wit and cleverness that I myself was not. I
remember thinking that she was perfect, and I could not
understand how it is that I made her laugh, but I did, and I felt as
though I could listen to her laugh forever. She looks so much like
she did then, only now she has black bangs which drape along her
forehead, and elegant character lines that grow along her eyes
and lips when she smiles. She's still just as petite, and her high
cheek bones continue to make her look more European than
American. The past five years have aged me far more than her,
and I know it is because she has a way of letting difficulties go
whereas I obsess over them. Small details get lodged in my mind
and I twist them into my brain like screws.

For example, Philadelphia was the only city in the U.S. which
had Obcasus fall from an airplane. It was the only city, and I saw
it with my own eyes in utter clarity. Why? In each city the
attackers used different methods to disperse the chemical
weapons; in some areas they were thrown out of buses, in others
they were detonated on subways, some were synchronized to be
thrown out of buildings and into the streets, and notably in
Miami the gas was released inside the ventilation systems of two
hospitals as well as in the downtown area. But Philadelphia was
the only place that an airplane was hijacked to drop the gas, and
it is strange to remember. Sometimes when I remember it's like a
dream, like it didn't really happen to me but I'm just some
outside observer watching a news channel or a WCN
documentary. But other times, especially in my dreams, it is as
real as if I'm reliving every excruciating minute and cannot flee to
reality, to the present.

Philadelphia suffered a lot in the attack because it is also the
closest major city to D.C. After the smoke cleared, President
Powell established refugee cities in the Richmond outskirts and
Newark. Today those cities still exist but they are formidable

places, filthy, destitute, full of the poorer radiation victims of D.C. On rare occasions our hospital receives a caravan of them visiting for supplies and treatment, but for the most part they survive there on government allocations, only to one day die sad and lonely deaths. And Liz, marvelously, healthily perhaps, let's that go. But I don't. I don't let it go. I see it, I feel it, I acknowledge it, and my best attempts at suppressing it do not make it disappear.

When he awakes, Liz suggests taking him to the neighborhood playground. I don't protest despite the inevitable dangers, because I desperately need to escape the walls of our house. The playground has had an unmistakable thinning this year. Virtually all Philadelphian children younger than the attacks have been blighted by this point, but older children still play along the monkey bars and swings. A part of me still feels nausea at the thought of what transpired this afternoon, but Liz holds my hand as we sip hot chocolate and look upon him. He giggles with each swing, steam clouds rolling upward in the frigid air from the heat of his breath. He holds the chains tightly in gloves far too big for him, and his black locks trail with the cold wind, flowing backward and forward, backward and forward. It seems so natural for him to play, as though the links of freezing fitted chain belong in his hands, and it occurs to me that someone must have taught him how to kick his feet and lean at the right time. Retrospection on this morning's events fades away, and I become nothing more than a man with his wife, watching a boy play. She remarks "He's like you in a way, I think. Bold, brave, capable of facing reality without reprisal." If only she knew.

The sun just begins to set, casting divergent colors against each other in the sky. Golds and greys decorate the horizon and the air becomes noticeably unkinder. Suddenly, something unthinkable happens. Violence, but not from him.

"You're not like us." Three teenage boys spew from the sidewalk, maybe fourteen and clothed in only black. One has shaggy long hair exposed to the air, but the other two wear dark heathered beanies. They step onto the wood-chipped playground, and make a bee-line for him.

"You're one of them, an Inexorable, aren't you?" Shaggy hair yells, rapidly shoving the Inex off the swing. He slams onto the slushy chipped wood with a discernable thump and begins to cry.

"You're a menace, you know that... A spectacle of life!" Another one pummels his thick boot into his side. The three teenagers surround him, and I see through a crack something new in his eyes: panic. Unadulterated fear of being beaten, or murdered, or sent to an Assistance Center or who knows what? To them he's just some small, insignificant toy – something to torment for pleasure, perhaps. How ironic. I rise to break up their bullying, but as I'm walking I see one pull a reflective four-inch blade from his pocket, squeezing tightly around its handle. I see in the teenager's face a disturbed severity that tells me his knife is not just for threatening. He intends to use it, he's going to stab him. I see, as if in slow motion, the blade rising into the air above his neck, casting back a mirror image of the dulling winter sky, and then as if I'm frozen but the rest of the world is on full speed, he thrusts the knife downward.

I might never understand how Liz arrived at them so fast, but as I am still feet away she already has the Inex in her arms. She screams epithets at the teenagers, but they sprint away before her artful threats come to fruition. He presses his teary face into her shoulder, and that's all it takes. It is amazing the way in which you can sense a life-changing moment when it happens. Here, now, looking at Liz, lean but determined, holding the child in her arms, I know that our world has changed. Her straight black hair, his matching curls, and their intimate position as his body forms against her torso for comfort, all preach to me, "embrace." Under her flowing red coat, it is not her arms that embrace him – it is her. She embraces him, and that's something only I can see, because I know her. The same thing that made this altercation so terrifying for the boy is the same one that made it unbearable for

Liz: the thought that he, this tiny human, was entirely alone in the world. He isn't only a danger to the world, the world is a danger to him. If belligerent teenagers weren't seeking to kill him for fun, Assistance Center workers would be seeking to kill him for country.

"Ethan, I want to name him." She approaches me, the dulling sky lighting her from behind and highlighting our breaths as they float into the air. I shake my head in disapproval, moving to her side and wrapping an arm around her.

"I want to name him Arthur." She rubs her pale pink lips together, undoubtedly cold, and squeezes the Inex a little tighter in her arms. "Arthur. It means strong doesn't it?" she asks me, her voice sounding soft and sweet. She's asking me because Arthur was my father's name.

"Stone," I correct. "Arthur means stone."

CHAPTER 7

What sort of man leaves his wife home with an Inex? The tapping of my foot and compulsive checking of my chronograph watch neither soothes me nor passes time. I push a microwave casserole around with a white plastic fork, but never acquire a desire to eat it. One second. One second is all it takes for him to grab a knife and slit her throat, or to start a fire and burn the house down with her inside, or for him to stab her, or bite her finger off, or god, even worse things. Two hands squeeze my shoulders and jolt me for a moment.

"Ethan, you seem off. How was your weekend?" Jim's southern voice sounds from behind me. He skirts around the dark industrial table, two pristine Georgia boots resounding his steps. He sits down facing me.

"You wear those just to embarrass me, don't you?" I quip.

"Well now, they're perfectly comfortable, which you would realize if you would only remove the rod stuck up your ass." Jim is handsome, but he has the unfortunate condition of smiling like a demented clown. A half smile highlights crescent wrinkles around his mouth, a single dimple presses deep into his face, and half of his teeth peer out clenched so tightly that it makes his smile look painful. "Oh, I'm sorry, that's not quite proper now is it? Better said, you would realize it if you would only remove 'the obtruding foreign object from your rectal cavity.'" His voice gets nasally as he maims an impression of me, then he releases a short burst of satisfied laughter.

"I don't sound like that," I say.

"Sure ya do. You're way too uptight. Which brings me to what I was just saying, what's going on with you?" His head darts back and forth obnoxiously trying to catch my exhausted eyes, but I ignore him. I debate lying for a moment, considering that the less information others have the better it will be. If I don't tell him, however, he would probably just call Liz, and Liz would tell him in some sanguine fashion that would make the whole thing sound very innocuous and maternal.

"I have news," I state as quietly and monotonously as I can so as not to attract the attention of others in the break room. His face get a devious sense of delight, and he leans in marginally closer.

"On Friday night I took an Inexorable home."

"What!?" he exclaims under his breath.

"He's still there. We're kind of... keeping him for now," I say even-handedly. I gaze up to see thick greying wheat hair atop skeptical sky-blue eyes that say 'I'm pretty sure you're just jerking my chain, but I'll wait for clarifying information.' "I'm having a hard time turning him over to the AC. He's tiny, maybe four, and he talks! When I found him he was freezing to death."

"You've lost your damn mind." His excited smirk shifts to a serious expression.

"At this point, I know that. I know it. God, he mutilated a cat on Sunday – I mean," I begin to feel nauseated, like a snake of emotion has taken up its home in my stomach and is slithering up my throat. "He pried out its eyes and squeezed them like stress balls." I make a clenching motion with my fists, in several quick spurts, to illustrate. "'Red and red' he said, because he made art by pummeling the cat's organs into a red block of our living room rug. And the worst part is, that I covered it up. Liz has no idea that this happened, and she's home alone with him today." I let my head fall into my hands and I rub steady circles around my temples with my thumbs.

"Welp, no time like the present to tell her!" he says.

"I'm not telling her." I scowl. He flashes me a prototypical condemnatory face. I hear the grey door creak open behind me.

"Ethan, when you're done I need you for something," Singh says.

"Alright," I respond, and Dr. Singh exits without a noise.

"If you want my advice, then here it is: you can't keep the kid, and if you wanna protect your wife you better have her call a center now. Not ten minutes from now, but now." Jim rises from his titanium framed chair. I rise as well and toss my uneaten meal into the garbage.

The moment that I saw the boy his fate became intrinsically related, if not altogether determined, by my choices. Had I seen him and simply left him he would have died. Had I called the AC and had them take him away, he would have died. But if I took him, even if for only one night, he would live. The only option at hand where I did not directly cause the death of the boy is the one that I chose, and who can deny the propriety of that? It is this same choice that I have continued to make, each day, each hour. I choose not to kill. Even if the killing is legal, even if it would be better for us, I choose not to kill. But that's the problem, isn't it? The boy would never make the same choice. In a world where he could choose life or death for another, he would always choose death. Murder. Violence. Far from feeling conflicted about whether or not he should let another die, he would gladly accelerate the death of them and feel pleasure. He's sick. And this thing, this hellish creature, is at home with my wife, and who could deny the impropriety of that?

I push through the door, and turn to the left toward Singh's office. To the right is a patient waiting area, which has one of the only carpeted spaces in the hospital. Among the chairs, two blue suede couches sit perpendicular to each other, giving them views to two separate works of art. The pieces of art are so miscellaneous and atrocious that they might very well give someone an aneurism. The couch closest to me gets a straight view of a large multi-medium rooster. Rusted metal slivers form the beak and a few feathers, pressed chestnut leaves fill out the rest. The legs are painted on, and the background scene might be done in oil. But the most offensive part of this 'art' is the sticker eyeball, the kind where if you shook it the pupil would move around. If I served on the board, my first order of business would be to remove this piece from the hospital. The second painting is not much better, albeit, it is already superior on account of being uniform. Just canvas and paint. It is a portrait of an African American man that looks like an elementary school art project. One eye is much larger than the other, and his nose reaches from just above the eyes down fully to the lips. Red highlighting coats the left of his face, making it look as though he was a severe burn victim. Best of all, protruding from his face are twenty or so beams of rainbow color, as if he was moving at warp speed through rainbow space. In this room it's just him and the rooster, and they deserve each other, but it's unfair that the rest of us should have to see them.

I knock on Singh's office door, and he shouts a welcome. The office is a cramped square of forest green carpet, fiberboard cabinetry with cheap veneer, and a pseudo-walnut desk. On the desk sits a miniature glass obelisk, the Philadelphia Humanitarian Award, given to all first responders during the American Bioterror Attacks. I have the same one at home.

"Yes, Radheshyam, you wanted to see me?" I draw out slowly, annunciating each syllable of his name with a grin.

"Oh my word, Ethan. Don't call me that. I told you to call me John, or Singh. Or John," he insists.

"Yes, but John isn't your name. Radheshyam is." I wait for his glare.

"Sheesh, Ethan, you're acid. Call me Singh." I nod to comply, with no intention of actually changing our custom. Undoubtedly originating in some high school, the term "acid" became an expression to describe anything mind-numbing. The acids in Obcasus melted the brain, and so your dad joke is 'acid.' Your dumb roommate: 'acid,' your professor's boring lectures: 'acid.' I can't help but laugh to hear Singh use it.

"I needed to talk to you because I have to send you to the Assistance Center off nineteenth today," he says as he sips a cup of his usual Rooibos tea.

"What? Why?" I ask too rashly. He knows about Arthur, doesn't he? Somehow he found out that I took him. The security cameras, probably. He reported it and now Arthur is going to be executed, and Liz is going to be reprimanded if not arrested. Or maybe he hurt her, and she's here in the hospital and the AC took him away to protect everyone. My next swallow feels tight.

"When was the last time you saw a Polio case?" Singh asks, oblivious to my panic. The question surprises me. Just answer it calmly, I tell myself.

"Only once, in first year residency when I went to Turkey for the HID program." There hasn't been a domestic Polio case since I graduated from medical school. Our vaccination protocols are effective and mandatory, even for Inexorables.

"They think one of the Inexes there had Polio. They wanted to send the body here, but, I gave them the obvious 'hell no.'" He nervously giggles at his remark. "But still, they need it identified, so I am going to send you to take some samples and verify here, and then we can report back to the CDC – maybe gain a little more notoriety, no?"

"Uh huhhh," I say, seeing his angle now. My eyebrows furrow at him, creases forming beside my eyes. Anything to bring more funding into the hospital.

"It's a public health service. Do it for what's right." He smiles half-authentically.

"Fine. What sort of infection control do they have in place?"

"Not much from what I heard. You best go prepared."

"But the Inex is dead, correct?" I clarify.

"Right."

"That is helpful."

Polio is a virus which is easy to contain in the dead. The virus, like many others, is spread from mucus and feces only. If it turns out that the Inex indeed had Polio, which is a near impossibility, then it need only be sealed in a body bag and all that it came into contact with sanitized. The scary prospect is not that it might spread among the population, as virtually all people in the city are vaccinated and the truncated number of children has widely disrupted the spread of even the most common infectious diseases, but that someone brought Polio into the country in the first place. I mindlessly gather supplies from the laboratory: masks and gloves, vials and serological fluid, swabs, and one of the hospital's digital pads for taking pictures and recording data, and drive a quiet fifteen minutes with thoughts racing over what I am about to see.

I park on the street a short distance from the center. Something feels ominous about this day, this task, and this place, and I don't want to be seen parking directly in front of it. The Assistance Center is a three-story Greystone building with enormous white paneled windows on the second floor, but only tiny crevices for windows on the first. The front doors are large white-washed wood. Above the door the stones form a rounded arch, and on the corners and sides of the building pink and green ivy swathe the walls. It appears altogether quite beautiful, and antique, and welcoming. The east side of the building contains a hidden driveway for Inexes to be discreetly transported from containment bus to building. It's all rather clean and unobjectionable on the outside, but the inside is what concerns me. It's the inside that has given me nightmares, and, for the past four days, the greatest moral uncertainties of my life. It isn't that I think it's universally wrong to kill Inexorables, because, I truly don't. They're evil, and in some real sense they deserve to die. It's just that, I don't think it's universally right to kill Inexorables either. They are shattered brains that grew within damaged bodies. The fact that they have no chance of hope does not plague me as much as the fact that they *never* had a chance of hope. It's the permanence of the whole thing, that damnable quality that makes it hard to even look at them sometimes. They're just a pitiful existence, a biological error good for nothing more than eradication. I hate it. I used to hate it, but now I hate it more, so much more.

CHAPTER 8

W hen I enter through the doors I am greeted by the smell of lemon peels and a blast of dry heated air. A middle-aged woman with curly blonde dyed hair and thin frameless glasses is sitting behind a white plastic desk. She must be the office assistant. There are a few waiting area chairs, but no one else is in the room.

"Hi. How can I help you?" She says in a high nasally voice. She looks at me nervously, darting her eyes between my bag and my face, bag and face, over and over. It's making me uncomfortable, and I'm already uncomfortable.

"I'm Dr. Ethan King, I'm here to examine one of the Inexes for a possible Polio infection...?"

"Ahhh." She sighs with an amused smile and presses a button on a machine I cannot see. "Enaria, Dr. King from Philadelphia East is here. Would you like to meet him at the door?"

"No, I can't actually. My hands are kind of full. Just send him in," a raspy female voice responds.

"Sure thing," blonde curls says, releasing her finger from the button and rising to her feet. She buzzes open two automated wooden doors to my left, and makes hand gestures to accompany her instructions. "You see the second hallway? Make a right there, and then it will be the second door on your left. Enaria will be with you shortly." I nod, and she gives a warm smile to me as I walk through the doors.

I follow her instructions to a T, second hallway, second door on the left, pulling open a pale wood door with a silver pipe handle. I push my body through the frame, unsuspectingly into the mortuary of the building. In front of me are several silver tables, ones reserved for the dead even in our hospital. On three of them are tiny bodies, just children, two partially covered with blue disposable sheet and one entirely naked. The one that is entirely naked is only an infant, no more than ten months old. They look harmless and innocent, too tiny to do anything wrong enough to deserve death.

Don't look at the hands or faces, don't look at the hands or faces, I repeat.

They are just Inexes. Just killers. But how can a baby be a killer? What awful deed could it have possibly committed? As I inch closer the smell of methanol and alcohol intensifies and my hands begin to tremble. The small heads of the pale, rigid bodies have gauze taped securely over their left temple, with blood and fluid seeping through. That's curious.

The back left corner of the room has a wide metal swinging door with a sign that says "operating room." That is even more curious. I walk past the body-tables and peer through the screened window in the upper middle section of the metal door. Inside is an empty room with one table and a blue glow. I push through, the door swinging unabatedly behind me, and once inside I pause to take in every detail, every inch, every piece of information that this room offers me. I'm not sure if it's unadulterated suspicion that's driving me, or genuine curiosity, but in less than a minute neither are satisfying. The operating room is the most uninhabitable place that I have ever stood. An ice cold draught blows along my exposed skin while I look upon cramped stainless steel walls which are insulated to keep sound from escaping. The ceiling has a dismal blue glowing uplighter in the shape of a figure eight stretching from one end of the ceiling to the other, which casts an unpleasant hue onto everything. The floor, reflecting much of the painful blue, is a resin-coated white ceramic, standard in operating rooms because it's easy to clean. In the center of the room one reclining chair, like in a dentist's office, lays coated in tight clear nylon. Only, unlike a dentist's chair, it also has yellow belted restraints systematically placed every few inches along its frame. It's like a dentist's executioner's chair. Great, because that's never been a kid's nightmare before. Beside the chair is the most confusing piece. On a silver tray-table sits only 3 objects: gauze, medical tape, and a surgical bone drill fitted with an extended quarter inch bit. Why only those three? What would they need the bone-drill ....

Oh god. That's how they euthanize them. They drill holes into their skulls. They shove a bone drill into their brain and spin them around until they're liquefied.

The children are literally lobotomized to death.

The urge to vomit suddenly overwhelms me. How could they do that? How could they do such an atrocious thing to children, even sick children like these? It's despicable! We don't even euthanize our dogs in such a brutish way! The room spins fast to the right, and then upward and sideways in a snake-like slither across my vision, and suddenly, as if the room became animate, the steel wall to my left plunges upward crashing against the side of my face with a clang and a sting. Suddenly the steel panel is the floor, which I am laying on top of, trying with all of my might to slowly and carefully push myself up from. Each slow breath brings in a better picture of reality, the room beginning to form back into order: ugly blue lamp is up, chilling ceramic floor is down, tormenting horizontal steel parallels my sides. Did I pass out, or only almost pass out? I take one more slow breath while stumbling through the silver swinging door and back into the morgue.

The only pleasant thing about a room like this one is its silence. No one talks, no one obnoxiously chews, no one makes slurping sounds on straws, no one argues, no one coughs or sniffles, it's just quiet. Death is quiet. But tiny lobotomized bodies spoil even that small blessing. I take calculated steps toward the Inex closest to me, a girl from the look of it, making sure my orientation doesn't betray me and cast me into another wall. The girl in front of me is possibly three, black, presented with four elongated pale-pink scars along her abdomen, not from a surgical instrument, more like from an animal attack. She has thick eyelashes that fan up from her face like palm leaves, and wild chocolate ringlets which shoot off from her skull in every direction except for the few stuck in the tape securing the gauze to her temple. I grit my teeth until they hurt trying to suppress the image of white brain matter oozing from the hole under the gauze. It's repulsive. She has thin rounded eyebrows and a tiny button nose that reflects the overhead LED lamp which distributes even white light over the room.

I wonder if she's the suspected Polio case. Behind her on another table is a boy a bit older than her – he looks as big as Arthur, and his hands are permanently cast into fists as rigor mortis sets in. It flashes me back to Arthur clenching and unclenching feline eyeballs with a smile of delight. I jump when the door with the silver pipe handle pushes open suddenly, revealing a tan, freckled woman with an evenly-parted dusky brown bob tucked behind her ears. She looks much younger than me, thirty at the oldest, and is wearing peculiar pink scrub pants with a black graphic t-shirt, exposing her noticeably masculine arm muscles.

"I'm Enaria." She approaches me and shakes my hand with a painfully hard grip.

"I'm Ethan, it's good to mee...." She cuts me off.

"This is the body you need to inspect. Here. This one," she points at the boy multiple times, and her face glares at me irritably.

"Okay... Let me grab my..." I open my bag to pull out the tablet.

"He presented with partial paralysis, fever, flu like symptoms, and possible vision loss. It was difficult to tell. We weren't concerned about it, but protocol says we have to call and report it anyway."

"Ma'am, I need to document this for hospital record, can you pause for one moment?" I ask with an intentionally patient tone despite her obnoxious attitude. I glance up from my bag to see her rolling her blue-grey eyes at me. Charming. Once I swipe the tablet on, she repeats her exact words in the same detached tone as before. I only nod in response. I slide latex gloves over my hands, and begin to perform a standard exam on the Inex. I feel along his lymph nodes, examining his cool umber skin for rashes or degeneration, vocally reporting the details as I find them into the tablet.

"Male, possibly four years old, mild lymphadenopathy obfuscated by rigor mortis, but nevertheless not enough to indicate Polio," I state.

Miss Caustic begins impatiently tapping her foot as she stares, and I try to ignore her. The boy has flaring nostrils and foul-smelling short dreadlocks; the kind you get from inability to care for yourself. I lift the medical sheet and examine his legs and feet for anything notable.

"Unkempt toenails, altogether dirty presentation. Likely homeless, increasing the risk of standard viral and bacterial infections," I continue dictating. Enaria says something under her breath.

"What's that?" I ask irritably, unable to conceal my frustration with her.

"Yes. He was on the street. Look, I have things to tend to. I will send someone else in to help," she says numbly and, without acknowledging my nod, exits the room.

I pause the recording to simply stare at the boy. He's so much like Arthur. Not in the way he looks, but his condition: born broken, left out for exposure in winter, but unlike Arthur, executed. His clenched fists remind me why, but it's hard to understand, it's hard to accept when this tiny body is lying in front of me. One way or another this is Arthur's future. If he stays sick, if he stays an Inexorable, he will die. I stare his destiny in the face, and I feel it as my hands touch along this rigid body.

But what if he could change, or be changed? What if they all could? What if lying before me is not simply a dead boy, not simply a dead psychopath, but raw material to provide the cure? What if I just took a little brain tissue and studied only one slide of it to see if there's something I can discern, an answer hiding inside of it? If it's useless then no one would know. It would be one tiny, microscopic secret, but a secret that holds promise for an overlooked detail or a chemical reaction that could change the whole Inex cerebrum.

I pull out a vial and an empty metal syringe to extract cerebrospinal fluid for the Polymerase Chain Reaction test that indicates Polio. As I insert the syringe into the center of the spine a new woman enters the room. She is heavy, pale as snow with rosy red cheeks, and bright copper hair. She is not in any way what I would consider an attractive woman, but she is wearing a marvelously refreshing smile.

"My name is Lapis Muir, welcome to our facility!" Her voice is high, almost tiny in sound.

"Hi. I'm Ethan."

"Hi Ethan. How is your work coming?" she asks, and walks toward me with a light bounce in her step.

"Fine I'd say. Unfortunately, the rigor is more difficult to work around than I expected. It will take more time, especially to get the throat secretions." I empty my syringe into the vial, quickly sealing it and replacing it with a new one in my hands.

"I can help if you'd like?" she asks hesitantly, almost as if she is trying to be careful not to impose.

"Actually, that would be helpful. If you could hold the pliers between the jaw I could simply swab the throat and it would be simple from there." I feel an itch in my throat from the dry air.

"Sure, that wouldn't be a problem whatsoever!" she cheers and bounces over to me, step after step of considerable weight flowing as seamlessly as a ballerina.

"You have an interesting name," I state while shoving the pliers between the farthest back part of the jaw, where teeth have had no time to grow. I feel them tearing against lifeless gums.

"Oh thank you! I think so too, but most people never say anything about it. Not that I see as many people as I would like to, let alone get to introduce myself to. But... Do you know what Lapis Lazuli is?" She leans in closely to assist me.

"Not really, no." I pull the pliers with painful force and the jaw slowly cracks open.

"Oh, it's a gemstone. It looks like flickers of stars in deep blue space sometimes, or sometimes it looks just like the earth from space, and even sometimes it looks like an entire universe. I was named after that stone." Her voice has a wistful quality, like she is visibly seeing what she is describing.

"Why, if you don't mind me asking?" I gesture for her to hold open the pliers while I grab my several swabs.

"It's a bit complicated but I don't mind explaining it. My father studied art in college, he was an artist in fact – genius of a man and still would be if not for Obcasus, such a monster isn't it? Well anyway, he studied art and told me that blues used to be painted using ground up Lapis, a precious gem, because it was the only source of such a deep blue color at the time. No synthetics of course. But, amazingly, the Sistine Chapel was uniquely completed without using Lapis unlike all other frescoes at the time. My father, not a particularly religious man, was charmed by this. He thought that the Sistine Chapel lacked a sort of realism, a sort of truth. One day while contemplating what it was about this fresco that made it lose such touch with reality, one of his classmates remarked 'Lapis. It's missing lapis.' Or so he claims anyway. Lo and behold, Lapis became his encompassing term for all that is true. Lapis looked like the earth, like the universe, like water and the stars.... Lapis was the visible universe, the observable, the truth. So he named me that, and considered me a completed artwork so to say."

"Wow." I look into her eyes astounded, with one swab fully engulfed in the stale Inex's mouth. Never in my life have I heard a name given with more thought or meaning, even if the sound of it is pitifully grisly. Lapis, I repeat in my mind. The more I hear it, the more the word sounds ugly and not at all peppy and pleasant like the person standing before me.

"Oh yeah well I'm sure I'm boring you," she says with almost a sense of shame.

"No, not at all actually. Real fast, I need to grab some brain tissue sample for testing," I lie.
"How long since this one has been... was... euthanized?" I struggle to remember what the politically correct term is for killing them.

"Oh, you mean *resolved?* Quite some time, at this point. Hours."

"I see. In that case, it will be necessary to take a sample from another in order to compare and contrast." Another lie. But the more samples I can examine the better my chance of finding something of value.

"Oh that's quite fine!" she encourages.

"Thank you. Can I ask you something, Lapis?"

"Sure thing."

"What is with the blue color in there?" I gaze over to the operating room.

"In the OR? Oh, that's color psychology. It's supposedly the case that blue makes people feel trusting, so it helps the Inexes trust us and cooperate. I don't know if it really works on them though. Their brains aren't like the rest of us, they always seem discontent – but I like to think that they're happy when they're resolved."

"Why not sedate them?" I ask, my nausea returning to me at the thought of conscientiously trying to get Inexorables to trust them before sticking a bone drill into their brains.

"Expense, really. It's just far more cost effective to use the drill. It's painless, humane, instant, and not very much clean up. It's all around the best approach. If I had to die in an unnatural way, this would be top of my list!" She answers each question with off-putting ease, as if we were talking about books or music, or pot-roast recipes.

"Mind if I ask you another question?"

"No, sir. Please. Ask as many as you'd like! It's great to have a friendly face in here. Jeanne's okay, but Enaria is, well. Unique let's say."

"Ha!" I bust out, unable to control my response.

"She just takes her work very seriously." She nods to herself while saying it.

"Don't you?" I ask, stuffing the official test vials into the black square bag. I pull out two spare vials, and begin retrieving brain tissue from the drill hole in the boy's skull.

"Oh sure. But I sort of see the beauty and positivity in everything! Enaria sort of does the opposite, and she seems quite proud of that. And, honestly, that scares me a little bit." She does a dramatized shudder.

"How do you see the beauty in a job like this?" I pry.

"Well. I think we're helping people, don't you?"

"It would seem to depend on which people you're referring to." I touch the stiff clenched hand of the unnamed boy.

"Inexes you mean?" Her face for the first time doesn't look unabatedly pleasant, but confused. I sigh deeply.
"Well, perhaps not. But don't you ever wonder if you're killing a real person, a human, and not just an Inex?" I say somewhat quietly, while using a thin blade to cut a wider diameter around the hole which is crusted with blood and white brain matter.

"Oh we wouldn't just take anyone. Not surprisingly there are a few freaks who try to get rid of their healthy toddlers. Makes me sick! No, in order to use the AC the Inexes have to be verified by a CT scan. It's super easy to identify. Not all of the scarring is the same, but it's always very widespread." She smiles and moves her head in affirming ways while she speaks. It's not at all what I had meant. I remove a small sliver of brain tissue, somewhat undamaged by the drill, and carefully place it into the vial.

"I need to gather a sample from a healthy brain to compare with the results of this one. A control group, since the tissue is older." Another lie.

"Sure, do you need help?" she asks, as I turn around to face the female body.

"I don't think so." I quickly make the same extension of the open tissue, and search for healthy segments to thinly slice and place in my vial. When I finish, Lapis is twirling the ends of her copper hair and staring at me a little too affectionately for comfort.

"I'll tip my hand here and say that I don't see the signs of a Polio infection, at least from my paper knowledge of it. However, as a precaution I do think we need to contain the specimen so that if Polio is present it isn't spread any farther," I try to speak as professionally as possible.

"Sure. We do use body bags, they are just here," she traces along the aisle formed by the silver body tables toward the Operating Room. She then makes a jaggedly sharp right turn, and from the wall pulls out a silver drawer, sifting through it quickly before pulling out an envelope-sized black pouch. "They're small so we have size-appropriate ones." She meticulously unfolds it, layer by layer.

"But is it effective protection against contagions?" I ask quickly.

"Oh sure. It might not look like much, but it's designed for bio-hazard, and has the added benefit of EPA burn specs. It's a win-win: they're good for transport and then they're tossed right into the fire without issue!" she says while unzipping the unfolded material.

"You cremate them?"

"The Inexes? Yes, of course! Twelve at a time at the facility just a few blocks west. Once we have enough here we place them in an amazingly small box and set them outside for bus pickup. It's very light because the Inexes are still small. It isn't going to be so easy when they get older. But thankfully there will be very few older ones as time moves forward." Her perkiness, despite the solemnity of the topic, is becoming not only unusual but annoying. I try not to let my agitation show. Lapis and I both lift the boy into the bag and zip it shut. Afterward we sanitize the room and dispose of all the materials used in a biohazard box.

When Lapis is escorting me out of the room she surveys me head to toe so conspicuously that it is impossible to pretend not to notice. I avert my eyes to the back of the room and take one final gaze at the operating room with its fuzzy blue light. I hate this place with its apathetic coldness, I hate this world for requiring such a place to exist, I hate this detestable existence that we're all participating in and cannot escape from. I cannot and will not keep swallowing this horse pill of a reality that is being shoved down my throat. One day, like these Inexes, I am going to die. And when I die I want to look back on my life and say that I fought with marrow and might to fix reality... or even to simply make my city a more habitable place.

CHAPTER 9

Before my father died he used to play a lot of baseball with me and teach me all about the glorious Orioles, and the "Stinkin's" which was what he called the Nationals. Some years he'd take me to games and we'd sweat out the salt from arena hotdogs and yell obnoxious insults at our own players when they'd miss a catch. Other summers we would frequent a bar where he'd be glued to the forty-inch plasma while I played darts with old drunks. Dad was a tall muscular man who worked contentedly as an electrician, and who was was patient even under circumstances in which most men were not. He was the kind of man who was loyal to a fault, and who'd give his left arm if it meant for peace.

But he died when I was twelve just two blocks from our Oldtown Fairfax home. He wasn't struck by lightning or hit by a car, he just stepped off of a curb the wrong way, hit his head and never woke up. Neither doctors nor the coroner had any reasonable explanation for it. He didn't have a stroke, or a brain bleed, his heart was fine and his organs were healthy – he just slipped and fell and died, and there was no rhyme or reason for it. The tiniest error, in the most ordinary of circumstances, cost me a father and my mother a husband. She always said that when he died it "ruined her" and she was all too right. She constantly lamented that every aspect of her life was altered, leaving her no opportunity for comfort and no room to heal. The way that she woke up every morning and went to bed every night changed, the amount of people she cooked for and did laundry for changed, the familiar face that she looked for in crowds changed, and no one said her name "Sophia" affectionately anymore. Even though she loved me, she struggled with me. In the beginning she would hold me when I cried, but in short order she became distant, busy with full time work and with avoiding the look of my face which was a replica of my father. Sometimes it even pained me to catch myself at the right angle in a mirror.

In one afternoon I lost my dad and half of my mom, and I became angry and hard. I stopped letting myself feel pain, and life became easier again. I had this impenetrable shell around me, and it made me feel like I could breathe and live and that life wasn't overly serious. Sometimes I could almost see it, like a silver metal orb surrounded me and kept me from feeling anyone or anything.

It was an unhealthy way to live, but it was also easy and safe, and it later protected me from the travails of being a nerd in high school. In my mind, even though I had acne and straight A's, I was not a nerd. I knew myself, and the person I knew was different than the nerd that everyone else knew. I was a dark soul whose father was dead and whose mother was broken, and who didn't care about anyone else's opinions. I had found that a lot of people pretended to be like that in high school, hard and disaffected, but they actually weren't. In a way, that made making friends difficult, and so I didn't put much effort into it. Instead I tried to content myself with my metal shell, disconsolate loneliness, and punk rock. I sometimes think that if it were not for punk rock I would have killed myself in high school. That angry cynical music was enough to keep me going because it showed me that someone else existed who saw what I was seeing: that life was really screwed up. That solidarity was enough for me.

And thus, because someone understood, I kept going, until I finally met my first real friend in Elizabeth. Liz. It took years of her patience and stability to show me that she too, like my hard, jagged shell and uncannily sagacious bands, was safe. She was safe. When she vowed that nothing but death would take her away from me, I believed her. I thought on that day that it was impossible to love her more, and I have gladly accepted the revelation of how woefully ignorant that was. When you've been a student of another human being for fifteen years you absorb their preferences and priorities, their pitfalls and proficiencies, their wishes and whims – and in all these ways I now know her, and she knows me. It's the maturing of perspective and the depth of growth in the knowledge of another that only comes with time, and pain, and sacrifice. It's that day when you look at your wife's naked aging body and you don't feel any primal sense of passion or heated attraction but you still want to be with her because she is elegant and she is yours. And the excitement of newness is invariably replaced with safe familiarity, and so she doesn't expect some ravishing performance but just our routine, and it is sweet and wonderful, even if altogether ordinary.

It seems to me no small tragedy that the term ordinary, indeed the concept for which the word stands, has become an undignified and pitiable expression of humanity. "Ordinary" is for lesser beings, and everyone and his mother is exceptional in some way. I'm not exceptional and I don't care to be. I want an ordinary job, and an ordinary marriage, in an ordinary world. A desire, that I might add, is very much not going according to plan. I can say assuredly that I never saw myself sneaking misappropriated brain matter into a hospital because some psychopathic child at home with my wife has spurred me into a rash desperation for change. Change for Liz and I, change for Arthur, change for anyone who could have it; the world, if such a thing were possible.

Before I walk into the hospital I call Liz, who tells me that everything has been "fine" and "not to worry," and that Arthur has said many more words today such as "garbage" and "food" and a name "Lailah" over and over. Her voice soothes me as much as the relief of knowing that everything is safe at home.

Once in the hospital, the brain matter goes blessedly unnoticed into bio-material refrigerator. As I suspected, Singh would not dare risk Philadelphia East notoriety to some inexperienced technician's mistake, so he directed me to perform every step of the laboratory testing myself, giving me an excuse to be in the laboratory for the rest of the day with my "materials." The testing for the blood and throat secretions is routine and mundane, completed almost entirely by machines over the course of several hours. The spinal fluid, on the other hand, requires significantly more personal engagement which makes it a task I more or less enjoy. I'm familiar with PCR testing thanks to exciting yet infrequent bacterial meningitis case. I love meningitis cases because they are serious, time-sensitive, and because for whatever reason, I am very successful at treating them. There is a rush in being presented with a medical mystery, and a life that is utterly dependent on you, while having confidence that you can cure them. There is, of course, a corresponding horror when a medical mystery and dependent life are presented before you and you have no confidence that you can save them. It's what I feel like every time I look at Arthur, and it's a weight that pressed against me on every side at the assistance center.

I take the vial of spinal fluid and add the enzyme polymerase, which will synthesize the DNA of my sample so that it can be copied and rebuilt over and over until it forms a structure large enough that the computer can scan it and I can compare it with PCR Polio. I carefully place the vial into the thermal cycler and adjust the settings for my test. As I turn it on, I begin to process how I will spend the next two, unmediated hours of laboratory time while I wait on my results. More than anything I am curious as to how Dopimazipal interacts with Inexes. Unfortunately, dead tissue will not show me much because there are no living cells to carry the dopamine, but it seems rather obvious that there is a connection in the Inexorables' deformities and the dopamine producer damage in their mothers. Since this is the case, it is a fair question as to what effect D-MAZ would have on the children. Even despite their scar tissue, there must be some effect. It is not, of course, the most scientific approach to throw a bunch of brain matter against the wall and see what sticks, so to speak, but since I am not a neuroscientist and since I am better at observing tissue degeneration and drug interactions, it cannot hurt to try something bizarre.

My tissue samples are not in the best condition, but I swipe them from the refrigerator and establish a work station in the lab. In the center of the sterile-looking room a long panel of desks with computers, microscopes, and centrifuges is attended by a few technicians. I decide to work at this panel despite the audience because it's less suspicious and more than likely the technicians, like me, just want to work in peace and quiet. The computer system at the hospital is unfortunately rather corporative, and rigorously logs your actions and research under your login code. This is immensely convenient when you are doing some legitimate business such as researching a patient's condition or making biopsy observations. In a situation such as this, however, it poses a problem, but I can't forego the computer since it allows me to view the microscopic images. For now, I login with my information and run the risk of it being seen. I comfort myself with the fact that if need be I could explain it away by ignorance of what is needed to test accurately for Polio.

I put on what feels like my hundredth pair of gloves for the day and lay out six Olympus slides on the carbon counter top. I add Mag-drops, open the drawers until I find the tools that I need including a D-MAZ pen, and I begin to work. After carefully tweezing the brain tissue out of the container, I grab a twelve-blade scalpel which is curved like a velociraptor claw and has a hearty recess in it. I slice the tissue into supremely thin pieces, each movement of the blade making the tissue feel more like tofu; tender firmness but ultimate frailty under pressure. After laying each slice on a different slide I add additional Mag-drops and squirt the smallest amount of Dopimazipal onto one of the center slices. I mark each slide carefully in marker: F3LH for "Female

Three Left Hemisphere," and a star for the one exposed to D-MAZ. I then place all six into the Olympus Infinity scope, and press "Run."

The Olympus is my favorite staple in the hospital, and maybe even the prize of modern technology. It holds up to ten slides, and automatically imports 100 images of each slide into the computer system at various magnification levels within sixty seconds per slide. The Mag-drops utilize a new bioactive luminescent dye that makes the images appear as if the neurons and neuroglial cells glow bright green, dendrites and axons shining yellow and copper respectively, bacteria blazing red, traumatic scar tissue and lesions electric blue, and most importantly it discerns between the final two through the varying fibrous patterns and contrasts everything with a black background. The end result looks more like a colorful inkblot than real material, but the way that it brings out easily missed details is unparalleled.

While the images are being scanned I casually peer down the desk to my right where a mild-faced woman with glasses is typing monotonously on a keyboard. Behind her sits an overweight technician who doesn't quite fit his lab coat. He has a soda can sitting on the desk which breaks protocol, which would frustrate me if I were not breaking the law myself. When the images are loaded, a viewing box pops up on the thin computer screen. I quickly scroll through the first five hundred images.

Slide one, dead brain tissue with fibrous scarring, neurons and axons and dendrites, and nothing whatsoever of interest. Slide two, three, four, five.... Dead, dead, dead, and dead. But slide six with the Dopimazipal is, remarkably, just at first glance, different. I cannot believe what I am seeing, and I anxiously search around the room darting my eyes to see if someone is playing a sick joke on me. But it isn't funny, it isn't even explicable. Inside of slide six, something is moving. Something is alive and moving spastically across the slide as I flip through each image. The more the magnification increases, the better I am able to see what the movement is. It is something thin, and long, and there's at least a dozen distinct shapes, maybe two dozen. When I get to the correct micrometer I pause and gape at the image. At .09 micrometer in diameter and 50 micrometers in length, corkscrew shaped spirochete bacteria are pictured spinning, barreling in and out of tissue like screws. But they aren't ordinary spirochetes, they are a more complex pathogen. I scroll through a few more images for greater magnification and stare harder. The bacteria looks like a four-strand braid that has been twisted into a corkscrew, with disgusting spikey fibers protruding from the exterior spines. Four sharp points mark the opening of its mouth, like teeth for a head. My screen turns into nothing but bright glowing red bacteria the more I increase the magnification, and then suddenly I am back to the beginning of slide one.

I scroll back to slide six and fix on a single image of one of the bacteria. What the hell is going on? How? Why? When a host dies, pathogens die, that's just.... That's how it works. But these bacteria are reacting chaotically to the D-MAZ, which makes no coherent sense. D-MAZ must be killing it somehow, maybe from the enzymes in the mixture, or else why would the bacteria be awakened so dramatically, and where did it come from? I don't see it anywhere in the other slides, but I rapidly swift through the other images again for comparison. Perhaps too quickly I move to inspect the Dopimazipal, adding a drop to an empty slide and inserting it into the scope, expecting to find the pathogen hidden inside of it. When the images arrive, however, there is nothing remotely unordinary: just colorful beams of Dopamine crystals and enzymes.

Hastily, I pull out slide one of the brain tissue and add a drop of D-MAZ in an attempt to duplicate the results of slide six. My heart begins racing, sparked by either confusion or dying skepticism. The images appear, and marvelously though perplexingly, again dozens of corkscrew bacteria inextricably spasm inside the solution. They materialize from apparently nowhere. No cells to hide in, no tissue to burrow out from. They weren't there, and now, they are. The presence of a bacteria is not surprising, especially in Inexorable children who are left out for exposure. Ticks bite them, transmit the spirochete that causes Lyme, and then the bacteria duplicates and ravages the tiny bodies because treatment of Inexorables is unheard of. The three problems are that this is not Lyme bacteria or any other bacteria that I have ever seen before. Secondly, the girl did not appear to be left out for exposure, and finally, the bacteria appeared from nothing as a response to Dopimazipal, which is impossible.

My hands begin to tremble, and I become immediately concerned that someone else might see these slides. I do not know what I have stumbled upon, but whatever it is, it's new. I minimize the images, sinking into my chair and I stare up at the white speckled ceiling panels. I anxiously rub my hand over my face a few times, and try to process how this could occur. My best guess is that the enzyme complex in the dopamine serum is awakening a dormant bacteria, and that the bacteria is hiding in such a way that neither I nor the most powerful microscope in the hospital can see it until it has been awakened. I impulsively tap my shoe against the ceramic flooring, which instantly unsettles the technicians. Sitting up straight, I begin the same testing for the male brain samples. Six glass slides, six less exact brain tissue slices on account of my trembling hands, and this time I douse three of the samples with Dopimazipal. I then mark them M4LH, for "Male Four Left Hemisphere," and star those treated with D-MAZ. I'm not expecting the same results, because the likelihood of these two unrelated Inexes contracting the same unfamiliar bacterial infection is desperately slim.

In the six minutes that I wait for the new images I prepare a bacterial screening on the female brain tissue exposed to D-MAZ. Because I have already identified it as a spirochete of some type, I am able to narrow the testing to only varieties of Borrelia, T. Pallidum, Trep Perinue, and Leptospira. Before I can test the samples, I must homogenize the tissue in a sample blender until it becomes a liquid and then I add it to the vials of gel. I walk in a consciously unhurried manner to the electrode chamber on the back wall of the lab and carefully insert the vial and enter my test codes, peering over my shoulder once to see if the technicians are watching but they are not. I return to my computer, and view the new images.

There are these rare moments when something so impacts the way you process truth and reality, that you know you will never be the same. The sounds of the men, women, and children choking during the attacks was one of these occasions. I knew at the time that I would never forget those sounds or images, and that I would carry their suffering and deaths around with me for the rest of my life. I don't think about them often, but every few months something will spark a memory of their faces and it will remind me that they don't exist anymore, and that they died in such a horrific way. And here too, hidden within these images, is a category shift that I can never go back from. Inside the brain tissue of this Inexorable boy, staring me in the eyes, are pointed, squirming, living pathogens. Some could consider it a mere coincidence that these two samples of brain tissue contain the same mysterious pathogen activated by Dopimazipal, but I don't believe in coincidence. This is anything but probable, yet anything but coincidence: it is suspicious and frightening and inexplicable.

I continue to inspect the microscopic pathogens, one by one, magnifying and demagnifying for what could be minutes or hours, when without notice, right before my eyes, the images disappear. Vanish. My heart skips and I race through my files and hidden storage folders, even the recycling bin, but they are gone. In an instant, 1200 images disappeared from my account and I am left staring at an empty screen. It isn't a computer issue because in a moment the blood results for the Polio test appear on my screen: no antibody response, and thus no active sign of Polio. But the images are gone. They're gone, deleted, disappeared from my account without my doing. Someone is in my account, reviewing my actions, and they saw this and erased it. Which means, whatever this is, whatever I have stumbled upon is a secret. My chest gets warm, my pupils dilate, and I lift the Dopimazipal shot in front of my eyes. Someone has been lying, either about Obcasus, or Dopimazipal, or Inexorables. Something isn't adding up. Something has been concealed, hidden away, protected and now, whatever it is, I have a piece of it. I discovered a secret, and now someone has discovered me.

I clear my account logs as much as I am able to, leaving only those documents associated with the Polio testing, and then shut off the computer. I dispose of the brain tissue discreetly in the biomaterial bin, covering it with some paper towels and my latex gloves, which we're not supposed to do. I adjust the settings on the electrode chamber to report the results of the female Inexorable bacteria type through print only. The machine warns me multiple times that this is not recommended and that it could lead to permanently losing test results. I consent twice before it processes my request. The bacteria cultures finish much faster that I would have expected, and magnificently, they came back with a family match: Leptospira.

Leptospira is a family of bacteria that causes biphasic diseases like Anthrax or West Nile, sometimes Meningitis. What is hard to account for, however, is that the type of antibody that reacted positively to the Leptospira is not a kind that exists in humans. L. Noboru exists only in rodents, and more frustratingly, L. Noboru doesn't look like what I saw. What I saw had been mutated, covered with long sharp spikes that shot out from its multiple spines. The bacteria was not normal, it was malformed. It makes no damn sense whatsoever.

I mindlessly fold the positive culture sheet into my pocket, while shredding and tossing the rest along with the sample material, covering it again with paper towels. I walk over and check on my final Polio test, which still needs some time. I exit the bright quiet lab to plant myself in the break room for a while. I just need to caffeinate and think and maybe slam my head against a wall until something clicks. There are many break rooms in the hospital, but I always use the one closest to the ER because it's typically emptier and because it's the one Jim uses. What makes it the destitution of break rooms is that it does not have a true coffee maker, instead it has a vending machine that spits acidic black sludge into a Styrofoam cup for two bucks, and that's if you get a cup. Sometimes you're lucky enough for the machine to have run out of cups, and for your sludge to be properly disposed directly into the drainage system. Nevertheless, as I push through the swinging door I march straight to the rectangular machine, which produces the ulcer-causing concoction just as expected, and into a cup this time. I pull the cheap plastic door to retrieve my coffee and sit down at the same table as this afternoon. The room is empty, allowing me to carelessly support my feet with a second chair before slugging down deeply into the cheap plastic.

With the cup held tightly in both of my hands I stare down at the aromatic vapors wafting into the air and it reminds me of the attack; the gas rising into the city from giant metal cylinders. I swallow a gulp that's a bit too hot and it slides down my throat in a burning knot. I inhale deeply and refocus myself. Obcasus. Nerve gas. A gas which causes Parkinson's-type symptoms in those exposed. A gas which has only one successful treatment: D-MAZ. A gas which causes extensive brain scarring in offspring. D-MAZ, a concoction of enzymes and dopamine needed on a daily basis to treat the effects of Obcasus. Bacteria, hidden away, possibly in scar tissue which comes alive with D-MAZ. I set my coffee down and drag my hands down my tired face. Obcasus means chemical acids which cause Dopamine producer damage. Dopamine-producer damage means fetal scar tissue, and fetal scar tissue means what? Bacteria?

Oh my god. I know what it is.

CHAPTER 10

Home is strange now, like my place most marked by rest has been swallowed up in the mouth of chaos and gnawed on until unrecognizable. What is rest? Every single action at home is marred by constant rigidity as I safeguard Arthur's movements. If I brew a pot of coffee I have to meticulously survey the kitchen to make sure he isn't climbing onto the counter to reach the stowed away knives, or taking a vase to shatter on the tile, or beating his own head into a window –which apparently he likes to do. If I get dressed I have to physically restrain him with one arm while doing so or he finds some creative item to throw at my skull. But I marvel when I see him with Liz. She seems able to somehow process the change in lifestyle with ease. Sure, the first time I was home alone with him he mutilated a cat, but the first time she was home alone with him it went "fine" and she even progressed his language skills. The contrast in our natural abilities is laughable. The most peculiar thing is that he seems to genuinely enjoy being carried on her hip, and instead of biting her neck or clawing at her face like I would expect, he strokes her shiny black hair like he were petting a family dog and says "Lailah," to her. It leads me to believe that he once had someone who protected him, who fed him and carried him on their hip, only to abandon him to a parking garage to die alone in the cold. It reminds me of yesterday, and the boy about Arthur's age who had lain rigid and maimed on the AC table. It overwhelms me with the sense that unlike Liz, and unlike me, he is alone in this world.

The first beam of golden light streams through the east window and casts an imprint on the ceiling. I shove another russet pillow behind my back, sitting up in bed, and the dazed picture my eyes present to me tells me that I'm desperate for caffeine.

"How do you do that?" I gaze at Liz curiously, while she adjusts Arthur on her hip in front of the bed. She bounces on her feet, gracefully shifting weight from one leg to the other.

"Do what?" her voice is still quiet and tired like my own.

"Carry him like that? Get him to listen to you?" Get him not to slice open animals when you're not looking is what I'm really thinking. She purses her lips while she thinks.

"I don't know. I think he just likes me, like I look like someone he knows. Lailah or whoever." We both nod.

"I've thought that as well. But how do you get anything done when he's with you? He's constantly trying to injure me."

"Oh I didn't get anything done yesterday, I called yesterday a sick day and skipped out on work." She laughs. Liz works from home reviewing quality control audits for the monopoly energy supplier, Ecore. She is one of the most focused and efficient workers I have ever seen, which allows her to work part time hours for full time pay.

"But he didn't attack you or anything?" I clarify.

"No. Maybe it's maternal instinct or something, but he seems to be okay with me. Also I found that he likes this." She pushes her thin fingers through his thick curls and scratches along his scalp. His small face scrunches together around his nose, with a subtle smile curling up his left cheek. I can't help but smile. The scene looks so natural, her bare morning face beautiful in that ageless way, a lavender silk nightgown flowing behind each of her dancing movements, a smiling child still sleepy in the eyes from the night before, and a room full of warm colors on this cold winter morning. It's like a normal home, but I remind myself that it's just some strange façade of one instead.

"Do you want to go to Kerrigan's before work?" she asks me. Kerrigan's is a diner one block from my work that we frequent together.

"With him?" I raise my left eyebrow high at her.

"No, I thought we'd leave him here and just you and I go." She squints her eyes at me like she does when she's being sarcastic.

"He doesn't even have his own clothes, and he might hurt someone at the restaurant," I press.

"So two things, or well, more than two things. First, he does have clothes. Actually, he has a lot more than clothes because I may or may not have gone shopping yesterday, and by that I mean I did. So he also has an age appropriate car seat, special drinks to help put weight on him, a bed that I brilliantly plan to put into this sophisticated play area, which really it's a large animal cage, but I'd like to call it a play area. Two, we went out yesterday and he seemed okay. I mean, he freaked out in the store, but I bought some toys that he likes – he really liked these squeezy slime ball things, and I thought what could be more harmless than that?" Heat forms behind my eyes but I blink it back. "And three, I'm hungry and you know I don't cook. So what are we going to do about that?"

"About your cooking disability? I've been wondering that for years."

She smiles and throws a decorative pillow from the edge of the bed at my face. Arthur bursts out with a full belly laugh, throwing his head back while he does, a few stray curls sticking over his face. Liz and I lock eyes, sharing a moment of pleasant surprise, and then we laugh too.

"Don't you feel bad for always getting what you want? Like you're plundering me and my good cheer?" I ask.

"Good cheer? Since when in the history of *ever* has Ethan King had 'good cheer' hmm?" She squints at me again but this time with a grin.

***

Kerrigan's is one of those crapshoot diners whose food is hit or miss but whose coffee is always excellent. It's a block away from the hospital which makes it a no-brainer for meals before work, because the only other option is a twenty-four hour cheesesteak shop that is guaranteed to give you diarrhea. We're known by name at Kerrigan's, and we know all of the waitresses plus the one gender dysphoric waitress or whatever that is called. His... her...their name is Sun. The other waitresses are Eloise, Karissa, Jane, and Sophia. As Liz and I park our separate cars on the street, I wonder how they will react to seeing a child with us who we've never mentioned having. Suddenly we say, "Oh, did we mention that we're parents? No? Surprise! We kidnapped an Inexorable and we're raising him like an ordinary human!" The whole thing feels ominous.

I hold the shiny chrome door open for Liz, who's bundled in layers of fabric underneath a purple coat. Arthur waddles in behind her in the orange inflated ensemble she dressed him in. It's somewhat adorable to watch. The bell attached to the door makes a twangy ring when it shuts, and we seat ourselves at an open booth against the right wall windows. Liz sets Arthur between us, and he does a little nudging bounce on the red vinyl cushion. The smell of grease and coffee wafts through the air. Liz and I instinctually flip our mugs top-up, but then she unusually pushes every item on the table to the far side, out of Arthur's reach. A burst of chilly air courses over us and the twangy bell sounds again. Suddenly a southern voice intrudes on us from behind.

"Well what do I fancy here? Friends in the morning patronizing the same very restaurant that I am now myself patronizing?" It's Jim. He approaches our booth with a blithe smile and sits down opposite us.

"You called him?" I glare at Liz. My heart begins to race thinking that he might have told her about the cat.

"Well, I thought he might want to meet him. Don't you?" she whispers to me, as if Jim cannot hear us.

"Uh huh," I respond, trying to catch eyes with Jim, who simply smiles and shrugs his shoulders.

"So this is the little critter.... Er. Kid. Thing." He bites his lower lip and tilts his head back and forth while inspecting Arthur. Karissa, a curvy twenty-something with bright pink lipstick, pours our coffees as she passes by. She gives Jim an inquisitive look about his facedown mug, and without words exchanged, he flips over his mug and smiles awkwardly at her while she fills it.

"Jim, meet Arthur!" Liz says proudly, and rubs her fingers through his hair again.

"Arthur? What? You guys named it!?" Jim bursts out with shock. Liz pulls back in an offended fashion.

"Liz named him," I correct.

"Oh just *me*? *I* named him?" Liz asks with visible displeasure.

"Well, just factually speaking, yes," I say at a dreadfully slow pace fearful of her reaction. Arthur begins trying to poke holes with his fingers in the air-sealed padding of his coat.

"Arthur is *your* Father's name," she spikes back at me.

"Yes, this is tru..."

"And the last time I checked, I wanted to turn him into the AC and you wouldn't allow it." The words come out quick and smooth like a dagger.

"Well..." I try to come up with a defensive response, but I know I have none.

"So this is our life now, I'm glad you get to see its full scope." She winks at Jim, who adjusts his position in discomfort at our tiff. I take a quick gaze around the restaurant which from the inside looks like one long chrome cylinder of booths with a parallel diner bar top. The red and white checkerboard flooring could use a deep cleaning, and one section of the white under lights are broken, but it is otherwise orderly. Then I notice something peculiar. Everyone in the diner is staring at us, or pointing, or whispering.

"Y'all can always change your mind. It's not written in stone," Jim contributes, locking eyes on Arthur, who is now fiddling with the zipper on his coat.

"Well, maybe so. But I went to the Assistance Center yesterday, and I would never let Arthur die that way."

"You what?" Liz gasps.

"Singh sent me in to test an Inex for Polio. All of his results came back negative, he didn't have Polio, but I had to collect the sample anyway, and the place was more horrible than you can even imagine." They both grow wide-eyed only to be jolted when Karissa asks for our order.

"The usual for us, Karissa. Plus some hash browns for the little one." Liz answers while giving a side hug to Arthur.

"Yes, I have been wanting to ask since you walked in - who is he?" She looks at him with concern.

"He's our nephew," Liz responds seamlessly.

"Oh! Okay, phew! I seriously almost thought you brought an Inexorable in here!" Karissa says, doing an illustrative wiping of her brow. Liz fakes a laugh without responding, and Jim and I stare straight-faced at each other.

"And for you, sir?" Karissa addresses Jim.

"Corn beef hash casserole, please and thank you." He smiles widely at the waitress, and hands her the menus before she skirts away. I continue seamlessly.

"They don't euthanize them. They strap them to a table and stick a bone drill into their skulls. That's the whole process." I want to convey every horrifying detail to them, the seeping of blood and brain matter down the sides of their tiny heads, but I don't. There are images that many of us carry around which scar the mind. They are sights, sounds, and experiences that so defy the natural order that instead of our brains metabolizing the vision they shut down instead, inadvertently trapping the image there forever. It often feels like if we only shared them with another person that the burden of the images would be reduced; that the other person would take half, and we would take half, and from then on we'd carry a lighter load around with us. Unfortunately, that is not the reality of things. When you share scarring images with another, it doesn't heal you, it only scars them too; far from cutting the burden in half, it doubles it. And the image of brain matter dripping out of holes in the heads of little human bodies is one of those scars I would never intentionally give to my wife or closest friend.

"Drill? Drill?" Arthur suddenly asks, and looks up to Liz for answers.

"A drill is a tool for building things," she tells him with a smile.

"Not this drill," I correct, but she rebukes me with her eyes.

"Look. Ethan, Liz, I don't want to be a pessimist here – but you're not the ones in the ER seeing the awful things these creatures do to people. Nietzsche said that man is the cruelest animal, but it's only because he didn't live to meet an Inexorable. Last week we had to amputate three fingers off a man's hand because an Inex maimed them too much for repair when it tried to bite them off. The week before that we put 38 stitches in a woman's face and neck from an Inex knife attack that killed her seventeen year-old daughter. Two days before that we had three burn victims because an Inex burned down his house. I get it. He's cute, right? He looks like your normal everyday kid. Maybe he even talks, and learns things, but I promise that if you keep him around he is going to hurt you," he speaks in a kind and quiet tone.

"What are you saying? That we should let them shove a drill in his head?" I respond tersely.

"No, that isn't...." Jim begins.

"I don't think we should talk about this in front of him," Liz interrupts quietly, tears filling her eyes. Clanging plates and murmuring conversation sound while the three of us uncomfortably sip from our coffees. Jim begins fiddling with the salt shaker, turning it around in circles on the table over and over. I scan the diner again, still full of suspicious eyes barreling in on Arthur.

"So get this," Jim begins, putting his elbows on the table and leaning in close. "Last night Mary and I went out to Leonardo's, so we're walking in Washington Square past that nice brick University area, ya know? And these three cars drive by us, just normal looking cars like a black pick-up truck, a yellow smart car, a grey SUV, when out of no-where they all slam on their breaks, and one of them drives up onto the sidewalk in front of us. Then out of nowhere SWAT looking guys with black vests rush out of the cars and one yells 'GO GO GO.' So this middle-aged white guy walking in front of us, who's holding a small package or something like that, they slam him face down into the ground! So he's on his stomach and they take the package from him and put it into one of the vehicles. They handcuffed the guy and threw him into the back of the black truck, and then just like that they drove off like nothing happened. The whole ordeal was maybe twenty-five seconds, maybe less! How crazy is that!?"

"Oh my gosh! I would freak out!" Liz exclaims.

"Yup! We figured it must've been a drug sting."

"Oh my gosh!" Arthur imitates, and then throws something across the table with remarkable speed. The tiny object rebounds off Jim's eyebrow and falls to the table with a clang. It's round, and metal, and reflective. It's the metal clip from Arthur's coat zipper.

"Ouch!" Jim makes quick short rubs over his eyebrow with two fingers. When he removes them from his face they are red with a small amount of blood. The entire diner sounds with gasping terror.

"Jim, I am so sorry! Here!" Liz hands him two paper napkins.

"Arthur, what you did is very wrong!" Liz squeezes Arthur's jaw tightly with one hand, forcing his head to face her. He resists, and makes biting motions at her so that I hear the collisions of his teeth. A silver haired couple rushes out of the diner with frightened expressions directed at us. All conversation in the diner dies, there is only quiet staring at our spectacle now.

"He's healthy! Okay!? He is a normal little boy, and like normal boys he sometimes disobeys and needs discipline! Not that it's any of *y'all's* damn business!" Jim yells over his shoulder to the onlookers, holding a napkin to his forehead. When he turns back, Liz mouths him a thank you.

"Nope, no, that's just for their benefit. Really the critter is Satan. No two ways about it," he emphatically whispers, holding the zipper hook in the air and staring at Arthur through it. Arthur jerks his head away from Liz and stares back at Jim with a crooked smile and lifeless eyes.

"Are you guys seeing these Acheron eyes?"

"Acheron?" Liz asks.

"The underworld, hades, the abyss? Honestly, how do you expect him not to kill you in your sleep?"

"Liz bought a cage that his bed is going in," I say.

"It's true. I did. But we're not calling it that. We're calling it a play area," Liz qualifies.

"Ah yes. The infamous yet underrated play area that locks from the outside. My Uncle Jed once locked me in a stable overnight for listening to rap music." He chuckles to himself.

"This brings me to my next question, how are y'all pulling this off with Social Services?" He dabs the napkin to his forehead twice more than sets it on the table. I make a quintessentially uncertain shoulder shrug.

"I don't know. Here is how I am processing this: Did I make it through today without death or dismemberment? Is my wife fed and happy? Do I still have my job? If I can affirm all of those things at the end of each day it's a colossal success," I say, pausing here and there to take sips of my coffee while it's still hot.

"I'm really very committed at this point," Liz says. "Ethan spends less time with him, so he doesn't know him as well as I do, and I think that makes it harder. I feel like I understand him, and yes I see the evil Acher-whatever it is in his eyes too. But he is small, and I am not, and I think that at least for now, I can do this- we can do this." Liz looks to me with great brown eyes of hope, and blushing cheeks like she's embarrassed to show it.

"To your credit I'll say this: you two are the only people I know who might be capable of doing this, besides Mary and I of course. But we own a lot of guns," Jim states his consolation unenthusiastically.

"Actually, it's funny you say that. Now that you've met Arthur and everything I was hoping that you two might be interested in babysitting one night soon so that Ethan and I could go on a date?"

"Sure, of course. The moment you have a baby, we will happily babysit." He winks.

"I didn't know that Liz was going to ask you that, but, all of my cards on the table - we really need it. There is no one else we know who would watch him, and the thought of never having a minute alone to process, or a semblance of normalcy, very well might make me insane," I submit.

"Oh! I see. Well in that case, just let us know a day when the sun rises in the west, and we'll be there." His tone is sarcastic but his blue eyes gaze out the window laced with a veil of defeat. He's going to do it.

CHAPTER 11

I t's been two weeks since we've had Arthur, and tonight is our first night of ordinary. A night of not worrying about him, or Liz's safety, or Assistance Centers, or the nest of pathogens hidden away in Inexorable brains. An ordinary night of just me and Liz, food and fire, and maybe making love. But for some reason my stomach feels knotted and I can't tell if it's anxiety about leaving Arthur home, or if it's because I feel like over the past two weeks I've really lost touch with Liz. I feel like I'm living a life full of secrets that she doesn't know about, and she's living an entirely new life with Arthur that I can't fully understand, and our shared life is now something so fundamentally different that it has forced us to become new people altogether. Liz is very much changed, as am I, and we don't know these new changed people inside each other. So in a way, this is like a first date, and first dates have always made me sick with nerves.

To get ready in peace we put Arthur in his 'play area' which is in the first room across the upstairs hallway. Not surprisingly he began screeching and thrashing incessantly, biting his teeth at us like he does, accented with those vitriolic eyes that I'm becoming accustomed to. But we shut the door and ignore the chaotic sounds. In the bathroom Liz is applying her finishing touches, a swathe of lipstick, a spray of perfume, and two hanging diamond earrings. I always knew that I was a lucky man for having such a gorgeous wife, but this calls to mind just how lucky. Her plum dress clings tightly around her hips, cutting off above the knees to show off her long silky legs, and her straight glossy hair flows down off her shoulders and over her breasts. She's the archetype of beauty, but she's never understood that. She can find a pimple on her face in the reflection of a puddle from ten feet away, but she can't see how charming I find her character lines. And we look good together, really good together. I'm wearing a tailored navy suit, accompanied with brown leather belt and shoes, and a classically muted red tie. While I am not the weight I was when I had this suit tailored, it hangs nicely enough to forgive the change, one of the benefits of being so tall. Liz is wearing a pair of silver heels, which helps to offset our height difference. I use my palm to smooth over the top of my short hair, and as I stare at myself in the mirror I notice that between my eyebrows two vertical lines are permanently imprinted, from focusing, or stress, or genetics, or who knows. They don't look bad, possibly they only make me look more established, experienced, trustworthy, sophisticated. And this is a quintessential example of why Liz and I see appearances differently; she thinks we look worse with age, and I think we look better.

When we're finished getting ready I grab Arthur. His room is the smallest in the house, which is why we had only ever used it for storage space. It's roughly the space of two elevators, and it is beyond bland – white washed walls and ceiling, no art, just a children's bed close to the ground with a large metal cage around it that uses a physical lock and key. It looks like we're either in some psychotic cult, or that we're pedophiles. I unlock the cage, fully expecting Arthur to enact some schemed retaliation for his imprisonment, but he doesn't. He simply glares his violence at me and then runs left out of the room and down the stairs, making tiny little thumps on each wooden step. I follow behind him, smelling a faint trail of Liz's perfume in the air, and before I reach the bottom step the doorbell rings. I glance down at my black-faced watch, they're right on time. The wooden door makes a subtle creak as it opens, and to my surprise only Jim stands in front of me, wearing blue jeans, a white t-shirt, and some sort of military vest. Around his waist is a tightly fastened leather tool belt with obscure items dangling from it. I welcome him in, and hear the click-clack of Liz's heels approaching from behind in the living room.

"Jim, you look like you're going to battle. What is that?" Liz asks, gesturing at his tool belt.

"Just precautions."

"Precautions?" her voice reverberates with concern.

"Just the essentials." He begins systematically pulling each item from its hanging position on his hip and displaying it proudly in the air. "On the left we have Mary's moderately low voltage lipstick stun gun. Moving around the front we have rope for obvious reasons, then two perfectly weight-regimented tranquilizer darts, and last but not least, my personal favorite the hundred and thirty-decibel defense alarm which works like a grenade! Pull the pin, throw the alarm toward your enemy, and boom!" He ends with an exalted grin of self-satisfaction. Liz's face, in contrast, instantly lost its warmth, and what remains is a stare of scorn so piercing that only a woman could achieve it.

"Smooth, Jim. Now Liz is going to be thinking about what torturous things you're doing to Arthur the whole time we're out!" I say.

"Now now, that's as backwards as a field mouse swallowing an eagle. If anyone is going to be doing torturous things to another around here, guaranteed it's the tiny devil over there. Besides, these are all just last resort precautions, and as you can see I didn't even bring a gun. I said, 'these are my friends, and they care about this heathen, so I would rather die than shoot the kid.' So there you go, you have nothing to worry about!"

"Are you kidding me? Where is Mary?" she asks.

"I didn't think she should come. Trust me, I can handle this!" he insists. Liz grabs Arthur off the couch, and rejoins us, shoving a sheet of paper into Jim's hand.

"This is the guide. It's extensive. It tells you everything you would need to know, what to feed him, where medical supplies are, what items to keep away from him, when to put him to bed, how to use the play area around his bed, what to do if he needs to go to the bathroom, he sit-pees okay, so you have to hold him up there or he likes to do weird things in the toilet bowl. I put his favorite toys on there, and he likes to watch movies – so I set it up for you, I thought it might be easier than trying to do something else. If there's an emergency, call us, no one else. And you can call us for any reason, our phones are on. When you have to go to the bathroom, just take him with you – but watch him carefully. He's not as good with men, and he has no boundaries with what he will or will not bite. If he tries to hurt you, I squeeze his jaw and tell him that what he did was wrong. Please don't use your weird weapons, Jim. Seriously." She kisses Arthur on the forehead and lets him down.

"Wow. You're a momma alright. I will do my best. Promise," he affirms.

"And... thank you. I know I'm a pain right now, but you have no idea how much it means to us that you're doing this." She rubs her hand along his shoulder for a moment, without making eye contact.

"Yes, thank you," I agree. He makes an appreciative smile, and walks into the living room to follow Arthur. Liz throws her grey wool coat over her arms, and takes a deep anxious breath before exiting through the door, and as I am shutting the door behind we both hear from inside:

"I'm your uncle Jim. Have you ever read Aeschylus before?" and we smile.

***

Adega & Flor is a bourgeois piano bar just three blocks from the Delaware River. It's one of those cramped candlelit restaurants that smells like dessert wine and reduction sauce. It has aged brick walls, rounded granite tables with oil lamps and flowers for centerpieces, and small black wooden chairs that sit too upright for comfort. The twelve elbow-to-elbow tables are typically reserved by flashy New Yorkers from the financial district or grey-hairs on their anniversary since a meal costs a month's worth of uptown rent. But Liz and I have never come here to celebrate. We have come twice, and both were occasions of solemnity. The first time we came as a consolation to our decidedly final failed fertility treatment, and the last time we came to commemorate making it through the first year following the attacks. And though tonight is properly a date, and though she looks so beautiful, we both know that we have a lot to talk about, and little of it is leisurely. We are seated at one of the small tables pressed against the brick wall in the opposite corner of the baby grand. A large-chested woman with tied-back brown curls approaches our table. She's wearing a pristine black vest and tie with the uncouth accompaniment of cigarette odor.

"How are youse guys this evening? My name is Mia and I'll be lookin' after you tonight. Owr specials are bacalhaua appetizer, which is a salted cod and sweet peppah dip served with crispy Mediterranean pita, and for owr entree we have baked red-trout in a lemon crème reduction over mashed yucca and served with a roasted vegetable medley. Of cowse everything that you see on our menu is fantastic, but my recommendation is for the trout. While youse look over your options can I get some cawktails owr wine stawted?" she says, Philadelphian as they come.

"Sure. We'd like a bottle of the Arinto blend please," I respond.

"You got it. I'll be right back with that." She brushes away from the table with a genuine smile.

"I have to say that this place has memories for me," I begin.

"I know. Hard ones sometimes, but I still love it here," she says, gazing around the space.

"Me too." I give her a half-smile, nervous of the conversations that we're going to have.

"I have to confess something, love." She looks at me with a mask of pain. "I quit my job. I put in two weeks' notice just a few days after Arthur joined the picture, and yesterday was my last day. I quit because I couldn't do it. I literally couldn't do it. I couldn't constantly watch him and work at the same time, and instead of being fired I chose to quit. So, I don't have my job anymore." She releases in a quick nervous unit, diverting her eyes from me.

"What? Why didn't you tell me?" I can't fight the shock adhering itself to my face.

"Because. I have no idea what we're doing. What are we doing? With Arthur I mean. Are we keeping him, or are we not? Should I love him, or should I not? Am I his mother or am I not? And I didn't want you to make the choice *for* us, if I told you that I could not care for him and keep my job at the same time. But now I just feel ashamed, and I'm so sorry." Her voice gets thin. I fight the sense of betrayal boiling up in me, not because it's anything big, we've always talked about how she doesn't need to work, but it's that she deliberately deceived me for weeks, so that she might trap me in some life-path without consulting me. And I know that I've kept some things from her. I hid the cat. I hid my brain-tissue discoveries, discoveries that have cataclysmic ramifications for our nation. I haven't told her about someone deleting my files, or my plans to continue researching and publishing my results. But, it isn't the same. Everything I hid from her I hid to protect her. She hid something from me to trap me. It isn't the same. I can tell that my quietness is bothering her because my peripheral picks up her anxious searching for eye contact.

"I'm not a savant of art," she fills the silence, "I'm not a student of music, I don't even know what it means to taste wine in the front of your mouth or the back. Like really, what does that mean? I feel like a simple Missourian who pretends to be high-class, a wife who can't cook, a worker failing at their job, a mother who can't control her child, and now, I don't know, a criminal maybe, or maybe something more hopeless than that. Maybe I'm just a woman, such a desperate foolish woman, that I'll take a demon in place of the child I've longed for. And in this mess of what I am something had to give." Her hands tremble as she fidgets with her wedding ring, and her eyes get glossy.

"Baby," I sigh and reach across for her hands. "You are a tender, unendingly patient, brave woman. If you give up a job to stay that woman then you will have painted the most beautiful picture, written the most melodic song, identified the most sophisticated wine, and not the one we ordered because I just ordered the cheapest one on the menu." She chuckles in response. "I'm upset that you would hide that from me. You know you don't need to work, I would have supported you if you just told me. I support you now. As for Arthur... Here's what I think. When you have family and that family gets physically ill you don't shove them away, you take care of them. When you have family and that family gets mentally ill, you don't shove them away, you take care of them. Here we have a boy who is heart ill, soul ill. He isn't body sick, or mind sick, but he is still sick. And so, if he's family, we take care of him. But if he isn't family, then we don't. We have to make that choice. We have to decide if he is ours or if he's someone else's, and if we decide that he's ours then we have to decide that dogmatically, with resolution."

Mia interrupts with her approach, verifying the bottle with me and waiting for my taste approval. She pours the bright golden blend into our glasses, while Liz and I both order the trout on her recommendation. When she steps away again we sip our wine too eagerly, giving it no room to breathe.

"Well, what do you think then? Is he family?" she asks with that sense of desperation in her voice that tells me she doesn't want to simply know my thoughts, she wants to depend on them. She wants whatever I say to be correct. I pause before answering, and look over her familiar face, glowing and dimming in the oil lamp light. Her alert careful brown eyes, rosy high cheeks, long thin Cleopatran nose, darkly stained lips, and of course her long black hair reflecting light and flowing over her shoulders like wings.

"I don't know," I admit, which she laughs at slightly.

"I know you know, ideologue that you are. I'm sure you made up your mind long ago," she presses.

"I thought that I had. I thought the moment I walked through our front door with him that my mind was made up. I thought that if I was doing the right thing that I could just muscle through it, as if it would be hard but not painful, or require sacrifice but not doubt. I didn't expect to doubt so much whether I was doing the right thing."

"What makes you doubt?" she asks, pressing her plum-red lips against the wine glass.

"The news. Jim. You." *The cat*, I think but don't say.

"Why me?" She raises a sharp eyebrow, and returns her glass to the table.

"I love you. I couldn't live without you, and I couldn't live with myself if something happened to you."

"Oh Ethan, I love you so much, but you're going to die long before me." She winks and I flash a toothy grin at her.

"What do you think we should do?" I ask, and her voice is hushed while she speaks.

"Arthur is violent, but he isn't all violent, and I think it's easy for you to overlook that because of fear. It isn't so easy for me to overlook, because I am with him, just him, for hours every day without you. He loves macaroni and cheese, but he hates tomatoes. He loves to be touched, but he hates to be constrained. He loves to talk, and to learn new words, and this is really the seal for me: when those boys attacked him I realized, maybe for the first time, that everyone else in the world is violent against him. The boys would have killed him, Ethan. They would have! And the assistance centers, they'd drill holes in his brain, you said?" her voice cracks, and she pauses for a deep intentional breath. "Love, he has your father's name. He already is family." Her chest blushes a warm red, and I restrain tears welling up behind my eyes. It hurts, everything she said hurts, like a cement cylinder pressing down on my chest making it impossible to breathe. It hurts that I don't know how to have affection for him, it hurts that the world treats him like refuse, it makes me want to vomit that every day of his life is an avoidance of death by drill bit in that metal torture chamber. It hurts that he has my father's name. But mostly, it hurts that she's right, because she is, and the flood of consequences for that is hard to anticipate.

"Then he is. I love you," I say again, and lift my eyes ceiling-ward, letting the vent dry the tears accumulating in them.

"I love you," she echoes. We sit in contended silence for a moment, sipping our finally aerated wine and listening to the melancholy overture the pianist is playing. I look at his comical appearance. He's unusually short, with Teddy Roosevelt-styled glasses and a full tailcoat. The sad-sounding music floating through the air is not unusual. America's music changed after the Day of Destruction. We all suffered and instantaneously understood what it was to lose something, and our music reflected that. Happy melodies were overtaken by minor keys and it seemed like the timbre of voices changed too. Electronic overlays disappeared and you heard everyone as they really were: raw.

"You remember the last time we were here and that strange Asian man kept staring at us, and then it turned out he actually had synthetic eyes?" Liz breaks our silence, and I almost spit wine out my nose.

"I had forgotten!" We laugh together, remembering the utter absurdity of it. By our second glass of wine we're musing about our vacation gone awry from two years prior, where our Chesapeake Bay cruise had been booked entirely by Kitty Crochets, a national group of 70-90 year old women swathed in their itchy creations. One woman in particular, eighty years old at least, solicited me for sex while Liz sat directly beside me, "A dying woman's wish!" the woman said, to which Liz responded "We're all dying, Grandma."

As we eat flaky, cream-saturated trout, Liz and I reminisce about how much easier life was when we had met in college, despite my difficulty of navigating a relationship with Liz's father, Mike. It's probably true that no man-on-man relationship can be easily navigated when the complication of sexual interest in one of the men's daughters is introduced. It didn't make things easier that Mike was a fire-fighter, a stout block of muscular ferocity, who in my mind probably drank blood for breakfast and ate bone marrow for dinner. The walls of their hundred year old house dripped with an inordinate number of hanging firearms and specialty hatchets which Mike kept in pristine condition. But no wall of hatchets or fatherly threatening can begin to compare with the intimidation I feel coming home every night to an Inexorable, to a son, to Arthur.

After Mia takes our final order of steamy black coffee and roasted red grapes with rum mascarpone to split, Liz asks me to dance with her--causing me to visibly grit my teeth. Ordinarily, I love dancing with her, especially slow dancing where I can feel her curves slowly sway against my body, but the only open space in the restaurant is four square feet against the piano that I earnestly doubt is intended for dancing. But she gives me that vulnerable "please," and the grounds that "we haven't danced in so long," and "who knows when we might be able to again?" which finally persuades me to stand, pulling her by one of her tender hands to the space near the piano. A gentle resonant melody plays behind us, and I inch in toward her, sliding my left hand firmly around her petite back so that I can barely feel the beginning of her hips with my fingertips. I pull her in as close as I can, gazing down at her exquisite face, which in this scene looks young again – occupied with an innocent glowing smile. As we sway and step, I stroke the skin of her hand in mine, and whisper with my eyes how I love her, and how deeply moving her years of loyalty to me are. And though I can sense the stare of onlookers, I commit to caring only for the eyes of my bride in my arms. In a moment the song ends, and I move from looking at her eyes to her sweet lips, leaning down to kiss them briefly – but long enough to breathe in that familiar smell of hers. I don't know what it is, if it's her skin, or her breath, but she has a scent unique to her that I can only smell when we kiss. It's like the smell of spruce in the rain, and skin, and fog.

***

When we arrive home, Jim is sitting on the couch whistling and reading one of his esoteric conversation partners.

"So! How did it go?" Liz is the first to ask.

"Oh, I would say it went exactly how you would expect one of these shin-digs to go." He shuts his book.

"Care to elaborate?"

"Well, he was fed and went to the bathroom in the toilet and is in his own bed, so those are huge successes, I'd say. If I was grading this whole thing, I'd say B+."

"But...." I anticipate.

"Well, there was an incident."

"What kind of incident? Are you both okay?" Liz asks.

"Oh yeah, we're finnneeee. It's just that, well, he's a little sedated right now." He shrugs and flashes his unapologetic blue eyes at her.

"Sedated? You tranquilized him!?" she exclaims.

"I panicked!" he defends.

"You panicked!?"

"Look, it's a perfectly regimented dose for his body size. He's going to be fine," he explains.

"B+, really?" I add sarcastically with a small laugh.

"Well, what happened was this: the kid is mental. Look, I wouldn't give him my little sound grenade, and so he began screaming at the top of his lungs and throwing things at me, and then I'm sitting on the ground and he's running at me with something in his hand and I couldn't see what it was so I thought it might be a razor or weapon or a nail or who knows what, but he was definitely heading toward my eyes with it so I just pulled the little dart out and anyway. He's fine! He's just going to sleep really well tonight, and he will need some more water tomorrow than normal."

"What did he have in his hand!?" Liz asks in concern.

"Oh, well. So. It turns out he didn't actually have anything in his hand, but how could I know!?"

"B+?" I refrain, with a grin plastered on my face, even if he only panicked because I had told him about the cat. It's still funny. I join him on the couch, and pat his back a few times.

"Jim, you did good, I'm just pulling your leg. We're very thankful for you watching him tonight. Can I get you a scotch?" I offer.

"Naw, buddy. I better get home to Mary, she's been a nervous wreck all night."

"Understandable. Thank you again, I owe you! I'll see you tomorrow at the hospital?"

"You got it. Goodnight, Liz."

'Thank you, Jim," she says in a forced manner, and rushes upstairs, undoubtedly to ensure that Arthur is still breathing.

"Night, Jim," I add while shutting the oak door. I join Liz upstairs, where Arthur is definitely sedated but also unquestionably alive; loud snores escaping from his wide nose.

The longer he's lived with us the more I'm persuaded that he's ethnically Egyptian. Tanned olive skin, wide centered nose, shiny black curly hair, and large almond eyes. But for the first time, as I look at him through a crack in the door, through the holes in his cage, I'm thinking about him not in terms of his origin, but in terms of his belonging. Tonight he becomes to me a son, one of the faces I look for in a crowd, one of the people I've vowed to protect. Tonight, we cease as simply Ethan and Elizabeth. I become a father, she becomes a mother, and he becomes our son. It's impossible to conceive of doing this with anyone besides her, the strongest woman I know, the most gracious woman I know, the only woman I know who could simultaneously build a cage for a monster and smother kisses on that monster's boo-boos. She's someone innately capable of the task we've bound ourselves too.

When Liz and I are finally in bed, unclothed and touching in all the familiar spots; her leg draped over my thigh, our arms brushing against each other, reading our various literature, warm and routine, she interrupts with the grazing of her fingers along my thigh. I drift my gaze to her, and uninhibitedly smile at her inviting eyes. Who knows how long it's been? A month at least, which makes it physically impossible to resist her advances, and so we wrap up the night together. The only way I can describe it is like an unmasking, a being known. I'm naked in front of her all the time but it's only here, in this scene, that I ever *feel* naked in front of her. It's somewhere in the glory of her skin, and heat, and the movements of her hips, and her breathy sounds that she's seeing me, responding to me, knowing how I operate in deeply personal ways. It's our unabated squeezes and grasps that say "You can see everything, instincts, humanness, dependency, and all."

CHAPTER 12

In the past three weeks I've learned an unfathomable amount about Arthur, about Liz, and about myself. Arthur, as it turns out, is really bright and verbal. We bought these children's shows that teach speaking and reading at the same time, and he is glued to the television whenever it's on. He is curious about everything, what a television is, or flowers, or spaghetti, or a child. And he wants to understand who I am, and who Liz is, and what it means that I go to work. He also responds well to physical touch, and now that he's more comfortable with me he will let me hold him when he's hurt or tired, and it makes physical contact an important positive reinforcement. Unfortunately, his responsiveness to things physical works in two ways, serving not only as an effective positive reinforcement but also as an effective negative reinforcement. Inflicting physical pain on him is one of the only ways to get him to stop being violent, so we have to constantly issue a threat of force. Liz has mastered a painful thigh pinch, which is pretty innocuous but always makes him cry, and at first I struggled to find a harmless method that worked. I tried to spank him but he would just laugh hysterically, almost like I was tickling him or something. But then I found these pain pressure points in his face that hurt like a tooth being sliced up through your gum. I only know how painful they are because I had to practice them on myself until I got them right. When I do it to him the venom in his eyes tells me that he would, even still, murder me the next time it seemed expedient. And while I don't enjoy causing him pain, we have to have something by which we can manipulate his natural behavior.

Bright and cruel are characteristics that you never want paired together, but they're bonded quite happily together in this little human. And even with all of our progress, every few days we still have a new police-level crisis with him. Six days ago he threw stone coasters through the front window, and sliced up his own hands while attempting to escape through the fractured glass. Thankfully they were not deep enough that I needed to stitch them. Then three days ago he tried to scratch his own eyes out, and still has scar-looking scrapes from his fingernails imprinted there. I can't begin to understand where Arthur's fixation on eyeballs comes from, but he truly is obsessed with them in a depraved sort of way that marks any Inexorable's fascination. He runs beside me at full speed, catapulting himself into the air and flopping onto the couch face first. His body slowly slinks off the side, making an uncomfortable squeaking noise as his skin makes friction with the leather.

"What are you, a whale?" I grab him by his rib cage, and tickle along his sides as I lift him easily over my head. A spontaneous laugh bellows from his tiny lungs. I bend my knees for support over the wooden floor and fling Arthur's entire body into the air, where for a flash of a moment he's flying, and floating, before falling back into my arms with thunderous laughter. His ear to ear beam unveils glistening teeth, and his eyes look, if for only a second, healthily amused. I continue the motions, and in every throw and fall a corresponding wave of giggles escapes from Arthur. I grin compulsively, even laughing with him every few seconds. The sound of joy echoes downstairs, as if everything is normal, but it isn't. I sense that as Liz enters my peripheral, returning my mind to reality. I set Arthur down, and my heart begins pounding with a new type of stress. The type of stress you might feel standing before a judge knowing that you were most certainly guilty of the crime.

Today is the day we find out the legality of the matter as we meet with Philadelphia's adoption specialist, Jace Hill, about the deranged prospect of adopting an Inexorable. Jace Hill is a pasty bald man with a fat rounded nose, loose jowls, and thin framed glasses that accentuate his girth. He is a man we've had contact with in the past, when we were first considering adoption through foster care, contact that he, conveniently, doesn't remember. His office is decorated with an outlandish cacophony of mismatched taxidermy and vinyl albums. He sits on the other side of a flimsy wooden desk, clicking his pen and looking over paperwork. Occasionally he glances up at us quizzically, as if he's trying to replay our questions or discern some unethical underlying intention behind them.

"Here's the good news," he begins, setting his glasses down on the desk. "You are not unique. Last year when the Inex situation became so severe, you remember those assistance center protests? Well, some of those crazy people actually tried to run Inex shelters." He releases a nasally laugh. "But basically they all died. The Inexes, the adults, everyone. It shut down pretty fast, but that's a little beside the point. The point is, that the government had to develop what we call a protocol of abandonment so that those exposed to the elements could legally be taken in by the shelters. What they came up with was pretty smart. Soooo." He reapplies his glasses to examine a center page, running his finger over the lines, then he takes them off again.

"Right. Any government or charitable organization, or individuals in good legal standing, are legally able to begin providing care to an Inexorable immediately upon finding them in the state of exposure, so long as they provide notice to police which includes a photograph, a physical description, and any special details such as articles they had on them when they were found. That information gets inserted into the police database to find a match with missing person reports in the continental United States. It operates on a cycle, so it automatically refiles a search once a day for twenty-one days and then once a week for six months. If a match is found, then they verify the details and the police reunite the Inexorable with its family. Of course that's never happened here." He raises his eyebrows as if to say "obviously, who would want an Inex back?"

"However if no match is found, at twenty-one days, whoever provides their care can receive an admission of temporary guardianship, which allows them to do things like interstate travel, take them to the hospital—well, used to—but as you know, hospitals have since stopped receiving Inexorables as patients." He pauses emphatically, as if he hopes this detail will change our minds. "Basically, ordinary temporary guardianship rights. Then at six months, if still no one has filed a missing person's report, then there is a TPR, or termination of parental rights, and you only need to sign a consent of guardianship and get issued a decree of endorsement. So, it's fairly easy to get an Inex I suppose. Not so for real children, I'll tell you that much."

"So then, if we've had him for three weeks you're saying that we could be issued temporary guardianship already?" Liz asks.

"No. No, sorry. You would have to supply the police notice, and I can get you the information on that, and then the timer begins. It'd be three weeks from then, and then six months from then, that you will be granted temporary and then permanent guardianship respectively." He begins clicking his pen again.

"Yes, we will need that information. Can you also give us a copy of whatever legal statutes you're looking at there?" Liz gestures to the stack of papers laying on his desk.

"Sure, that won't be a problem. I have to admit that what you're asking for, how do I say this.... That your desire to adopt an Inexorable is not exactly normal. It concerns me, frankly. It doesn't mean I won't help you, that's my job is to help you. I will be here whenever you have questions about this stuff, but, for my records, and this will appear before the judge if you guys do decide to work toward permanent guardianship... why are you doing this?" his deep voice sounds cautious and serious. When I look over Liz's eyes nudge me to answer. I organize my thoughts, and take one large breath before beginning.

"Have you ever been helpless Mr. Hill? In a position where there was not a single person who could help you, but whatever the circumstance was you were doomed to it and no desperation or cry for help could fix it?"

"I can't say that I have," he half grunts.

"In the hospital where I work we see that sometimes. Cancer patients who are too far progressed to treat, car crash victims who are gone before they come in, AIDS patients who have caught pneumonia... and these people are so utterly desperate for your help, and there is nothing that you can do for them. They cry out for help, they beg you to save them, but it is completely out of your power to do so. It would take some form of a miracle, and we live in a world painfully devoid of miracles. So when I saw this little boy freezing to death, and I knew that it was in my capacity to save him, how could I not? So many people beg for help that is out of reach, how then could I deny helping this child who was at arm's length?" I become emotional while rehearsing it, and Liz reaches for my hand.

"It's moving what you're saying, but, and this isn't to interrogate you two or anything but it's important for me to understand: at the hospital don't you also see the victims of Inexes? The mutilated people, the people 'out of reach' on account of Inexes, to use your own words?" He sits more rigidly in his chair. I pause, calculating his words, considering how apt they are. That's the dichotomy of the whole situation. It's true that Arthur is violent, but that doesn't change the veracity of what I've said. At the end of the day, broken or whole, sick or healthy, Arthur is human. He belongs to us. It's difficult to consider that we've been subjected to live in a society where monsters exist and they require our care. But that's reality, so how can we be condemned for facing that reality and accepting its difficult calling?

"I do see them, and I think what they suffer is unbearable. It's just the case that I find it equally unbearable, to my heart, to turn this child over for execution. We have to live in a way that our consciences will afford," I finally respond.

"And we're teaching him," Liz adds, with sweet affection in her voice. "He's learning things, like how to speak and write. He has food preferences and he likes to cuddle, believe it or not. He has more to offer the world than just his natural tendencies, I think."

Mr. Hill makes undiscernible grumbling sounds, while typing up a few notes on his computer.

"Very well. I see that you both are made up in your minds, which is good. Your naïve optimism, on the other hand, will impress no judge. But I'm fairly certain you'll be less optimistic when I see you again in three weeks with legal. Here's the copies of the information you need." He pulls out a small stack from behind his desk and hands them to Liz. I grit my teeth to resist responding. "And though I'm cynical about how this will work out for you, I reiterate that I am here for your questions at any time, my information is in the letterhead of the first and last pages there." He stands to brush us out of his office. Liz and I give unqualified thank yous, though mine are through gritted teeth over his lack of decorum.

We exit first his office and then the sixteen story glass and iron government building. The grey winter sky breaks with a single beam of sunshine above the block, casting tiny shadows to the side walk from the bundled bustles of city men and women. This block is the most freely spaced in the city on account of the historic Philadelphia City Hall, now a protected landmark. Being that this massive cut of stone artwork is the largest municipal building in the world, it ceased from practical use after the Day of Destruction. It now serves as a historic Philadelphian museum, complete with the largest memorial exhibit of the Day of Destruction in the U.S. An exhibit which possesses my name in two inscriptions of first responders and their duties on that day, an exhibit which I have only been in once and will never return to again.

Inside they play videos of the attacks, the bombs dropping in center city, the screams of people being trampled in fearful pandemonium, the tornado sirens, the yellow cloud of Obcasus rising up from the metal cylinders to flood buildings and fill streets. Sirens and panic play over and over, with flashes of our dead lying on pavement. Scenes that I hate to remember, scenes that I desperately wish I could bleach from my brain. The exhibit is progressive, so it documents all of the attacks in chronological order, following the recovery to the present. It starts with the nuclear attack in D.C. and moves forward, charting the events of the day and the fallout: the freezing of the market, the refugee cities for those from D.C. with radiation poisoning, the fast-thinking heroic moves of President Powell, the post-exposure effects on Obcasus victims, Powell's team developing Dopimazipal, the intricacies of government funding for the drug – moments of reprieve, moments of hope, moments of rebounding before the discovery of the state of Inexorables. All things which I now have to reinterpret, apart from hope.

The exhibit then documents well the confusion of the medical community as we looked upon these infants with brain deformities whose mothers were exposed to Obcasus and had no satisfying explanation for it. I understand why now. I can see how deceptive publications kept us from investigating in certain directions, fed us frameworks that kept us from asking the right questions. But the motivation for these things I still don't understand. Next in the exhibit you see the pain it's all caused, as women weep in videos knowing that they can never again have a healthy child, or that they can never hold their child in their arms again because it was too murderous to stay with them. One video in particular broke Liz's heart. It was of a woman who had not been exposed to Obcasus, who was healthy, and who has had three healthy children since the attack. This woman described how ostracized she felt in her community for having healthy children, how her friends abandoned her because it hurt them too much to see her have what they couldn't. I remember Liz weeping as she watched, telling me later that it was because she was healthy, she had never been exposed to Obcasus, but she still couldn't have a child. The exhibit, miserable as it is, is supposed to leave you with a sense of hope. Excerpts from President Powell's eloquent speeches broadcast morsels of hope and promise of recovery overhead. I can still hear his stately voice announcing the opening of Assistance Centers. The speech was replayed so often on the news that I have it nearly memorized.

"Today, we stand as a nation greatly healed from the wounds of our enemies. Today, our citizenry has experienced remarkable recovery in health, in prosperity, and in security. In health, the wealthiest to the poorest of our country are able to live normal lives thanks to the government sponsorship of Dopimazipal, and our continual efforts to make it more accessible for all people. In prosperity, our market is recovering, experiencing just in this last month the greatest growth we have seen since the Day of Destruction. In security, we avoided a bloody war with the Mujahedeen, which could have destroyed our already fragile nation, and yet we have continued to watch their disestablishment by other Middle Eastern forces and the support of our allies.

But our security, I am sad to report, is being severely threatened by the most unsuspected of enemies. Inside our borders we are dealing with the difficult reality of Inexorables, who incur murderous brutality against our people with no sense of remorse, and regrettably, without the possibility of ever possessing remorse. Due to the exponential rate at which Inexorables are being left out for exposure to the elements, putting more human lives at risk, today we open Assistance Centers in every major city which was directly affected by Obcasus. Today we provide a safe and effective way for our society

to respond to these grave threats. And because I understand the
sensitivity and the unimaginable grief with which parents will be
faced, we will never make it mandatory for the American people
to give over the Inexorables born to them if they do not desire to.
But for those who are desperate to flee to safety, we provide you
that safety in these Assistance Centers. The great Thomas
Jefferson who wrote our Declaration of Independence, penned
these words: 'The chief purpose of government is to protect life.
Abandon that and you have abandoned all.' Though there are
many who find the presence of Assistance Centers troubling, I
simply say to them this: That my calling as the leader of the
American people is to provide us with protection, to preserve
lives. The threat of Inexorables has reached an unfortunately
unbearable level, and should we leave our people in danger? I
promised day one that I would never do that. I will never do that."

***

When we arrive home, relieving a hostage Jim from his
babysitting torment, Liz completes the police notice, calling the
local headquarters and faxing them the necessary information.
She resounds a "Happy Holidays" to them, reminding me that
deathly ill flu patients are about to flock to me at work, and that I
have yet to purchase a single gift. I pull Jim down into the
basement with the promise of scotch, descending through the
door hiding in the side of the first floor staircase. What I need is a
confidant, because it's time to tell someone what I know, and
what I plan to do with that knowledge. Our basement has the
musky scent that I suppose accompanies all underground spaces.
The smell reminds me of childhood, in the Fairfax basement,
sneaking processed sugar and watching adult comedy shows
when I was still too young for them to be appropriate. My favorite
show, Sour Lemon, had these hilariously profane skits such as
Dear Tranny Granny where viewers would write in for advice and a

black transvestite in their sixties would answer with the most incongruous remedies. I can picture with immaculate clarity the scene, as Tranny Granny sat center stage as if on a talk show, reading card after card of sad stories: "Dear Tranny Granny, I'm struggling with an overbearing manager who constantly takes credit for my work, what should I do? Signed, Pouty Pushover." To which Tranny Granny would respond in the vein of "Ooooh baby girl, or boy, or whatever you feel like today, this is so easy. Mmm hmm, so so easy. I could solve this problem with nothing more than the end of a flashlight and some duct tape, ohkaaaay, but I won't say how. Look child, here's what you need to do: you just march right into that job and you become the most mediocre worker you could ever be. Guess what? If your work sucks he ain't gonna steal it anymore now is he? Problem SOLVED! Next writer!"

Our basement is far less entertaining. The right half of the rectangular room is sectioned off by navy blue carpet, signaling the beginning of my 'office' space. The left half of the rectangle is marked by grey speckled laminate flooring, and now the two dozen storage boxes that used to keep home in Arthur's room. My 'office' is a pitiful excuse for a research center. It consists of one aged, but fairly well maintained, maple desk upon which are microscopes, a computer, a stack of journal publications I've been meaning to read, and a half drunk bottle of scotch. The microscope set is archaic, bulky, and requires an arduous amount of manual reporting instigation to replicate even one image into a digital copy. It is painfully far from the efficiency of the Olympus Infinity at the hospital, but for my purposes it suffices. Two stiff leather chairs sit on the carpeted section near the desk, chairs which Liz had purchased for the living room but later decided she hated. Jim hands me two artisan glasses, and I pour the medallion colored liquid evenly between them, its smoky particles wafting up and stinging my nose. I had once considered myself a connoisseur of scotch to the point that I began distilling my own, ꞟ quarter-gallon barrels to test my flavors and to learn how ꞟlend without the need for long-term aging, then to half-gallon, and even once the costly five-gallon barrel, at which point Liz informed me that my acquiesced hobby was due for a timely death. Thus the scotch swirling around in Jim's glass is some unexceptional import. We adjust in the uncomfortable leather, squeaking accompanying each movement.

"Jim, when I was at the AC I found something unusual," I sober my tone.

"What do ya' mean?" He takes his first sip, and surveys the pale grey textured ceiling.

"I tested an Inexorable for Polio, but I also secretly tested two of them for something else. I accrued brain tissue from two non-relative Inexorables, one who was home-kept and another who was out for exposure. I used the microscope at the hospital to inspect the tissue both with and without introduced D-MAZ, and for the samples introduced to D-MAZ, I found an anomaly. Only it can't be an anomaly because it happened twice, in both Inexes. When Dopimazipal was introduced to the scar tissue in their brains, something happened. Leptospira materialized out of nowhere, from nothing, and began corkscrewing around in distress, like it was being killed by the D-MAZ." I wait for a response but his face is mortared with confusion.

"I'm sorry, Ethan, ya' lost me at 'accrued brain tissue.' So let's slow down. You're sayin' you stole Inex brains from the AC?" A crescent wrinkle impresses his cheek as his face stiffens in discomfort.

"I wouldn't call it stealing, I mean, they were dead, and it was just small segments. There was a woman assisting me the entire time who had no qualms about it," I qualify, thinking back to the strange cheeriness of Lapis.

"So you're cuttin' open little monster heads, and the Assistance Center freaks are A-Okay with that, but, friend, can you explain to me in that moment what is compelling ya' to do this? Because it's out of character, and I want to make sure you're okay." He talks in a slow and careful way, making me feel like he thinks I'm going clinically insane.

"Why is it always like this with you? Why do you psychologize things? Seriously, you are an ED doc, you deal with straight facts and blunt solutions, but the second you're out of the ER you're quoting Shakespeare and asking about what? My id and ego?" I respond with agitation, and take a sip, feeling the sharp alcohol slip down my throat, warming it along the way.

"First off, I'm offended that after all these years of friendship you still think that I'd quote Shakespeare. He's whiny, girly, and on the nose, plus he lacks that philosophical pedagogy that I need from a writer. You should know that," he stares straight at me, fighting a smile. "Second off, I'm basically asking if you're okay, or if because of the kid you're having the understandable breakdown that I'd be having." He softens his prod as much as possible, but it still pisses me off because it's impertinent to what I'm trying to say. I see the supportive concern that he's trying to convey, but that isn't why I brought him down here.

"Jim. I'm fine. I took the tissue because I had opportunity and because I've been suspicious. I've been suspicious since before Arthur. Can I please tell you what's going on now?" I say tersely. He raises his hands in resignation.

"Do you know what Leptospira is?" I ask him.

"Nope!" he responds happily, trying to lighten the mood.

"It's a spirochete bacteria. But it's a special family of bacteria, making it like Anthrax. Well, inside the Inexorable scar tissue, I found a new kind of Leptospira. A mutant. Something I've never seen before, which is freaky enough, but that isn't all. It only appeared in response to D-MAZ, and it appeared from nowhere. It wasn't in the tissue, and then magically it was. So I began to think that the Dopimazipal injections were hiding this parasitic entity, so I tested it, and nothing. D-MAZ is exactly what they say it is, nothing special. So while I am staring at these microscopic images trying to understand what this means, all of the images are deleted before my eyes. Just like that, they're all gone," I snap my fingers. Jim sits upright, holding his glass tightly in both hands and listening attentively. "It wasn't a computer error. Everything else was still there, no other files were deleted. Only these. And there's no trace of them, no cache record, no recycling bin, nothing. I got rid of my samples and I stopped investigating on the spot, because whatever I had found was seen by someone else, and instantly concealed. I don't know who, and I don't know why – but I haven't pursued it any further, because frankly, I'm afraid of what repercussions Liz might face if I'm caught doing or knowing something that I'm not supposed to. But I haven't stopped thinking about it. What does Obcasus have to do with D-MAZ, or first exposure victims with fetal malformation, or scar tissue with an invisible mutated Leptospira? These things are intricately connected to why this bacteria lives in Inexorable scar tissue – are you following me?" I look into Jim's eyes which are still alert and concerned.

"Somewhat." He nods.

"So I went back to the basics. In order to survive bacteria must feed on something. Most bacteria utilize oxygen to metabolize sugar, which is how they nourish themselves. But, some bacteria are areotolerant anaerobes: they don't use oxygen but are also unharmed by it. What if instead of metabolizing sugar, like many bacteria do, this mutated Leptospira metabolizes Dopamine? I think this Leptospira is an areotolerant anaerobe. I think that it survives in oxygen rich realms, but doesn't use it or sugar for food – I think that it eats Dopamine. I think that, far from killing the bacteria, the D-MAZ injections feed it. "

"I'm still struggling to understand. So these Inexes have a strange bacteria hiding in their scar tissue that eats D-MAZ. And?" Jim urges the end point.

"No. That's just it. The bacteria isn't hiding *in* the scar tissue. I think, for a lot of it, the bacteria *is* the scar tissue. The

Inexorable brains are partially scarred, but the rest of the scar tissue is actually this dormant pathogen, bundled together and sealed off by a white biofilm that makes it blend seamlessly with the scar tissue," I explain.

"What is the implication?" His wide eyes beg for clarity that I can't seem to give. It's like a chain of domino blocks, each one relating to the other with a precise match only to change sequence and begin a new pair. I have to begin with the first domino.

"Walk back with me to the attacks. Obcasus fills the air, people inhale it, touch it, and their dopamine, a neurotransmitter, is obliterated causing mass system failures, right?" I ask.

"Right, because the acids in Obcasus cause its breakdown and burn their dopamine producers," he adds.

"Wrong. I think that's lie number one. Obcasus is not properly a nerve gas, it might be, but hidden inside it are hungry Leptospira ready to awaken at the first taste of Dopamine. Think about it, the Mujahedeen used Anthrax just before the Day of Destruction. Same family of bacteria, similar method of delivery. So people inhale an ungodly dose of this microscopic pathogen, which immediately goes after their dopamine, some even swimming to its sources and damaging them."

"Then why would Dopimazipal work? Think this through, Ethan. If what you're saying is true then it would keep the bacteria alive in people, causing further damage instead of curing them," Jim reasons.

"Yes it would. And so I think that the enzyme compound works to kill some, while the Dopamine works to feed some, and there's a high enough dose that enough Dopamine is still used by the body to alleviate symptoms." I can see the skepticism blanketing his eyes.

"It sounds crazy, friend." He takes a hearty swig of his drink.

"Just indulge me for one more minute. If it were the case that the dopamine producer damage was caused by a parasitic infection that feeds on dopamine, then I hypothesize that during fetal development, when the amygdala and surrounding cortexes are flooded with dopamine, it attracts the parasite which, until that point, is satisfied with the laboratory dopamine concoction provided by D-MAZ. But when it senses a new source of natural dopamine, the good stuff so to speak, it rushes to it and begins to feast. Unfortunately, because the fetal brain is still developing, it injures major cortexes of the brain: the anterior insula, the anterior midcingulate cortex, somatosensory cortex, and the right amygdala – all associated with empathy and emotion. When it is done eating, and when it seems that no more Dopamine will come around, it becomes dormant, bonding itself with the scar tissue and wrapping itself in some protective biofilm. And this is why the women become asymptomatic during pregnancy, it's why they feel so good, their infection is alleviated because it's attracted to the new tissue."

"So let me understand fully. Obcasus is released holding a pathogen that eats Dopamine, you're suggesting. The government, knowing this, creates a drug that doesn't actually resolve the problem but feeds and kills the bug *just enough* to make a society of life-long dependents on this drug? Why?" Jim squints at me with unbelief.

"I don't know. I haven't figured that out yet. So what do you think?" I ask, and finish my glass.

"I think what you found in your initial tests is compelling, but doesn't warrant these conclusions," he says, with a grin forming on the corner of his mouth.

"I thought you would say that." I stand from my chair with the intention of pouring us each a second round.

"But, like I always say 'measure what is measurable, and make measurable what is not,'" Jim says before taking his last sip.

"You've never said that," I laugh, pulling his glass from his hand and setting it with mine on the maple desk.

"Okay, it was Galileo. But my point is, that even though right now I think you're a little pitchfork-wielding crazy, maybe you're right about some of this, but you'd need to prove it. Which means you'd need to test it, and it also means that you need to be very careful, Ethan. Don't tell anyone about this," he finishes with encouraging eyes. It's what I was hoping he would say. But if I'm going to continue testing, I'm going to need more material, which means there's someone I need to talk to. Lapis Muir.

CHAPTER 13

December 24th, 2046

One time of year above all others makes me despise my chosen specialty: flu season. Flu season unhappily occurs at the same time as the holiday season, and in this way every year the bane of my professional life links arms with the archenemy of my personal life to drown me in mucus and cellophane wrapping. Liz has the stomach flu this year, the worst of years. She's vomiting constantly, while trying to care for Arthur, and it makes work even more miserable to know that she's at home alone in that condition. For most people flu season is marked by an increased intake of vitamin C and frequent use of hand sanitizer. For one fifth of the city population, flu season is marked by a week of eating canned soups and binge-watching television. For me, flu season is marked by dying elderly patients and on rare occasion infants. While healthy infants still exist, they are few and far between in the city. The city is heavily populated by women exposed to Obcasus. The women who weren't don't want to raise their children in a city of violence like ours so they move away. Healthy families live rurally, exposed families live urbanely, and it's as reasonable as it could be. So in addition to my usual patients I also receive exclusively elderly flu victims. Men and women who were too smart, or too busy, to get the recommended flu vaccination.

The flu is by definition a respiratory virus, not because all of its symptoms are respiratory but because it spreads through respiratory fluids. Most people don't consider how incestuous human bodily fluids are: in order to catch the flu someone else's mucus or saliva must enter into your nose or mouth. Since humans instinctually touch their faces three times a minute, one hundred and eighty times an hour, for every waking hour of their lives, I have no patience for the inevitable cry of "oh, I have no idea how I got the flu, I was so careful." Careful is getting the recommended flu-shot, careful is not wiping down your shopping cart with a sanitation wipe, old man. It's what I uncharitably think, but withhold from saying, to my fourth hospitalized flu patient of the day. And as if the day could not get any worse, bitchy Becca is the nurse on the rotation, and she hasn't stopped bemoaning the holiday "cheer" that has vomited itself on every square inch of the hospital. I too despise the banal decorations, the glorified salutations, the unnatural putrid invention known as the fruit cake, and the inauthentic smiling or, far worse, the authentic smiling. But the only thing I hate more than these seasonal ruinations is hearing Becca squeal about it: "Who do you think is responsible for this trash? I bet it's the board. Those animals are always looking for something to take this god-awful place from bad to worse. I hope they choke on the garland they're blowing all over the place."

I encamp in my office, sifting through monotonous paperwork to escape the sounds, the lights, the nurses, the patients, people in general. I review test results for my regular patients who I will be seeing again this week. A brain MRI shows stable condition in the lesion progression for Lorinda Marks, which is both good and bad news. It's good news, because it shows a fairly healthy condition of her brain, but it's bad news because it leaves the degeneration of her neurological symptoms a mystery. I note her file to test for mycoplasma, candida, ANA, and a hormonal panel. The blood results for Liam Ottoman came back with a startling low number of macrophages, which further suggest the suspected bone marrow disorder. I note in his file to refer him to Dr. Jones for further investigation. Finally, four other blood results for other patients all perfectly normal. I sign two dozen prescription refills, Low Dose Naltrexone, a few anti-depressants, extended release antibiotics for my bacterial infection cases, which awakens my brain to today's plans.

Today, I am pushing to leave the hospital an hour early to visit the Assistance Center. Once there I'm going to insist that the hospital would like to "follow up" with Lapis. If I can get her alone, I am going to persuade her to let me volunteer to handle bodies with her, in exchange for her looking the other way as I extract samples. Of course, all of this is dependent on how my hospitalized flu patients hold up. Healing a sick body is a practice in art, but healing a frail and aged sick body is a fall of the cards. You can have two flu patients, both male, both seventy, both the same weight and height, with the same lifestyle, equally infirmed with the virus, yet one will live and one will die. It's enigmatic; something science fails to explain. It can be added to the pile of inexplicable contingencies that cloud my thoughts: why did my father die from a simple fall, why is Liz unable to have children, and today, why is the government promulgating erroneous information to us?

When I'm finally able to escape the drudgery of the hospital, the snowy streets lengthen my drive to the Assistance Center by twice the amount of time. I flip through radio stations, stopping on APR - the Associated Press Radio. They are discussing the possibility that Bryan Powell will call for updated studies on D-MAZ, now that it has reached its fifth anniversary since development. The female-led commentary switches to an outdated clip of a press conference, where the commanding voice of President Powell can be heard answering press questions:

"Some have posed the question as to why we have restricted the testing of the Dopimazipal to government-employed physicians, namely from the Department of Defense. It's a really important question and the answer is remarkably simple: that proper preliminary testing required the use of Obcasus on laboratory animals. It seemed plainly unwise if not unethical to entrust chemical weapons materials to those untrained to handle such materials. Furthermore, once the studies reached readiness for clinical trial, our doctors, who worked with RemX to develop the drug, were the most qualified to understand its dosage, effectiveness, and even side effects. When we considered to whom we should entrust the care of the American people, we simply went with those who were most qualified, who devoted themselves in full immersion to the development of this drug and who had already walked through trial after trial with the laboratory animals. We wanted to have the purest, simplest, most effective treatment possible and today we now know with full acceptance from the medical community that this is exactly what we provided."

I turn it off as I street-park, rubbing my hands over my face a few times in an attempt to clear my mind and jolt myself awake. It isn't true, any of it. It's all one big pile of bullshit, and that's why I'm here. I'm going to expose it.

"Hello, Sir. How can I help you?" The office attendant asks me. She's the same woman as before, only she looks more unkempt than the last time. Her roots expose a mix of brown and grey, her blonde curls are dry and frizzy, her disposition is fairly unengaged, and under her glasses I see bland unmade-up eyes. I see she's taking the holidays as well as I am. I haven't shaven in three days so the thick layer of scruff is itching where it meets my neck, the bags under my eyes are finally reaching parental levels, and I'm altogether curmudgeonly in attitude.

"Is Lapis here? Can you tell her Dr. Ethan King is here to see her?" I ask. She makes the routine phone call, and as if orchestrated, Lapis skips through the double doors before the phone is even returned to its hold.

"Ethan! I've been expecting you. Here, come! Follow me," she says sprightly. Expecting me? Why would she be expecting me? She does a spastic motion with her hand for me to follow her through the double doors. I comply, and once through, make the familiar right turn into the hallway leading to the morgue.

"Nope, this way." She grabs me by the wrist, yanking me from my turn, and pulls me behind her to another hallway. She stops in front of a thick steel door with a small metal gridded window. She doesn't have to tell me what room it is. The blue glow emanating from the window tells me all I need to know; this is simply the front entrance. She opens the door and pushes me into the room, making sure the door fully shuts behind her. Instantly the cold air trickles past my skin and into my heart. The blue light distorts Lapis, making her hair look a luminescent violet instead of red, and setting her pale skin bright blue.

"I have to tell you something, some men came by a couple days after you were here. They said they were doing a quality audit, federal inspectors or something. Well, they interviewed me and they asked me some strange questions... about you." Her voice echoes in the steel room. She takes another step toward me, and I make a corresponding step backward. "Oh, don't worry Ethan. I'm a great secret keeper." She winks at me, and inches toward me again with a smile.

"What did they say?" I ask her. I examine her skeptically for a recording device, or a weapon. She's wearing only black scrubs today, which makes it all the more difficult to judge where Lapis ends and space begins. The only thing I am able to discern is the disturbing fact that she isn't wearing a bra. Anytime she moves or adjusts, which for Lapis is every thirty seconds or so, a corresponding jiggle waves over her chest, finally setting atop her distended stomach. I have rarely found it attractive when women walk around braless. Occasionally, some gorgeous woman with perky breasts noticeably bigger than Liz's will walk into the hospital to provide the exception, but Lapis is no exception. In fact, Lapis is painfully the rule, because her large size forces my mind to consider any jiggling on her body as a symptom of a health issue instead of a pleasant reminder that all women are naked under their clothes.

"Yeah, so, it's a tad bit strange. They asked if you had performed unnecessary testing on the Inexes. Specifically, and they kept using that word 'specifically,' whether you had taken brain tissue from them. The way they were asking, honestly, made me really uncomfortable. I felt like maybe you had done something illegal and I was a co-conspirator or something, and like I might lose my job, so I lied. I said 'no,' that you hadn't taken any and that I was with you the whole time. So, needless to say, Dr. King, you owe me. And I can't wait to hear all about why you took brain tissue that you didn't need, but first let me get to the strangest part. They told me that you might try to come back here, and that if you did that I should contact them immediately and let them know. Which I haven't done, so you double owe me and I have all kinds of ideas as to how you'll make up for it." She does a standing bounce of excitement. I can feel the blood leaving my head, beads of clammy sweat forming on the back of my neck, and the most painful headache instantly forms behind my eyes. Who are they? What do they want from me? Are these the people who saw my laboratory images? They have to be!

"Federal inspectors" repeats in my mind. For years the city has known about a group of federal agents that we neutrally refer to as "black coats." They serve as an anti-terrorist task force, and so occasionally we'll notice an increase of them in the city, but then they disappear for a while. I've always assumed they were just doing their jobs, investigating tips, and maybe making occasional arrests of terrorist suspects. Now I wonder if these "federal inspectors" are the same people, and if instead of searching for terrorists, they search for whistle blowers, for people with their noses in the government's business, for people like me. I wonder if they told anyone else here to contact them if I came in, if right now while we stand here the front desk manager is dialing them. I feel ill, and panicked, like I need to escape. As if Lapis is reading my mind she makes another small step toward me with a comforting tone.

"No one else knows about this, by the way! They were very secretive with the whole thing. They only talked to me and to Enaria, and so of course I asked Enaria what they said, because, as

I mentioned, I was a bit afraid. Turns out, they had only asked her if she had any direct contact with you and she didn't even remember talking to you, but they did say that all civilian interactions are explored for quality purposes and to let them know if you came around again. Lucky for you, Enaria isn't here today. Yes, apparently with Christmas being tomorrow even the wicked witch of the west has somewhere to be." She connects word with word at a pace more adept for a conversation with the Flash than an ordinary human. "Are you okay?" she asks, staring at my now trembling hands.

"I don't like this room," is all I'm able to whisper.

"Oh. But this is the most private room in the center. Here, maybe you should lay down." She gestures to the chair of death. I anxiously shake my head 'no' at her. "I don't think you have anything to worry about, Ethan, really! Now curiosity is killing me. Why did you take brain tissue you didn't need?" she asks, tilting her head sideways like a dog might if you tried to have an in-depth conversation with it.

"I... It. It's complicated," I say as calmly as I can, but with no realistic sense that such an answer would suffice for Lapis. I can't tell her about the Leptospira, or the deleted files, or the grand conspiracy I've begun to believe. For all I know she isn't actually on my side, and she's simply waiting for me to divulge my discoveries and report me to the inspectors. What can I tell her? A lie? A lie won't do, not with her. A truth? What sort of truth would be compelling enough?

Arthur.

"You might not understand the 'why' in what I am about to tell you, but my wife and I took in an Inexorable almost two months ago. We're working on adopting him. At the beginning I just wanted to understand him better, and since I'm a doctor the only natural way I could do that is through research, examination. I thought it would give me a better understanding of who he was. And it did, in a way. It really did." I hear my voice echo back to me across the steel walls. Lapis gawks, before biting the inside of her cheek and swaying her hips in a bouncing motion like she does. But her eyes, which are glued to mine, look new to me. Like for the first time I'm seeing underneath the fabric of her personality and into something penetrable – something afraid.

"You're lying," she asserts, regaining confidence in her features. "You're lying, Dr. King. I just know it. You wouldn't take an Inexorable in, would you? You're one of the good guys. Good guys don't feed the animals." She places her pale hands on her love handles, standing in a posture of certitude.

"Why not?" I ask.

"Because, Ethan, they hurt people. Do you really have an Inex in your house?" Her tone is skeptical.

"I do." I nod while pushing out the two difficult words. Her cheeks begin to flush, and she stills her movements, causing me to focus on her falling, sad eyes--not sad, disappointed. For some reason I don't want to disappoint Lapis. I want her to continue finding me charming, and faithful enough to lie for. And the fact of the matter is that, I don't just want it, I need it.

"Why did you come here to see me, Ethan?" she asks in a defeated voice.

"I have this masterpiece painting that I've been working on, it's in my head, not on canvas. It's of a Philadelphian street, filthy and forsaken. On the street there are many poor people, an elderly homeless man, a D.C. refugee with burn marks along her face, a drug addict trying to sell D-MAZ. But on the street one is poorer than them rest of them. This person, the poorest one, is small, barely clothed, and so skinny that you can make out the shape of his heart beating behind his ribcage. He's an Inexorable. The image is bleak, it's real, it's what I see day in and day out. But, in this scene, there's a break in the skyline that offers hope. It lets warm sun beams through to shine down on them. The problem is that I can't finish that skyline, because, it's lacking something absolutely essential. You see, someone recently told me that there's this special type of blue color that I need to finish the skyline. It, uh, it provides the answers, it gives the whole painting meaning. Do you know what that color is?" I urge the last line at her. She looks up to me with a blooming smile.

"Lapis Lazuli. But that doesn't really answer the question, now does it?" she responds, still beaming and now bouncing on her toes.

"I would like to volunteer with you in disposing the bodies here. I'd keep you company, and provide a helpful hand as needed, and in exchange I thought you could look the other way if I took a few more samples. It would obviously need to be kept a secret. I just want to understand my son better." I submit my proposal, and look into her eyes with a sense of desperation.

"Oh, well, I like the idea of spending more time with you, but you can understand me feeling a little queasy, because, honestly your story doesn't add up. I'm not saying that to be mean, I would never intentionally be mean to you. My father used to say that I'm frenetic and that meant asking questions that weren't always appropriate but that were almost always correct. So, I'm just thinking to myself that if you were only using this brain tissue for personal growth to understand the Inex, why would government black coats be so interested in it? I don't need you to answer, I'm just pointing out why I'm feeling a little uncomfortable with the idea." She smiles for her remarks, except for the term "Inex" which she scrunches her face at.

"That's understandable. I think they found out about it because I used the same hospital lab for both my personal and professional tests. That is, I think someone was examining my progress in the actual Polio testing and noticed me examining Inexorable brain matter and perhaps became concerned. That isn't a mistake that I would make again," I assure her.

"I would hope not. If I'm going to make lying for you a regular thing." She winks.

"So, is that a yes?"

"Yes, it is. That is, if you can tell me what's different about me since the last time you saw me!" She makes a fairy-like giggle to herself. I look over her again, seeing nothing unfamiliar besides her black scrubs.

"New scrubs?" I ask.

"Close! It's what's under the scrubs that matters. I've lost twenty pounds! Can't you tell?" She does a spin to show me her profile. What a trap. If she lost twenty pounds it would have to be that she had an inflamed kidney removed or something, because even in black I can see the same exact rolls jostle to and fro with her steps. But to her credit, the more time I spend with Lapis the more compelled I am by her, not physically, but something deep. I think it's possible that her unabated optimism is something I need in my life. Positivity, energy, passion, characteristics I'm not prone toward, but that I am growing to enjoy in this other person.

"I hadn't noticed precisely, but I believe it. You're always up to something new and exciting. I suppose next time I see you, you'll tell me you've taken to skiing," I jest. She lets a snorted laugh.

"Why, would that surprise you?" She steps nearer to me, and my corresponding step back finally pushes me against one of the cold steel walls.

"Nothing would surprise me with you, Lapis. But I have to go. I'm running late as is," I admit, scooting to the side and closer toward the door.

"Oh, that's too bad. In that case, I hope you have a very Merry Christmas, Ethan." She skips over to the door and opens it for me.

"You too. And Lapis?" I look back, catching her eyes one last time. "Thank you."

CHAPTER 14

Arthur whips his head around to take notice as I push my way into the house. I dust off my snowy shoes with a few quick stomps, and let the warmth of the house exude into my body layer by layer. Liz has the fireplace going, bright flames twirl behind the tree-gilded metal screen, casting its flickering shadow to the floor. Arthur sits directly in front of it, his hands touching and shrinking back from the hot metal episodically. His mesmerized attraction to the fire scares me, and it must scare Liz too, because the screen is accessorized with a reflective silver padlock. Poor Liz is lying on the couch, cocooned in a blanket, watching Arthur with the most disconnected gaze.

"Hey sweetheart, how are you feeling?" As I approach her she bends her knees to make room for me on the couch.

"Uhghruh," she mumbles out.

"That good, huh?" I affectionately rub my hands over her blanketed knees. The only thing that could be worse than Liz having the stomach flu this bad, is if Arthur contracts it at the same time. I'll have to sanitize everything once they're in bed tonight.

"You just can't even believe the day I've had," she barely makes out, a glassy layer of tears welling up in her eyes. The pasty complexion of her skin reminds me of the way people look when they've experienced something traumatic. Her eyes are plagued with dark bags below and puffy redness above, her cheeks are hollowed, and her lips are pale and chapped.

"What's wrong?" I ask.

"Nothing. Everything. I don't know." She shakes her head and barely raises her shoulders to display a defeated shrug.

"Did he hurt you?" I turn to Arthur, who is still fascinated with the burning sensation of the metal screen.

"No, he didn't. It was just a hard day." Tears fall upon her cheeks. I lean over, wiping them away with gentle strokes.

"I'm so sorry, baby." I hug her knees, as if to infuse happiness into her.

"You just wouldn't believe it," she says again.

"Tell me about it."

"Tomorrow. Tomorrow." She nods, showing how tired she is.

***

Christmas morning is something foreign today. After my father died I never regained a positive sense of the holiday. That first Christmas without him served as nothing more than a painful token to my mother and me that the most important thing in our life was gone. The second Christmas was slightly better, not so formidably sad, but it instead highlighted the schism forming in mine and my mother's relationship. The third, the fourth, and the fifth Christmases, I can't remember a single familial thing about. I only remember avoiding home, the cold walks through snowy Main Street, and the Christmas lights glittering inside store shops at night.

Before Liz and I were married she tried to redeem the occasion, to make it something celebratory for us. Her parents invited me to share in their annual Christmas party before returning to Fairfax each year. They'd stuff my arms full of gifts, my mouth full of homemade cookies, and they'd laugh as Liz and I would dance like stereotypical white people to the holiday music. They crammed so many neighbors and friends into their miniscule home that Liz and I would have to escape to the frigid back patio just to breathe. Each year we would sit there cuddled against the firepit, sneaking absinthe and laughing about her father's idiosyncrasies. Sometimes we'd talk about this day, the day when we'd have Christmas morning with our own children. We shared that innate knowledge that when you have children Christmas becomes something magical again, something full of wonder. But as Liz and I move tiredly around the kitchen with resonate thankfulness that Arthur is still sleeping in his cage at seven-thirty, I am overcome with the sense that our first Christmas with a child will not be how we had imagined it.

Our living room is devoid of the potential dagger-producer that other people call a Christmas tree, there are no Christmas lights because we had to plaster over most of our electrical outlets, and of course, the gifts we got for Arthur are exclusively therapeutic: chew sticks, language videos, and lavender-infused everything to calm him. I pour our first cup of Christmas-morning coffee, hot steam fills the air to reveal each sunbeam piercing through the kitchen windows. I push Liz's mug toward her on the marble counter. She looks somewhat healthier today, her complexion warmer, and no impending signs of vomit. She has her hair pulled into a disheveled bun on the top of her head, and she's swallowed up in a puffy pink robe.

"I love you. I love coffee." She softly laughs, her naked eyes connecting with mine as she gathers the mug into her hands. I smile back at her.

"Before Arthur wakes up, would you want to exchange our gifts? It might increase the chance that they don't get destroyed," I say.

"You're a wise man." She nods tiredly, and points to the back counter of the kitchen where she's already set two pristinely wrapped presents, presumably for me. She mosies to her feet, before sifting the gifts over to me.

"I only have one for you," I say, pulling the purple envelope shaped box from my back pocket.

"That's alright, love. I'm sure it's wonderful whatever it is. Since you have two, you should open one first, then I'll open, and you can open your second gift last."

Leave it to Liz to systematize something as innocuous as this. I chuckle at the proposition. She pushes a shoebox-sized gift toward me, with gold wrapping paper and a carefully crafted blue ribbon. As I take it in my hands to liberally unwrap it, Liz returns to her coffee, cautiously sipping it from both hands. The unwrapping reveals a brown wooden box which I set carefully on the counter. I expect a bottle of scotch or a row of cigars, but when I flip the lip open, it reveals a large diamond-shaped glass plaque contrasted against black velvet. I pull it out and hold it up. The glass contains a detailed image of the anatomy of the human heart, which glows in soft color when there's light behind it, giving it an antique quality. It's beautiful, but I don't entirely understand the gift. I smile down at Liz and lift a curious eyebrow.

"It's because really, foundationally, you're all heart." She winks. "And ... it's more than it seems." She takes the glass plaque from my hands, and tits the bottom of it toward me. She runs her finger over the bottom of the glass until we both hear a click.

"Ah. See!" She shows a distended end in the bottom of the glass where a reflective material is slightly exposed. She pulls it out with two fingers revealing a brilliantly disguised memory chip for laptops.

"I loaded this with pictures of us; you, me, and Arthur, so that even when you're at work, we're with you – hidden away in your heart. You get it?" I gaze into her excited eyes.

"Liz, it's brilliant. I love it." I pull her in for a slow soft kiss, before returning the nearly indiscernible chip inside of the plaque, and placing the plaque carefully in the box.

"My turn," she declares with a veiled sense of enthusiasm. I hand her the small purple box. She opens it with intentionality, unfolding each tab of paper one by one, until it reveals a thin jewelry box atop a sealed envelope.

"Open the envelope first," I suggest. She sets the wrapping on the countertop, and grins skeptically as she slides her fingernail under the envelope's seal. Inside is our grant of temporary guardianship of Arthur. We had been told that we would need to meet with legal to undergo scrutiny, and the idea had been making her a nervous wreck. It wasn't too difficult to persuade them to meet with me alone, and so this envelope will tell her that she, Elizabeth King, is a temporary guardian to Arthur King. As she reads the first few lines her face develops a scowl of concentration, her smile fades, and the paper begins trembling in her hands. When she finally meets my eyes again, she begins to cry.

"It's our guardianship?"

"Yes." I gently caress her arms.

"But I thought we had to..." she begins, and I interrupt: "I found another way."

We share an emotional smile and a few breaths in silence. She hastily sweeps her tears away and embraces me with a tighter squeeze than normal. I wrap her up firmly in my arms, kissing along the top of her head and feeling her smile against my chest. When she pulls away I give her nudging eyes to open the jewelry box. Inside she finds a necklace to commemorate the occasion. A one inch rose-gold pillar which hangs vertically from its chain, is inscribed on the left with "Mom. EST Nov 1, 2046," the first day she met Arthur. An inscription on the right side of the vertical pillar reads "The pillar that makes us strong." Liz lifts it from its box, turning it left and right to read the inscriptions, but then begins crying again, and harder this time. I hold her for a few minutes, feeling her chest expand and shrink with each shaky breath. She tells me how much she loves me, I tell her the same, and when she feels composed enough she kisses me and hands me her final gift.

"You remember, love, yesterday, when I said that you wouldn't believe the day I was having?" she asks, as I go through my same routine of tearing paper.

"Yeah, why?" The question hangs in the air as I open the shoebox-style lid. The object inside makes my heart skip a beat with confusion. No, it isn't just confusion, it's unbelief. I stare at the object, not sure if it's real. I don't, I can't... It's some sort of joke.

"What?" I barely whisper, but she nods in affirmation as tears stream unremittingly down her cheeks.

"You're not sick?" I ask with overwhelming trepidation in my voice, my hands beginning to shake.

"No." She forces a smile. I look inside the box again, unable to speak, unable to inhale a single breath of oxygen. My eyes fill with heat, but inside my stomach I feel an ice cold brick pulling me to the floor. I lift the white thin stick from the box, my hand making it tremble in the air uncontrollably. She looks up at me with a mix of desperation and joy, and tells me plain as day: "We're having a baby."

CHAPTER 15

June 18th, 2047

I can map exactly where in the brain emotional experience originates. I can perform a CT on Arthur and point to the specific scar tissue which caused him to be emotionally disturbed. I can reduce our emotional experiences to the hormonal concoction that floods our brains when we're introduced to something supra-ordinary, something startling. But emotions are a complex thing, and it is this complex piece of personhood that separates us from Inexorables. When we found out that Liz was pregnant, I should have felt overcome with joy. This was the realization of all our hopes, it's what we have sacrificed unquantifiable pain and time and procedures for; a baby. Our baby. Our sweet, healthy, human child. But emotions are a complex thing. Right after she told me, I didn't hug her, I didn't kiss her, I didn't tell her that I loved her or that everything would be okay. Instead, I ran to the bathroom and vomited.

After years of desperation and preparedness to hear that Liz was pregnant, why now? Why, when we had altered our lives in such a way that the prospect of a baby is horrific to us, would it at last appear? The impossible, it seems, only happens in the most desperate of circumstances. It descends *deus ex machina* to tip the scales for deliverance or destruction, and we couldn't tell which one this would be. Emotions are complex because they often reflect complex situations, like this. We felt momentarily paralyzed. We cried, a lot. We knew in our hearts that we were not going to give up the baby, but we also knew that we couldn't handle Arthur and a baby. The worst news stories are of Inexes slamming bricks into their newborn sibling's heads, or biting their fingers off, or drowning them in the toilet. In Philadelphia a few weeks ago, a mother found that her newborn Inex had bled to death because her toddler Inex had fully castrated the infant with a pair of scissors. Images like this became a constant source of nightmares for Liz and me. Nevertheless, the thought of turning Arthur over to the AC or dropping him in the forest to die, was unfathomable.

And so, we had agreed that we were going to find a new home for Arthur, somewhere, with someone, who would care about him like we did. Liz devoted herself to finding a family, and to detach from him emotionally. But even in a city as big as Philly, there was no one who wanted him. She called orphanages, religious shelters, every woman from her old adoption group. When she switched to online efforts, she discovered what we should have suspected, that she was not alone; that many mothers were begging for families to take their Inexorable children. Like us, they knew that they couldn't control the violence but did not want to see their children resolved. But persistently, Liz posted an advertisement for Arthur. She included a picture, and a glowing list of his abilities, interests, and tastes. She detailed our training methods, and how he hasn't seriously injured anyone or anything since he's been here, which isn't exactly the truth but it is as far as she knew. Then, a week later, a miracle happened. A man named Lewis Little inquired to Liz about taking Arthur in. He accompanied his inquiry with a sad story about how he lost his wife and son in the attacks. He said that he hadn't been ready to move forward since then, but that lately he has felt the need for companionship, or to do something good in the world, just something to fill the void. Liz bought it hook, line, and sinker, but I had reservations.

We invited him over to meet Arthur, so that we could get to know the man who might be taking him in. When we opened our front door, he was older-looking than we expected. He had told us that he was fifty years old, but he looked at least a decade older. He was bald, wrinkled, and age spots stained his cheek and forehead. He had these piercingly dark green eyes that felt ominous and insincere, but we invited him in anyway. The moment he laid eyes upon Arthur we knew that something was very wrong. He got a look in his eyes, not the kind that a father has for a son, but the kind a man has for a woman; a lustful, desirous look. He all too quickly scooped Arthur into his arms, as if to hug him, but Arthur squirmed and screamed. Lewis just held him tighter and whispered in his ear with an off-putting smoothness: "That's alright, angel, you're okay." Liz ripped Arthur from his arms, and yelled at the man to "get the hell out of our house!" Arthur repeated Liz's phrase, yelling at the man in his tiny voice "get the hell out of our house!"

Liz watched Lewis from the window with a face of repulsion until his car was out of sight. She turned around, and then with a sense of calculation, got down carefully on one knee, and then the other, and finally dropped forward until her face was on the floor. She began to sob and make frustrated screeching sounds in between. Turning her hands to face the ceiling, she clenched her fists, occasionally beating them on the floor. It's a position I have never seen Liz in, like she was praying, crying out in desperation, but her sounds of agony were so raw it told me that she didn't expect anyone to hear. It's like she was expressing everything pent up in my heart, everything that hated this cruel world and needed help. I didn't know what to do, if I should comfort her, or if I should let her be. And so Arthur and I just stood there watching her weep and mourn all the excruciating details of our circumstances.

"Mommy was bad?" Arthur looked at me with the most sincere eyes I had ever seen. We taught him to connect pain with punishment, and so he applied that knowledge to the best of his ability. Liz was hurt, and so she must have been bad. And when she heard it she whipped her head up from the floor, with bloodshot puffy eyes and a wet face. She stared with breathlessness, first at me, then at him. He's never called her that before, "Mommy." We haven't even taught him the word. She rose to her feet, and knelt to take Arthur into her arms. As she held him, scratching along his scalp, she wept on his tiny shoulder.

"I'm sorry, I'm so sorry," she whispered over and over. Her face was as readable as a billboard: He's our son, he belongs to us. He always did. It broke me, having my betrayal to my own promises exposed. I joined them, holding Liz from behind and kissing along the top of her head. We swallowed that we would become a family of four, and we tried to imagine what that would look like in with our situation. We formulated plans for how we would keep a protective barrier between Arthur and the baby at all times, how Liz would work feedings and diaper changes, and how we would handle bringing them out in public. We knew that no amount of preparation would be sufficient, and that the likelihood of tragedy increases every day. Even so, two days ago we stood boldly on the 13th floor of the government building in a run-down court room, Arthur propped up by Liz's belly, and we swore ourselves to him. Before granting us permanent guardianship rights, the judge, who was a freckled man with warm eyes and an unprofessionally large beard, looked at us with a contemptible amount of pity while asking for the tenth time if we were sure this is what we wanted. He was quick to remind us that as his guardians we would have responsibility not simply to keep Arthur safe, but to keep the world safe from Arthur. His crimes would be our crimes, and his restitution our restitution. Though he never verbally condemned our actions, as we signed the court stationery the judge looked at us as if we had signed our own death certificates. We patiently accepted his warnings, and then we brought our rescued malefactor of a son home.

Today, we celebrate it, our adoption of Arthur Carmine King. Jim and Mary join the three of us for a summer picnic at Neshaminy State Park, which sits directly along the Delaware River. The park is host to innumerable animals, which scurry around the natural drinking pools, skeptical of their human onlookers. Liz carefully selected a picnic table with a wide view of the river which reflects sunlight in fragmented flashes. The table is shaded under draping oak branches, which makes the heat barely tolerable for Liz; I can already see beads of sweat congregating along her hair line. The table is decked with a quintessential red checkered cloth, chopped watermelon, a cool layered salad, and a pitcher of lemonade.

"Wow, a girl. I always wanted a girl, but we just ended up with T.J. What are ya'll namin' her again? It's pulling teeth tryna' get anything out of this guy." Mary thumbs in Jim's direction. Liz laughs, rubbing over her belly a few times.

"Alice. We're naming her Alice." Liz smiles.

"That's just lovely, Liz. Oh! Arthur and Alice? How sweet," Mary says with a rosy expression.

"Thank you," Liz responds. Mary looks quite a bit older than Jim, though they're the exact same age. She has sagging cheeks, shoulder length salt and pepper hair, and I have never seen her apart from a full-length skirt of some kind. Even in this heat she's wearing a thick yellow striped one that drapes loosely around her ankles.

"So how far along are you again?" Mary asks.

"I am 36 weeks, so we only have four weeks to go. Wow, it's strange to hear myself saying that. I've never had time pass so quickly while also having so much dependent on time. We still have so much work to do at the house, but I am so ready to not be pregnant anymore. Pregnancy is not as happy clappy as I would have expected." Liz adjusts uncomfortably on the wooden seat.

"Morning sickness got ya' good?" Mary pats Liz on the shoulder.

"Morning sickness, brain fog, fatigue, mood swings with no wine. Not to mention sharing my internal organ space with a whole other creature that just keeps growing and stealing more room. And gosh, my pelvic bone... what is that pain? Long story short, I'm a miserable pregnant woman. I love my baby girl more than you can possibly imagine, but pregnancy, it turns out, is not for me."

"I've forgotten, because it's been so long and because you kind of idealize the whole thing when you're done having babies," Mary adds.

"Welp, after all the red meat I'm grilling, we're all going to know what it's like to have a baby later tonight," Jim intrudes, standing from the table while proudly lifting a cooler of raw animal flesh.

"Oh, now that's real nice, dear," Mary remarks dryly.

"Hey, I'm a doctor," Jim qualifies. It's his classic excuse when he wants to say something filthy. He's a doctor, so he's seen it all, and therefore the rest of us must excuse his impropriety.

"I'm a doctor, and I think that's disgusting." I make sure to stare him right in the eye while saying it, my face grinning wide.

"Well now, thank you, Ethan." Mary nods at me.

"Yeah, some sissy doctor....." Jim whispers under his breath. I continue to grin, but roll my eyes dramatically for him to see.

"Well if you two are going to start cooking, I'm going to head down to the water's edge with Arthur." Liz's voice sounds tired already.

"I'll go too," Mary adds, and the two stand, Liz requiring considerable more time and leverage to do so.

"Watch him with the stones," I warn Liz.

"Of course, love." She casts a glowing smile at me. She doesn't see the glow in herself, but I see it. It isn't some magical state of bliss, but her dignity as she does everything she normally would, in miserable conditions, all while carrying that gorgeous belly around and still forking over the energy to flirt with me. The women walk down toward the water, Liz's summer dress trailing in the wind behind, while Arthur runs circles around them with insurmountable energy, spewing angry growls at them--a new and unappealing trait of his.

"So let's talk." Jim switches effortlessly into a sober tone while pouring charcoal into the primitive state park grill. "What more have you found?" He makes a quick look over his shoulder for passersby. I pull a microchip from inside my wallet, and tuck it into his plaid button-up pocket with a pat.

"With my last set of samples, I continued to feed them and all they did was stay active. They never reproduced. They don't breed, ever! It explains why each person is in a sense stuck where they were from first exposure. I was wrong to think that the enzyme complex kills the bacteria. Nothing in D-Maz kills the bacteria. The bacteria just doesn't reduplicate," I say.

"How long before we can go public?" he asks in a hush.

"I still need time. We have enough to prove only that the administration is lying about the cause of the brain damage. But Jim, if I don't find a cure for it, if we can't publish a treatment, then no one will be convinced. It will be censored and never promulgated, and even if people believed it, who would care? So they lied about the source of the damage, but they still provide an effective treatment for it. It wouldn't be enough!" I exhale frustration. Jim rolls a piece of printer paper and sets it ablaze using a zippo-lighter, before stuffing it in-between coals.

"Can you find a cure? Is there a cure?"

"As I already told you: I created a sufficient protocol for eradicating the bacteria from the body. But the antibiotic protocol would only keep people from having Inexorables, it wouldn't actually cure anyone, because it can't restore damaged tissue. This is why stem cell treatments never worked on Inexorables when we used to treat them. The bacteria would just attack the new material. We need both, we need the bacteria to die and the tissue to be rebuilt."

"Dammit, Ethan. The information you have is already enough to tumble the house of cards. It's enough! It is enough for people to have normal kids, people will listen for that!" His voice rises.

"We've never tested it, Jim. You're being hasty," I insist.

"Tested it? We can't sit on this forever. How long have we known about this? How long have you been hiding your AC work from Liz?" he almost yells, his voice deep and firm.

"Why are you panicking?" I ask as calmly as possible to ease the tension. The second he and I go public is the second my research ends. Which means if the day we go public I don't have a cure for Arthur yet, then I will never have a cure for Arthur. It isn't time yet.

"They are going to find out," Jim insists, while shakily pulling zip-lock bags of marinated beef from the cooler.

"They are not. We have laid low, we are off the map with discretion. We have copies, and backup systems. We're okay."

"I see more black coats in the city by the day. Something is up, and we have no back up if we both get taken." His blue eyes flash a mixture of desperation and irritation.

"I want to find a cure," I restate, calmly again. Jim throws a few steaks onto the metal bars of the grill top. They hit the grill with a sizzle.

"What if there is none?"

"I don't believe that." It's the truth.

"You're a misanthrope, Ethan, but now, at the most inconvenient time, you're suddenly an optimist?" He clenches the metal spatula so hard that veins begin popping outward from his grip. I look about our surroundings, sun-cast shadows of tree branches land upon the raw earth, birds fly to and fro disinterested in our affairs, and a brilliantly quiet rustle of leaves that makes me feel unshakable.

"My baby girl will be born in four weeks. I am going to heal Arthur. I am going to heal everyone. I can only research so fast, and it's convenient that you're busy with ED matters and don't even know what the hell Leptospira is."

He glares at me with a palpably disgruntled expression. I know that he's tired, I know that he's afraid, I know that he is not handling these secrets with composure or patience, but he has to man up and swallow it.

"It's hard, Ethan, not knowing," he says, restraining his anger through gritted teeth. He's right, it is hard not knowing. It is hard not knowing why this lie exists in the first place, or whether a cure can ever be found, or how our families might be affected by it. Liz, gorgeous and pregnant, mother of two, has no idea and could easily watch me dragged away to jail for meddling in this administration's secrets. What if we are charged with treason? What if she finds out that I'm spending every Thursday evening at an assistance center with Lapis, cutting out Inexorable brains? She would not, could not, understand. Innocent minds never do. So yes, it's hard not knowing.

"I understand everything you're saying, and we are on the same side. I just want our strikes to be fatal when we make them," I say. Jim stares fixedly on the grill to avoid my eyes and doesn't speak a word in response. I watch him, his greying wheat hair being pushed upward by the hot jolts of breeze, his watering eyes from the smoke of the grill, and his stiff angered face slowly flattening into normal with each passing minute.

"How do you turn a free market into an oligopoly?" Jim asks with a smooth, southern, rhetorical voice. "You buy out or eliminate all small competition, and make a pact with a few large competitors so that you all secure your power. How do you turn a free democracy into an oligarchy? The same way: by eliminating all small competition and making pacts with a few powerhouses so that you all secure your power."

"Where are you going with this?" I ask skeptically.

"You've figured out the *what*, well, I'm trying to figure out the *why*. We only hear about three main sources of power anymore: the president, the military, and the drug company RemX. They're a little incestuous don't ya' think? The government serves the interests of the drug company RemX by subsidizing billions of dollars for D–MAZ not to mention the revenue they naturally receive from it, therefore RemX serves the interests of the government. The military serves the interests of Powell by formulating a non-curing drug that a large portion of our population is dependent upon, making a change of power a frightening possibility. Powell serves the interests of the military by continuing to employ them heavily in his governance and in domestic affairs," he finishes hurriedly as we hear the women and Arthur approaching.

"Aren't you just glad your mother didn't name you Wolfgang?" Jim asks seamlessly as Liz and Mary near the grilling area. I laugh in shock, patting his shoulder twice.

"Those yuppies," I jest, shifting my eye contact to Liz.

"That's all I'm sayin'. Back so soon ladies?" he asks while returning his focus to the sizzling of the grill.

Arthur smiles ear to ear before charging at me with full force. His fists are clenched into tight balls, as each rushed step makes an imprint of his tiny shoes in the dirt. I squat toward the ground, assuming the grin plastered across his face is an invitation for my arms to open and embrace him. But as I open my arms, as the gap between us decreases foot by foot, I discern that dark conniving air boiling behind his eyes. His grin twists sideways, deadened unnaturally by something malevolent. The space between us shrinks to arm's length, and something reflective obtruding from his right fist casts a beam of sun against my face. My vision zeros in on his hand as he raises it into the air, a rusty metal shard squeezed so tightly in it that a drop of blood begins trailing down his arm. My heart has no time to race as his body slams into mine, his arm slashing the metal toward my face with undiminished speed.

I instinctually yank backward from the strike, feeling the metal barely scrape against the hairs of my cheek. He lunges toward me again, blade first, but is suddenly yanked into the air, constricted around his elbows by Liz's hands. She awkwardly jolts his arm, forcing him to drop the blade to the ground, while he kicks incessantly and screams bloody murder for the benefit of the entire park. My heart kicks its first dose of adrenalin through my body, too late to be of any use. It feels as though it's being deposited directly into my stomach, turning it and making me sick. As I rise again to my feet, Liz and I make that familiar eye-contact of shared horrified relief, and a shaky breath exits my lungs. Mary huddles defensively behind Jim, her mouth gaping open and her face devoid of color.

"Happy Adoption Day!" Jim exclaims with a singular sarcastic laugh. Liz and I don't share the humor with him, but Arthur begins laughing manically, before reciting in typical mimicking fashion:

"Happy Adoption Day!"

CHAPTER 16

I n my office I stare at the glorified paper weight Liz gave me
for Christmas. The cold, white ceiling light pierces through the
glass diamond illuminating the carefully articulated heart
anatomy. A world full of secrets is hidden away safely inside the
heart, a microchip with file upon file of demonstrated findings
proving the existence of an unknown parasitic bacteria which
invariably inhabits Inexorables' brains. It's a poetic portrait of my
own heart, deceptively ordinary to the human eye but full of
destructive secrets. Images of tiny dead human bodies under my
hands often disrupt my thoughts like metal sparking in an
otherwise functioning microwave. Swarming bacteria flood my
dreams like the yellow clouds of Obcasus which brought them
here. Sleep has become elusive, work has become a blur of
monotonous insignificance, and the pressure I sense to find a
cure for Arthur is insurmountable. I am certain that I can
eradicate the bacteria with an extended intravenous antibiotic
amalgam, and I've already set aside the proper dosages for
Arthur's body size. Unfortunately only one treatment in the world
exists for the restoration of underdeveloped brain regions. It's
surgically invasive, and the materials needed for it are rare,
expensive, and undoubtedly reserved for the healthy elite of the
world. The only conceivable way of accessing the materials
necessary for the treatment would be to procure them myself, an
undertaking so painful that I doubt redemption could grasp me
there.

The ringing vibration of my pager startles me as a message
from Dr. Singh scrolls across for me to come to his office. I rise
from my chair with a stiff grunt, bending my knees a few times
before exiting my banal office. I take the familiar steps across the
hallway to join the elevator's empty space. Inside I see myself in

the recently polished steel doors, and I look like a haggard stranger. My white coat fits loosely over my slacks and button up, putting on display the weight I've lost over the past seven months of stress. I look frail in a way that I have never looked before, like a curmudgeonly homeless man or retired marathon runner, but not like the virile strong father or husband or doctor or any of the things I am actually supposed to be. Grey hair creeps backward from above my temples, waging war against its oak brown predecessor, and the crow's feet beside my eyes are beginning to descend downward from weariness. For the first time, I can see what I will look like as an old man and it scares me. It isn't what I am supposed to look like, or feel like. But I do look and feel it.

I exit the elevator and turn left toward Dr. Singh's office, making a polite knock before hearing his voice, "Yes, come!" I turn the cool metal knob and enter the faux-wood paneled office. Dr. Singh sits with a contented smile, his big cheeks pulling outward enough to scrape against the lobes of his ears. His features are all overly large: large eyes, large nose, large ears, large lips and cheeks. It would seem that the sheer number of large features would subdue them by proportionality, but they don't.

"Ethan! Come, sit, I have exciting news!" He taps his table with both hands twice in excitement.

"Oh?" I sit down in one of the two uncomfortably upright chairs.

"Next week University is hosting the federal D-MAZ program for an Obcasus exposure test in preparation for a reformulation of D-MAZ," he says quickly, his accent highlighting unusual syllables along the way. A knot of anxiety instantly forms in my stomach. The feds are in town, it explains the increase of black coats Jim has been seeing in the city. But why would they do an Obcasus exposure test? What even is that? And reformulate D-MAZ?

"Why would they need to reformulate?" I ask with a furrowed brow and anxious tone.

"I don't know. But that's what you're going to find out!" He points a chubby finger at me and grins ear to ear.

"How?"

"The University is taking research observers from local hospitals and the board selected you to be one of them after much encouragement on my part." He nearly bounces in his seat with excitement. I glare confusedly at him, and rub my hands over my eyes in slow meditative movements before responding.

"The board decided *what*?"

"You get to sit on a panel of observers while they do the testing! Is it not amazing!?" His face becomes discouraged from my response.

"Why me?" I ask, my heart pounding faster.

"You're invested, given your situation... I thought you'd pay extra special attention," he says with some hesitation.

"Given what situation?" I spit out too quickly. He knows about my research, of course he does. He's probably the person who saw and deleted the Leptospira from Inex tissue almost a year ago. It wouldn't be hard for him to have tracked me to the AC each week, and to discover that I'm a liability. He's setting me up to be found out. He's sending me into a military controlled environment to be caught.

"You know, your... your adoption. Your son, the Inexorable?" He says with careful pauses, calling him 'the Inexorable' as if to distinguish him from some other son of mine.

"No. You'll have to send someone else." I shake my head nervously in response and avert my eyes to the veneer peeling off the cabinetry behind him.

"No, Ethan, you are going," he makes his tone and expression somber. "What is wrong with you? You should be excited, you should feel honored to be elected for this. I pulled ropes, and whispered your name in ears – why are you like this anymore?

The light in your eyes is fading, your performance is off, and for fate's sake, you need a sandwich! This isn't something you can say no to, but I'm worried, extremely worried, as to why you would want to say no at all."

"My daughter will be born in a couple of weeks, and I need to devote my energy elsewhere. I'm not a good fit to observe right now," I respond concisely with a few supporting nods.

"I don't know why you would make me say this, Ethan, but you need to do as you're told. The hospital has been flexible, I've been flexible. I let you off early every Thursday, no questions. I've accepted the pathetic bedside manner reports I've gotten over you, I've even pulled ropes for you –like in this very instance. The dishonor you are showing is very real to me, personal to me, and it is not how an inferior should behave, yet alone a friend. So I'll ask once more, what is wrong with you?"

"Nothing, I'll do it," I respond tersely as I feel cold sweat forming on the back of my neck.

"Do you need help?" He lifts his palms to the ceiling in a desperate questioning fashion.

"I don't need help."

"Do you need a friend?" He presses with more kindness in his voice.

"I don't need a friend." I look up to him with dull, fiercely disinterested eyes. I don't need his lecture on religious stability that I know is coming.

"Perhaps, Ethan, you don't have the essential foundation for processing the change in your life." Here it comes.

"I don't need Hinduism, either." I cut to the chase, and skid my seat back in preparation for a swift exit.

"But maybe you need meaning, hm?" He leans back in his chair in resignation.

"Maybe I need to get back to work." I flash him a dead stare, and hide my trembling hands in my pockets before exiting the room.

Wafts of rubbing alcohol scent the air as I return to my office. I systematically rehearse the places my data is hidden: in the glass diamond on my desk, in a James Joyce book at Jim's house, and of course in my home office computer. It's exactly like Jim said, if we're both caught we have no back-ups, and for the first time the prospect feels all too possible. On the sixth floor I walk through the ugly yellow corridor toward my office, passing Becca at the nurses' station without acknowledgement, and unlock my door with a trembling hand. I reach for the glass diamond, and without a second thought lift it off my desk, lugging it in both hands across the hallway to re-enter the elevator. I press the third floor for the cardiac unit. The world would be a better place if almost all the cardiac doctors in the world dropped dead. They are the wealthiest, cockiest, most self-assuming creatures in the hospital world. Dr. Lexington, the head of cardio here at Philadelphia East, received fourteen awards in one year for his contribution of applying various stitch patterns to a porcine valve replacement. Well, la-di-dah, he can sew. The board elected him to Chief of Staff as a result, causing the entire hospital to suffer under His Greatness' reign for the next year.

When the doors open I do a quick examination of the warm-grey walls in the waiting area. God, even their interior design is better than everyone else's. To the right is the receptionists' desk, which I approach as slyly as possible.

"Hi ... Jane." I talk with a smile while reading her name tag.

"What can I do for you, doctor?" The silver-haired receptionist responds with a voice of radio-worthy smoothness.

"I wanted to offer this as a gift to the cardiac unit for their incredible work. I thought it'd be perfectly displayed in the reception area actually, because the windows let in enough light to make it glow – here look!" I tilt the glass diamond into a beam of sunlight to display the glowing heart.

"Oh wow! I love that, I am sure everyone else will too. What is your name, again, sir?" She stares with joyful green eyes.

"That's not important. It's just a token of appreciation. Have a great day." I turn toward the elevator before she can list me her goodbyes.

CHAPTER 17

Liz adjusts uncomfortably on her side, enveloped in her new husband: a pillow the size of an inflatable rescue boat. The long cylinder pillow curves over her shoulder, under her head, around her front and back, and through her legs with a snake-like quality that makes it unpleasant to look at. It's as though my wife has been slowly strangled by a python whose sole end is to keep her from making physical contact with me. I've taken to calling it "Bob," and I'll occasionally have dialogue with it for the sake of Liz. "Damnit, Bob, stop sleeping with my wife!" I'll say, and she'll laugh. This morning though I don't have it in me to be sarcastic, or flirtatious, or anything pleasant.

"Are you okay, love?" Liz asks me in a tired, cracking voice, "you seem anxious." I throw an extra beige pillow behind my neck and sit up in bed. Today I go to the University Bio-Medical lab to observe military men injecting Obcasus into specialized rodent containments. I am a wreck, certain that I've been on some watch list ever since my first visit to the Assistance Center. But I'm also sick thinking about how soon the baby is coming. I know I should be excited but I'm dreading it instead. It was one thing to have a child who I could throw in a cage and feel no guilt over, it's a totally different world to hold a tiny fragile baby in my arms who depends on me for everything and who has a natural right to that dependence. How do I keep her safe? How do I teach her about the world? How do I constantly care for a tiny growing human person, who is half me and half her mother? With Arthur it's just a matter of survival: if we've kept him alive then we've done our due service to him. Anything else is just extra, and he's really grown to embrace it.

He calls me dad now, and when he's really tired in the morning all he wants to do is cuddle with me, which is more than

I can say for my incredibly pregnant wife these days. But he's still a monster, and he displays that nature constantly. The past few days he's been peeling sharp wood chippings off his bedframe, and he'll try to stab them into us when we're least suspecting it. When he succeeds, he laughs hysterically, as if we just told him the funniest joke. I know it will be something totally different with Alice. It isn't enough that she survives, she needs to live, and that's my job. It's a job that I don't feel even moderately prepared for. But could I share any of this with Liz? What could I possibly say that wouldn't upset her? I want to be honest with her, I want her to see everything going on inside of my mind. I want to divulge to her all of my secrets, all of my worries, all of my hidden life in research and the Assistance Center. But I can't.

"I'm nervous about the baby more than anything," I respond with half the truth.

"So am I. Do you want to talk about it?" she responds softly, and caresses my hand.

"Not really," I respond with a lie, the thousandth one I've had to make this year. The loud clanging of Arthur's hands against his cage signals that he's awake.

"He's up early. What time is it? Six?" Liz asks, making a lame attempt to look over her shoulder at the clock.

"Five-thirty," I correct.

"Uhggggg," she mumbles while burying her face into her pillow.

"I got him for now. He can eat breakfast with me." I lean down and give her a kiss on her forehead.

"Thank you, love," I hear her, still muffled through the pillow. I throw my feet over the side of the bed and feel the wood floor under my toes, rising carefully so as not to aggravate the morning pains of my aging joints. I exit our bedroom, shutting the door quietly behind me, and walk across the hallway to Arthur's room. I open the door and see him hanging from a corner of his cage, tiny hands gripped tightly around the bars and feet propped up to support his weight. He looks at me with blatant confusion, probably because Liz normally gets him in the morning. He lets out an ugly hissing sound and lends me his favorite dead stare. It looks like a scene out of a horror movie: the demon-possessed child is hanging sideways upon the wall, hissing, with evil intentions in his eyes. It ought to be scary, but it isn't anymore. If this were a game of man versus beast, then I have officially tamed the beast to the best of my ability, and though I still respect the power for destruction of that beast, I no longer possess a personal sense of fear when I'm around it.

"Want to go get some breakfast with me?" I ask him tiredly. He climbs down from the corner of his cage and stands in front of the locked door.

"Yes!" he says enthusiastically with a big nod. Before unlocking the cage I examine his blue space alien pajamas, his hands, his messy puffy hair, and any other hiding spot for slivers of wood that he might use against me. His middle and pointer fingers are held too tightly together, which makes me suspicious.

"Arthur, what's between your fingers there?" I point to his left hand. He glares and shouts his response.

"Nothing!"

"Drop the wood, Arthur. Let's not start this day with a fight." I make the hand movements that I use for his pain pressure points, and he winces even though I haven't touched him. He presses his left hand against the cage and then separates his middle and pointer fingers slowly, exposing the fact that nothing was hidden between them. Huh. Strange.

"Thank you for showing me, little man." I push the thin key into the padlock, twist, and let the lock fall into my hand with an inaudible thud. Arthur races beside me, pushing through the door and down the stairs, anxious to find a weapon before I arrive at the kitchen, but he won't find any. Liz and I have turned this house into something one step below a padded psych room. Sharp corners? They've been filed. Electrical sockets? They've been rewired to the ceilings. Light inanimate objects? Sealed in cupboards and drawers by coded locks. Even so, he'll try. He always tries.

The stairs creek underneath me as I step. The thought of hot coffee becomes more than desirous to me; it's a need. I need something, anything, to get me through this day, to get me through this morning. What I really need is a bottle of scotch, and an alternate reality to live in. One where fathers don't die from simple missteps, and terrorists don't release areotolerant bacteria into human populations, where children aren't shattered in the womb by something outside of their control, and where governments don't lie to their people. A world where I am the good guy. A world apart from fear. A world where I'm not so utterly exhausted. As I turn the corner from the staircase into the living room I scan it for Arthur, who isn't there. I take the usual six steps to pass the threshold of the kitchen, the temperature changing under my feet between the wood and tile. I flip the light switch which casts white beams against the shiny countertops, temporarily blinding my eyes. I rub them a few times before examining the kitchen for Arthur.

"Arthur? I'm making your breakfast," I yell in an intentional hush to allow Liz to sleep. I peer under the wooden kitchen table, gaze past the tiny locks on each of the cupboards for any missing ones, and decide that Arthur isn't in the kitchen. I turn around to re-enter the living room and am startled by Arthur standing directly behind me.

"Ouch," he says with a satisfactory smile, dead eyes rising up to meet mine. He shifts them quickly back to my thigh and erupts with unabated laughter, throwing his head back with bellows, and struggling to take in full breaths. Ouch? What's ouch? Suddenly I feel it. A sting. A pinch. A pain begins radiating upward from my thigh, but I can't see anything through my plaid pajama bottoms.

"What did you do?" My voice is irritated. I quickly strip them to the ground, feeling them tug against whatever he's just inserted into my thigh. With my pants around my ankles I am able to see a single stream of blood flowing down my leg, slowly making its way to the floor. Sticking out from my thigh is a piece of wood about twice the size of a matchstick. Great.

"Red," Arthur giggles, and claps his hands.

"You're going to be punished, Arthur," I tell him with intense solemnity as I slowly pull the sliver out from my skin. Thankfully it's only about a quarter inch deep, but unimaginably sharp. I wonder how he crafted it. I twist the blood-dipped sliver in the light, wondering how he was able to make it so sharp, yet alone conceal it from me. It must have been a bait and switch this morning, like good magicians do. He caused me to look to one place, his left hand, while concealing his trick in the other. He's becoming cleverer and that makes me profusely tense, especially with Alice coming.

I throw the sliver into the sink, and walk over to the bottom of the stairs, a few drops of blood finally making their way to the floor.

"Liz, honey, I need you downstairs." An echo of my shout floats back toward me. In a moment I hear her tired grunts as she slowly descends the stairs. I quickly shove Arthur away from the blood on the floor with my foot, but he already has a couple drops on his hands. When Liz turns the corner she's holding her heavy belly with both hands, and she makes three calculated eye movements: to my thigh, to the floor, and then to Arthur.

"What happened?" she asks unenthusiastically and waddles over to me.

"Wood sliver."

"Ethan, you're supposed to check for those!"

"I did!"

She gives me that glare women give when they know they could have handled a task better than you. It's that quintessential expression that says "It's your incompetency that has us in this mess." It's not what I need this morning. She hands me a paper towel which I quickly swipe up my leg, catching the slow line of blood in one movement.

"Can you watch him? I need to get ready." I rush past her without waiting for an answer, ascending the stairs with hot anger in my chest. I don't bother bandaging the wound, it bleeds a little more in the shower but clots quickly afterward. I carefully shave the homeless veteran look off my face, each scrape of the razor against my thick black scruff irritating tiny nerves. I dress myself with what feels like lightning speed, shoving my light salmon button up into my grey slacks and fastening them with a brown belt before putting a brush through my thick hair a few times. It seems due for another haircut, but then, it always seems due. When I check the clock again it's already six-thirty. I rush downstairs and go directly to the kitchen. Food isn't important to me, but coffee is. I am pleased when I see Liz sitting at the kitchen table with a steaming mug in her hands. Her eyes are still red and disengaged from sleep.

"Is that coffee?" I gesture toward her red and brown glazed mug. Arthur sits beside her eating cereal.

"No, it's decaf tea." She doesn't make eye contact with me.

"Did you make coffee?" I ask almost desperately.

"No, did you ask me to make coffee?" Now her eyes meet mine in a biting sort of way.

"Forget about it. I have to go." I walk over and give both Arthur and Liz a kiss on the tops of their heads. This isn't how I wanted to end this morning.

***

University hospital is only twenty blocks away from Philadelphia East. I street park eight blocks away from the hospital, near the largest street market in the city. It's full of underpaid grocers who sell produce from government-owned and mechanically operated farms outside the metro. Even though it's still fairly dark out, the shadowed vendors are already stocking their shelves under huge striped awnings, thuds of heavy boxes being dropped synchronize perfectly with the grunts of their carriers. The market is also home to intermittent hoagie stations and wannabe artists, but they won't show up until at least an hour after sunrise. And of course, every third vendor or so, a D-MAZ dispenser stands fully stocked for the day's needs. I walk past the market and down one of the more trafficked through streets. Taller and shorter buildings encroach on every side of me, some brick, some stone, some no more than metal shells of buildings in need of demolition. The smells of old garbage and piss fight for dominance as I walk past the sleeping homeless, many of whom are trembling in their sleep, not from coldness but from Obcasus exposure. They'll hold up signs during the day that say "PLEASE D-MAZ," but then they sell the injections for money to buy controlled drugs.

I wait at an intersection, watching the bright shine of headlights drift past me, left to right, right to left, making me feel dazed and sleepy. I wish for the darkness to overtake their light, but the sun begins peeking over the horizon, adding to it. Once through the intersection, I read the blue and gold banner which hangs from alternating street lamps: "Cradled by Liberty - Cleansed by Fire - Cured by Love. Philadelphia Strong." The same banners have hung in Philly streets since the first anniversary of the Day of Destruction. At three blocks away I can already see University Hospital. Philadelphia East is a short, blocky formation of tan cement with sparse windows, virtually indiscernible in design from the parking garage attached to it. University, on the other hand, is a twenty-story glass skyscraper of impeccable geometric design – making it appear more like a glorious castle's steeple than a hospital. As the sun surfaces past the horizon, pink and purple hues reflect off the blue silver glass, causing certain panels to shimmer rainbow reflections into the city. For a moment, I understand what Dr. Singh feels every time he hears the name "University": resentment. He once called them "ostentatious money fiends," and he isn't altogether wrong. The amount of grant money that pours into University every year is sickening. Their Infectious Disease department gets two million in research grants annually, without ever having to submit a specific proposal; meanwhile Philadelphia East is viewed as the dirtier, under-achieving, lower-class hospital which is evidenced by the fact that our hospital is the number one hospital for gunshot wounds in the city. In Philadelphia the vote for which hospital ought to receive research grants is fairly obvious, and if it wasn't, I'm sure University would just add more sparkly glass to the outside of their building until it was chosen.

At the base of the building it's disorienting to look up. Just above the main entrance a giant enlightened sign reads "University Hospital." Glass rotating doors greet me with interim bursts of cold air. I push through one of the quarter-wedged doors, and enter into a serenely quiet lobby. The white tiled floor is spliced with trails of glinted gold and turquoise which reflect the ceiling lamps in different directions. The sound of smooth jazz plays softly in the background, while a janitor cleans interior windows to the right of me. The front desk is a white and turquoise semi-circle, so large that ten people could sit between the space of the two women stationed there. As I approach the desk both women smile at me with bright gleeful smiles, perfectly straight teeth, and seemingly innocent faces. The woman on the right has dimples pushing into her cheeks.

"How can I help you?" Dimples asks.

"I'm here for the, uh, the Obcasus trial," I say mutedly, leaning down toward her. The other woman answers with blistering enthusiasm.

"It's in the second floor basement. Right wing once you're down there, all the way at the end! If you just take the elevators to your right up ahead, they will take you down. Do you have your identification?" Both women are still smiling. Smiling so big their teeth show. Teeth smiling. It's seven something in the morning, what impetus could there be for smiling this early in the day? I flash the two women my hospital tags while moving beyond the desk in escape of their merriment.

There is a large waiting area to the left, parallel with the elevator. The waiting area is filled with blue and yellow cushioned chairs of various hues, not stationed in any logical way but placed in imperfect circles to give the room a lounge feeling. When I enter the elevator I confusedly stare at the inestimable number of buttons aligning its wall for some time before locating the second level basement button. There's absolute silence in the elevator: no music, no voices, no sound of movement, just quiet. I can feel my heartbeat accelerating. With each inch of descent I am one inch closer to meeting the enemy, to looking upon their fabrications, to being within their steel-armed reach. I don't want to be here. I want to be home, I want to be feeling Alice kick against Liz's belly and throwing Arthur into the air. I want to be drinking coffee, and watching sunbeams through the window which change the entire mood of the house. When I was studying for my board exams Liz was working full time at a marketing firm while I worked two days a week at an immunologist's office. Work sucked, Liz and I never saw each other, and when we did see each other my nose was so stuffed in a book that I could smell its previous owner. The only communication we had for several months was that of me begging her to quiz me, and her tiredly refusing. She was growing to resent me, and to resent the medical profession that I had chosen.

One day my brain, my stamina, my resolve had reached their limits and I broke down in front of Liz. I punched our ugly apartment wall, I screamed, I got on my knees and wept, and she was there to behold it all. For the first time, I saw how much of a failure I truly was. I was failing as a husband, I was failing as a provider, I was failing as an intern, I was failing in my studies; I was failing. At one point she joined me on the floor, wrapped her arms around me and asked, "Why do you want to become a doctor?" It wasn't what I had expected her to say, I had expected the only words to come out of her mouth to be "I love you." I considered her question for a minute, and I told her "I want to help people." It was the truth. "Hold onto that," she whispered. And I did. And I do.

The rear doors of the elevator open revealing a wide, empty hallway lit brightly by unmediated industrial lamps. It's one of those uninhabited spaces that kids yell into so that their echoes reverberate back, and it's the type of sterile environment I've come to expect from a research or surgical wing. I follow the hallway to its end and turn the corner in the hopes of finding a sign of direction. When I turn the corner, however, I no longer need one, I know I've arrived. Two black coats stand stiffly in front of a set of swinging doors. The one on the left is six foot five, with a blonde military buzz, and his black jacket propped open enough to show off his government issue Glock. The one on the right is bald, a few inches shorter, and his shoulders are shrugged upward by his ears as if he slept wrong and is in pain. The three of us exchange eye contact, their expression an indiscernible blur between stoicism and wrath. Then I notice a devious smile growing on the corner of Baldy's mouth. Instantly my heart spasms, inflating and constricting with difficulty, making my eyes dilate and throwing the scene into a dream-like blur. There's no one in the hallway, just black coats and me. No one to hear, to see, no one to know what happened. And it occurs to me that there is no Obcasus study, that it was no more than a plot for my extermination.

"Dr. King?" Baldy says, his voice gravelly and authoritative. My heart thumps rapidly in my ears. I try to control my breathing, but my body begs for oxygen. This is the end for me. This hallway is where their secrets will be kept, my research proven meaningless, and the world left just as it was before me.

Run, run away, run back, get into the elevator and run out of the hospital. No. Breathe, stay calm, answer them.

"Yes? How do you know my name?" I ask hesitantly, but force myself to take one step closer.

"It's our job to know. The study will begin shortly through these doors. As a procedure we need to see your identification," Military buzz says flatly. I take each step toward him with a preoccupied carefulness. Step, breathe smoothly, step, don't let your hands shake, step, don't let your face flush, step, don't begin sweating. I pull out my badge and hand it to him. He examines it for a moment, hands it back, and pushes the left door open for me. I enter through the door into what is clearly an observation room. Set half a level above the laboratory and separated by plexiglass, rows of movie theater-style seats are stuffed too closely together. A few individuals, two of whom are wearing white coats, sit on opposite corners of the room, one in the front left and the other two in the back right. They all turn, as if coordinated, to watch me as I enter the space. The door swings shut behind me, and they return to staring stiffly at the lab. I stuff my hands in my pockets as I fight their trembling, and sit in the second row directly in the middle – a perfectly neutral spot.

I look through the plexiglass, admiring that the lab looks remarkably similar to one of my labs in medical school. Three rows of silver steel tables, one lining the entire length on the right wall, computers on plastic desks lining the farthest back wall, and doses of color in the form of hazard signs: one to mark the emergency shower, another marking a hazardous waste bin. On the table against the right wall sit several air-controlled mice cages, each one fostering a lone white mouse. A few military specialists march around the lab, arranging certain containers, syringes, micro-cameras over the cages, sensor pads, and computer analytics. It begins to feel strangely normal, like I'm back at one of Philadelphia East's annual training seminars, crammed into seats with strangers, half sedated by the dullness of the material and distracted by the smell of Middle Eastern co-workers. A few more individuals join behind me and quickly begin making small talk about a patient case they're working on together. University doctors, no doubt. By the time the room is full, my anxiety has calmed, and a man in a marginally decorated military uniform stands in the front of the room near the glass, silencing our group.

"Hello ladies and gentlemen, my name is Lieutenant Collins, and I will be your avenue of information for the duration of the day. Like the individuals working in the lab now, and like yourselves, I am an MD by training. I have been working with the federal research team responsible for the formulation of Dopimazipal since its inception. I will be narrating for you the process of events today, and answering questions periodically. You may have noticed the security outside. This is not to make any of you feel uncomfortable, this is a precaution implemented during these events as we do not allow for any video recording, including surveillance, of anything within the testing area excluding the mice themselves. We hope you understand. As we begin, I will introduce you to our staff and the mechanics of the testing being done today."

Lieutenant Collins looks a lot like me. His brown hair is in an immaculately tailored crew cut, greying along his temples, he has hazel eyes which are browner than mine, and deep tired darkness underlies his eyes as if he hasn't slept in a few years. He tells us about each of the doctors within the laboratory, and their decorations. I try to commit their names to memory by rehearsing their names in my head and watching their actions carefully, critically. Laura Dones, MD and PhD in Chemical Biology from Cambridge. Liam Davis, MD and PhD in Chemical Biology from Harvard. Michael Roberts, MD and PhD in Pharmacology and Experimental Therapy from Cambridge. Carvin Lutz, PhD in Molecular Toxicology from the University of Denver. All of the researchers are decorated in some fashion in the United States Armed Forces.

Lieutenant Collins explains that the general premise behind today's testing is to find out whether a new formulation (which they insist be called a "reformulation") of D-MAZ will have any negative effects, either short-term or long term. We as observers will only be able to view the short term response in the mice. As the other doctors prep the Obcasus exposure, he explains that they have a very restricted reservoir from undetonated bombs during the initial attacks which they use sparingly and carefully in their experiments. Today, six miniature aerosol cans filled with small doses of Obcasus sit next to each of the mice cages. This is the closest I have been to Obcasus since the Day of Destruction. Memories rush back, distracting me from the study at hand. The tiny boy, his shirt, "Play Ball," the choking sounds, the woman holding her dead child, the heat, the sweat, the smells, the vomit, my vomit. The horror of the next several months. All of it comes to me, suddenly, in flashes. I can tell that other doctors in the room are experiencing the same thing. They adjust uncomfortably, or look down in a dazed manner, as Lieutenant Collins continues speaking about the Obcasus being used only a few feet away from us. When the researchers begin the exposure, Lieutenant Collins tries to catch our moderately preoccupied attention.

"They're beginning to inject Obcasus into the cage. If your heart bleeds for mice this would be a good time to exit the observation room."

A uniform laugh fills the room. I force awkward laughter out of myself to mirror the crowd. One of the researchers, Lutz I think, inserts a pointed nozzle into an insertion catheter attached to each of the cages. He presses the dispenser slowly and watches a tiny monitor attached to the cage until it's filled with the proper amount. What follows is difficult to watch. The mice begin to run around in chaotic motions, then turn on their sides and writhe in pain, some more, and some less. Some clearly exhibit seizure like activity, and I'm there. They're in my arms. She is. He is. They are, they're in my arms. And I'm lifting them into wheelchairs, and I'm placing stickers on their robes. They're seizing, and I'm trying to rinse their bodies, their eyes, but I'm breaking down, and I'm screaming in my suit, and I'm watching them die. The overweight man. He dies. The boy, I'm holding him, but he dies. His face, their faces haunt me for the millionth time.

Then I'm back, and they're using a cleansing system to clear the cage of the gas, before pulling the mice from their cages, limp and unconscious, and injecting them with the new drug. The mice wake up, recovering instantaneously, and are replaced in their cages where they begin to behave as if nothing had happened. In the observation room we sit stunned, and then the questions begin.

"Why would you be testing on mice if it's only a minor adjustment? Why not skip to a human clinical trial?" A woman asks from behind me.

"In the past our mice studies have proven to be remarkably predictive of the human response to the drug. Given how quickly we can conduct them, it would make little sense not to test them first for possible side-effects before giving the reformulation to human patients," Lieutenant Collins answers.

"Given that D-MAZ is such an effective treatment for Obcasus exposure, why this reformulation? Have you discovered a bad long-term side effect from D-MAZ that needs correcting?" A grey haired man to my left asks.

"No. Let me be clear, I should have stated this before: the primary impetus for this reformulation is to create an extended release form of the drug that is still intravenous, but would reduce the number of shots required. Our mind is only to improving the daily experience of the American people. We have, to date, not found any unusual or concerning long-term side-effects with Dopamizipal," Lieutenant Collins states his answer calmly and compellingly.

"How do you create an extended release intravenous drug apart from utilizing some external mechanism such as a port or picc-line?" The same grey-haired man asks with marginal antagonism, "as far as I understand it, that's a clinical impossibility."

"It *was*. It *was* a clinical impossibility. This research team has discovered a unique compound that binds to the elements of the drug, but is metabolized in the blood over the course of forty-eight hours." Collins smiles for the first time as he answers.

"Could you explain that in more detail?" The woman from behind me asks.

"Of course. It comes down to this: the compound creates a protective film over the drug constituents creating an innumerable number of microscopic bubbles of the drug. In each injection, that protective compound is added in varying degrees so that the drug will be released at a continuous pace, as the blood metabolizes the film."

"What is the name of the compound?" Another person asks.

"That's classified," Lieutenant Collins answers firmly.

"Classified or trademarked?"

"It's classified," he states again, and the room becomes silent.

"Why?" I ask, suddenly very alert and engaged.

"It is the long-term goal to release the compound information to the public, however, because this compound is a limited resource the government would like to keep its sources protected until it can develop a sustainable way to reproduce it here," he responds with several pauses, carefully choosing his words.

"Here? Then where does the compound originate from?" The woman asks again.

"That's classified," he repeats.

"What in the blood metabolizes the film?" I ask. It makes sense that the Leptospira would metabolize it.

"At this time I am going to cut off questions. We will be opening up the laboratory to you momentarily, to come in, look at the data analysis, and ask our researchers some questions. Please be respectful of the university's property, and of the significance of this research by not touching anything in the laboratory," Lieutenant Collins finishes.

CHAPTER 18

Lieutenant Collins leads us down a miniscule staircase to the left of the observation room. I follow somewhere in the middle of the small crowd, and at the bottom of the staircase turn the full one-eighty to enter the lab. I sniff the air carefully, trying to see if the smell of Obcasus is anywhere in the air, but it isn't. It's fully contained. Huddles of enamored doctors quickly form around the researchers, but my attention is stolen by Dr. Lutz, who holds in his hand an aerosol can of Obcasus. At first I'm concerned, watching it carefully for release, but then it occurs to me that the nail in the coffin, the undeniable proof of government deception lies within that can. All I need is the smallest remnant of Obcasus to test under a microscope and I can prove that it's an areotolerant Leptospira bacteria responsible for all of the symptoms and the brain damage in offspring caused by Obcasus. Dr. Lutz lifts the lid of the hazard bin and moves to drop the tiny can into it when the precocious woman who sat behind me begins barraging him with questions, throwing him flirtatious smiles throughout. He pauses, setting the aerosol can on the edge of the silver countertop, away from the mice, and moves toward her. No one notices, he doesn't notice, no one in the room notices. I look through the observation glass and no one is there. Could I grab it? Could I take it? Could it go unnoticed that it isn't in the pile of hazardous garbage with the others? Maybe. Probably not, but maybe. But what would my excuse be if I got caught? "Oh, I was just throwing it away for him.... In my pocket." There's no time to think about it. This is life or death, again, as it always seems to be, and I need to act. In one swift movement I walk past the table, carefully snatching the can and stuffing it smoothly into my rear pants pocket. I instinctually want to leave, but I need to appear ordinary like everyone else. I approach the woman, Dr. Dones, who sits in a different corner of the room and join the mass around her.

"D-MAZ is really the best thing we could have imagined producing, and so now, to have discovered this compound, we feel incredibly hopeful for what the future holds," she finishes saying, a slight Hispanic accent coating each word. I join in asking questions, but mine seems to particularly offend Dr. Dones.

"What is your relationship to the pharmaceutical company RemX, and how has that influenced your research?" Her face becomes sour as she answers.

"My team does all of the heavy lifting, sir. We conduct all of the research, we invest all of the time and resources. We contract with RemX to mass produce the drug, but that is all." Her tone is full of resentment, which signals me to ask no more questions. Microscope images flash behind her on the computer, but none contain the iconic Leptospira I've become so familiar with. That's not surprising.

As noon rolls around Lieutenant Collins escorts us out of the research area. We take two cramped elevators to the lobby, and I am blessedly in the first. The can of Obcasus taps against my thigh with each movement, and I can't escape the hospital fast enough. Suddenly I wish I hadn't walked so many blocks, I wish I had parked closer. I walk at an unruly speed, bypassing workers on their lunch breaks, and bumping shoulders with unhappy frequency. A man wearing too much hair gel trips me with his shoe, I think on purpose, but I don't bother looking back. Then I hear a voice, one I've heard before.

"Dr. King! Dr. King, wait up!" I turn around, and see the two black coats approaching with unsettling speed – almost breaking into a run. I immediately thrust myself into an alleyway, and empty my pocket of the Obcasus, searching frantically for a place to hide it. I find the perfect spot, stuffing the small can into a deep crack of broken brick in the building's wall. I turn and begin running toward the end of the alley, hoping to make it to the next street before they approach me. But the tapping sound of their steps against the crated sewage piping informs me that it's too late.

"Ethan.... Heyyyyy. Why in such a hurry to get away from us?" Military Buzz draws out from behind me, all too quickly grabbing my shoulders and shaking them in a harsh, joking fashion. I turn to face the two of them.

"Well, you do have a reputation..." I say quietly.

"A reputation, for what? Beating down bad guys? Are you a bad guy, Ethan King?" he says my name again, tapping me against the cheek hard with two knuckles. I take a step backward.

"No," I say with a voice more sincere, more desperate than I expected.

"Then you won't mind us searching you, would you?" he asks, while baldy walks behind me. The two of them ravage through my clothes and pockets, tightly squeezing every inch of my body, my arms, my legs, pushing their hands through my hair, pulling my shoes off and throwing them away.

"Hm. Interesting. Do you think this asshole asks too many questions?" Baldly says from behind me. Then a sharp agonizing pain surges through my spine and I fall to the ground on all fours. In a moment I realize that the pressure I felt was from a dull metal tool he'd jabbed into my back. "I couldn't agree more," Military Buzz says, then his polished shoe flashes toward my face and collides with my right cheek. I fall on my side, and cover my head as kicks continue to pierce into my ribcage. I try to take in breaths but I can't. It feels like meat hooks are being sliced into me from different directions, tugging and ripping me apart. The muscles surrounding my chest constrict and I begin choking for air. I'm underwater, and a rusty spear is protruding through my spine, my chest, weighted and pulling me to the sea floor. I need to breathe, the bubbles of my last breath float up toward the surface but the surface is out of reach. I can't wait any longer, I gasp, agony ripping through my torso. The next thing I see is the sky between the two buildings, bright blue, blurry, confusing, but calm. Just a blue sky, on a normal summer day. Maybe I'm at a park. But then the pain begins emanating, awful piercing pain in my sides, in my cheekbone near my eye, and in my spine like I have never experienced.

"Stand up, stand the fuck up!" Baldy yells at me, pulling me up by my coat. His face, my surroundings, slowly coming back to me. I put energy into my legs and try to stand, but it's so excruciating. I gasp for breath with an agonizing whimper.

"Hey! Wake up! Can you tell me your name?" Military Buzz asks me.

"Ethan King," I slur.

"Good. Now look here, Ethan. Look," he grabs me by my beaten cheek and squeezes it tightly as he forces me to look at a bright yellow paper. Red pulsates through my vision, and I see him only in spurts. "This is a police report, signed by you, stating that you were mugged today by two homeless men. It's already been filed with the police, so don't bother going in."

He stuffs it into my hands, and I almost fall backward to the ground. The other one pulls my wallet from my pants pocket.

"You never saw us, and your questions about Obcasus end here. Do you understand? If we have to see you again it will be for the last time. You won't make it through that meeting. Are you listening to me?" He smacks my face a few times, while still supporting some of my weight by my collar. I nod to the best of my ability, and verbalize the faintest "Yes." He drops me and my body slams against the cement, scratching my face and elbows. I hear the sound of their footsteps exiting the alleyway, but then a pause.

"Oh and hey Ethan..." I hazily hear as I fade in and out of consciousness, "stay safe out there."

Then they're gone. I groan as I roll into the fetal position, moving my legs slowly toward my chest until I can find a position where the stabbing of my fractured ribs doesn't make an inhale of air impossible. I take the breath slowly, shortly, not deep enough to satisfy nor to spare myself some pain. My right eye begins swelling shut at an impressive speed, deep aching throbs taking over the entire right side of my face. The pain in my spine is like when you pull your back out so severely that you cannot move or walk for several days, only worse. Even the small vibrations caused by my body's trembling sends spikes of unbearable pain through it. The longer I lay the worse the pain becomes. I begin crying, and writhing, barely able to make out desperate whispers for "help." Help. I need help. I say it in my mind far more than what I can verbalize, but still hoping that someone can hear. I need to stand, I have to grab the Obcasus, and I have to get home. I roll from the fetal position onto all fours, and the pain in my chest and rib cage, in my spine, causes visible vibrations to roll over my vision. I feel myself losing consciousness.

I grit my teeth and try to take a deep breath, then pain like a pitchfork pierces into my lungs, into my heart, and opens up like a metal claw of pin pricks. I yell again, but force myself to stand, leaning against a filthy green dumpster for support. Its hard metal burns my arm from the sun it's absorbed this afternoon, but I don't pull away. While I lean against it I try to move forward, one foot and then the other, resolving to only take short shallow breaths. I process my injuries as I limp slowly toward the hole in the brick wall. I have multiple fractured ribs, possibly a broken rib, no punctured aorta or I would not be conscious, probably no punctured lung or breathing would be harder and my lung would collapse. Possibly lacerated kidneys, god, the pain is so intense. If he had actually stabbed me in the spine I would not be able to walk, so nothing is severed, I don't think I feel blood on my back, but maybe I do. It could be a spinal strain, somewhere thoracic, maybe between T3 and T7. I could have a facial fracture in the right zygoma. I really hope not. I look at the crevice set approximately two feet below my reach, and wonder how I could possibly retrieve it. I cannot bend down, not now, but I can't leave it either. I look around to ensure that I am alone, and I bend my knees slowly, inch by inch keeping my back as straight as possible, but an extreme splitting pain begins pummeling up my spine, like a bone saw is slicing my body in half. I can even feel it reverberating through my chest.

When I finally reach inside the hole, a world of relief rushes over me as I feel the tiny tin can at my finger-tips. I pull it from the wall and zip it in the inner pocket of my suit jacket. Now the difficult part, the remaining five blocks to my car. My first full dose of adrenaline hits me as I cross the first intersection, numbing my pain only slightly, but it's enough to allow me to walk at almost a normal pace. Every face that sees me stares in horror and confusion. Is it because I'm in a suit but shoeless, or because my face is so swollen that I can't see out of my right eye? I pull out my phone and dial Jim as I cross the third intersection.

"Hey, buddy. How'd the whole hoop-la go?" he answers.

"Jim," I barely make out, my voice raspy and frail.

"Ethan, are you okay?" He becomes instantly serious.

"I need to check myself into the ER. I'll be there in about twenty minutes." I have to stop walking to take several shallow inhales before moving forward.

"What happened!?" An undertone of panic is in his voice.

"I can't talk now. Be ready to help me. Twenty minutes. Don't call Liz," I whisper the last few words. The sun beats down heat on my skull but only cold sweat drips down my neck.

"Ethan, stay on the...." I hang up the phone before he finishes and slide it back into my pants pocket. I ignore the gawks of the strangers I pass by, and force myself to walk faster toward the car. Driving is more difficult than I could have imagined, each turn of the steering wheel rams through my sides as if I had been squeezed between steel beams. As I pull into the emergency entrance, Jim is already standing outside with a stretcher and a group of emergency specialists, all who I know by name on account of Jim's stories. I push the gearshift into park directly in front of the emergency doors, and Jim sprints toward the driver side and opens the door.

"Can you walk?" he asks.

"I don't think so," I respond faintly. He works quickly, unbuckling me, and carefully lifting me into his arms, something that could not be done if the roles were reversed. As he moves to lay me on the stretcher, I whisper in his ear to take my suit coat and put it somewhere safe, that it's of first importance. He nods. I hold on tightly to the yellow sheet of paper as the pain of my body decompressing on the flat surface barrels through me.

"Dr. King, can you tell me what happened?" Dr. Carolyn Hobbs asks me, her nasally thin voice exactly how Jim had described it. I hold up the yellow sheet of paper.

"You filed a police report before coming to the ER?" she asks incredulously, as the small crew rolls me into an evaluation room. I ignore her questions, and quietly try to voice the major health concerns, through pathetically shallow inhales and exhales.

"Ribs, spine, face. X-Rays." I whimper. One of the other doctors inserts an IV access line into my arm, and another begins cutting my clothes off.

"These are nice clothes," I try to protest. Jim rejoins the room, and asks if I would want a dose of morphine. My inarticulate groaning seems to be enough to persuade him to insert the shot into my IV. As soon as the morphine hits my brain it seems humorous to be a patient, or a doctor, with the strange things that they are wearing and the strange words they're using. My body begins to feel strong, capable again, but then in a moment the room grows quieter, dimmer, heavier, sleepier, like it's all pretend. It's all pretend.

CHAPTER 19

When I wake up, I run my hand along my face which instantly zaps with pain. A five o'clock shadow has pushed in along my jaw, and I feel extraordinarily sore. I stare dazedly at my IV and replay the details of the day slowly in my head. Jim is sitting in a chair next to me, and the sunset shines through the patient room window.

"Ya' just gotta wonder what sorta idiot gets mugged in the middle of the day?" He winks at me with a chuckle, but then his eyes grow more serious, indicating to me that he understands what happened.

"How are you feeling, buddy?" he asks, and pats my knee gently a couple of times.

"You remember that time we went fishing and you caught a trout, and those two birds of Satan immediately began pecking it to death?" I ask him with a hoarse voice. "I feel only marginally worse than the trout." He smiles at me and nods.

"The good news is, ya got no facial fractures, just four rib fractures. One in rib three, two in four, and one in five, and they're only posterior non-displaced fractures. Believe it or not these, uh, homeless fellows were pretty restrained, Ethan. Either that or they just don't know how to throw a kick, and I seriously doubt that second part. You're not going to have any long-term damage. Now your spine is going to cause you a lot of pain over the next several weeks. You have pretty severe spinal bruising from blunt trauma. It's clearly the result of edged brass knuckles, because there are four distinct imprints along your spine, but I noticed that wasn't in the police report." He pauses.

"I was mugged. That is all," I say through gritted teeth.

"I know," he assures me, knowing better than to say much more in this setting, but his eyes hold a full range of emotion: anger, and fear, and resolve.

"I know you know."

"Don't worry, friend. I wouldn't let anyone at the hospital know that you got mugged in the middle of the day. How embarrassing. Instead while you were unconscious I made sure to tell as many people as I could that today when you saw a woman choking to death at a restaurant, you performed the Heimlich maneuver on her and saved her life. Her husband, who walked in at just the wrong time, thought you were assaulting her, grabbing her breasts or something, and beat the crap out of you. I told everyone to praise you for your heroism. I would expect applause if I were you," Jim states amusedly.

"You didn't."

"Oh, but I did." A mischievous grin plasters his face. I chuckle once, but then wince in pain, and return to taking shallow breaths.

"I think I'd like to get home before dark. Let's get this back brace on me."

I call Liz to tell her what to expect when she sees me. She instantly panics, flooding the phone with a bombardment of questions, the majority of which I have to fabricate answers to: "Who did this?" "Did you call the police?" "Did they find the guys?" "What did they take?" "Why were you in an alley?" At some point I convince her to continue her loving inquisition once I'm home, and in the interim I begin plotting a way to tell her the truth, the whole truth, which begins with the contents of the tiny tin aerosol can hidden away in my coat pocket, now folded up and sitting in the passenger seat next to me. I can't tell her in the house, I don't trust that they're not listening somehow. But I don't think they've been in the house, because if they had been they would have come across my research, and today's beating would have been substituted by an execution. A knot forms in my stomach as I think about the way things have to change. I have to accelerate everything, finishing my research, healing Arthur, dispersing the information as widely and quickly as I can, and most importantly finding a safe place for my family to hide in the aftermath. And that is why Liz has to know. She needs to understand that our comfortable bed will not belong to us, and the modern convenience of being known by the world will have to end, not forever, but for a time.

As I push through the door I see the edge of Liz's white and blue striped dress skirting the bottom of the stairs. She is waiting on the bottom stair step, her modus operandi when she's anxious for my return.

"Don't over-react, okay? It's not as bad as it looks," I say, attempting some preemptive caution.

"Ethan, oh my god, are you okay?!" She hurries toward me, as fast as any nine months pregnant woman could. Her eyes instantly fill with tears, while she barely strokes the uninjured side of my face and evaluates my injuries.

"How could someone do this to you?" Her tear-filled eyes look up at me with a sense of helplessness.

"What? This? If you think this is bad, you should see the other guys." My voice is still weak, but carries the sarcasm well enough.

"Is now really the time for joking?" she asks, but I don't respond. I just stare into her scared eyes and try to muster up as much strength as I can for her. It isn't the time for joking, but it isn't the time for truth-telling either. It's an awful purgatory. It's a time for laying low until I can get her alone somewhere and tell her everything, until I have a solid plan for her protection. I look down at her belly, and feel over it with my hands, thinking about Alice, thinking about how hard this must be for Liz and how much harder it will be soon.

"I missed you today," I whisper.

"I love you." She embraces me in a hug, awkwardly trying to wrap her arms around the brace which takes up my entire torso.

Even her gentle squeeze surges through my chest, and I grunt in corresponding pain.

"I'm so sorry. Here, let me get you some ice. Do you want to go upstairs?"

"Where's Arthur?" I ask, it suddenly occurring to me that I don't see him in the living room.

"I put him to bed early," she says as she enters the kitchen.

"And he went down?" I half yell at her, the deeper breath required feels like an ice pick being shoved into my lungs.

"Apparently. I guess he knew you'd need some rest," she answers, and I begin a slow painful ascent up the staircase.

Once upstairs, Liz helps me undress the set of surgical scrubs Jim gave me, each inch of uncovered skin accompanied by another gasp of horror from Liz's mouth. She cries the entire time, a constant flow of tears descending her face as she looks at the bruises that I am only seeing for the first time. The skin of my chest is arrayed in deep purples and blues, significantly swollen with tender cushions of inflammation. It's amazing the way the human body responds to injury. The bruises are an unhelpful pooling of blood which forms as a result of broken capillaries in the beaten area, but the inflammation is an essential immune response. The body releases a concoction of chemicals, some of which widen the uninjured capillaries allowing for increased blood flow to the area, others which eat the damaged tissue so that surrounding tissue does not decompose or become infected, and then others which initiate tissue rebuilding by cells. The pain serves as a marvelously effective warning system for idiots, saying: "Whatever you have just done, do not do that thing again." Since I am not an idiot, the pain only serves as a reminder that the enemy is real, that my task is dangerous, and that I am just a man.

Liz works to carefully lay me in bed, arranging lightly-covered ice packs under my back, over my chest, and on my face. She sits up at the end of the bed and begins massaging my feet.

"You don't need to do that, baby. Really, I should be doing that for you." I make a lame attempt to pull my feet from her grasp. She holds on tightly to them, and ignores my comment.

"So you ran away shoeless? What a weird thing to steal, shoes..."

"Yeah, they were strange people," I concede. We both stay silent for several minutes, hearing nothing beside the overworked air conditioner blowing chilling air through the house.

"How old do you feel?" She finally breaks the silence.

"Decrepit. Maybe older." My voice sounds hoarse, illustrating my point.

"You look young to me. I can always see you young. See, if you ditch me and marry some young hot thing she'll never be able to see you young. She'll always just see you as you are right now."

"Decrepit?" I ask with a small laugh, but instantly regret inflating my lungs that much. Liz laughs, her big eyes becoming bright for the first time since I've been home.

"No. Just older, mature. She'll never be able to see you younger than you are right now. But I can always see youth in you. And it isn't just the virile muscles you've maintained." She winks at me with an adorable smile and pushes her long hair over her shoulder.

"You mean the muscles that so valiantly defended me today?" I grin at her compulsively, restraining a laugh.

"You did well today, love. You did all that you were supposed to do in a situation like that. You survived, you came home to me. I need you to be around, Dad," she says softly, making rubbing motions over her belly.

"I know." I know what I owe her, what she deserves from me. I know what Arthur and Alice will need from me. I have to tell her what's going on, she has to know, but I can't tell her here.

"Let's get out one more time, just you and I, before the baby comes. I really want some alone time with you," I tell her, holding out my hand for hers. She takes it, and caresses it gently.

"I'd love that." She moves cautiously to lay beside me.

***

The next morning I tell Liz that I have more police paperwork to complete at the local station and that I won't be back for a few hours. She doesn't like the prospect, insisting that I ought to be resting, but it's satisfactory enough that she lets me leave. I don't, of course, go to a police station, but rather to the Assistance Center, where Lapis lets me in through a side entrance.

"Oh my gosh, what happened to you?!" she exclaims as soon as I transition from the brightness of outside into the dimly lit building.

"I was mugged," I say rather unenthusiastically.

"Mugged? Ethan!" Her voice is filled with concern as she leads me quickly into the morgue as per usual, except that it's empty of bodies.

"I'm fine really..." I begin, as I stare curiously at the empty body tables. When the door shuts she rushes over, throwing her weight around me in a hug, and despite my squeal of agony she doesn't let me go. Instead her mouth hovers close enough to my ear that the smallest hairs can feel the brush of her lips. She whispers almost inaudibly: "Black coats watching. Questioned me. I made up an affair. They thought I wouldn't notice the cameras and so I acted like I haven't, but I saw them right away. Everywhere, in every corner of this place. Don't look for them, keep your eyes on me. This is the last time we can see each other," a few of her hot tears sink through the shoulder of my shirt. "You have to go along with what I do Ethan, and for goodness' sake, be a grown up about it and act like you're into it."

She pulls her face away from my shoulder.

"I've missed you," she says at a normal volume. I struggle to smile at her, I struggle to play along, I struggle to see her as afraid and wounded as she is in her eyes. She strokes along the right side of my neck, and places a few gentle kisses along the bruised portion of my face. I can feel her pale make up rubbing off along my skin. It smells like a mix between baby powder and old chalk. She slides her left hand down the center of my pants, and I reflexively pull back, but she holds on tightly to my shoulder and leans in to whisper: "It's two samples, the last I can give you," and suddenly I feel it. Behind my boxers I feel a cold round piece of plastic, a specimen container. I look into her bright blue eyes which are full of pain, and I mouth her thank you.

"I hate this next part," she says, and a tear strikes her cheek.

"It's the baby isn't it? Is that why you won't leave her?" Her voice becomes shrill as she quickly pulls back from me, crossing her arms over her chest. I wince in pain at the sudden movement.

"Lapis, I...."

I have so much that I want to say, an incalculable amount of gratitude that I want to clothe you in. If it wasn't for you none of my research would have been possible, and more than that, you've been a good, albeit strange, friend to me, I think but cannot say. I can't say anything that I want to.

"Forget about it, Ethan! You just use me for sex and I'm sick of it! You're never going to leave your wife, you're never going to be what I need you to be, and I can't do this anymore. It makes me sick, seeing the way you look at me, like you're so much better than me and that I'm lucky to have your affection at all," she bursts out louder, with so much conviction that I wonder if it's how she actually feels, minus the sex. Tears fill her eyes, and she screams at me to leave. I look at her for a long time, her fiery red hair just as bright as her personality, her mismatched scrubs, her body which seems thinner than when we first met. Her endless stories about her family, or art, or her views on morality, or television, or love. Her kindness toward me, her steel tight confidence for all of these months. And then I turn away, and I say goodbye to it all. I exit the Assistance Center for the last time, and drive home with the last specimens I will ever collect. Things begin feeling dark. It no longer feels like a noble endeavor to search out the truth hiding behind serums, or the purpose menacing behind publications. I crave normalcy in every fiber of my being. Just me and one damn normal day, just one day where it doesn't cost me anything to know what I do. One day apart from secrets, one day apart from fear. I'm going to create that world, and it's going to start right now in the basement.

Once I'm set up, I prepare the numerous tests, all of which I can perform relatively rapidly. First, I need to test the Obcasus on its own and then with D-MAZ. Next, I need to portion out the brain tissue carefully into four sides, injecting D-MAZ into two of the segments, with the intention of exposing all four samples to Obcasus. Fourth, I test my live blood and Obcasus, and finally my live blood with D-MAZ and Obcasus together. Strangely, the blood will paint the most compelling picture, because it will confirm the presence or absence of HVA in the blood sample, which is the byproduct of acids (supposedly the culprit) eating dopamine. If HVA isn't present, then it would prove that acids were not responsible for metabolizing dopamine, and another enzymatic byproduct would unveil itself, that of Leptospira.

I push through the tests as quickly as I can so that they finish before Liz and Arthur wake from their nap. For the first time since being beaten I forget the pain in my body, I forget the surrounding world, or the threats within it. It's just me, and the microscope, and quiet research and discovery. The results of the testing are perfect. The swab of Obcasus proved the presence of Leptospira activity, and furthermore, the metabolization of Dopamine in D-MAZ. In all cases where brain tissue was used, the tissue surrounding the injected D-MAZ is injured; but it is unable to produce swelling or scar tissue on account of its being hours-long dead. The injury, of course, could be done by supposed acids in Obcasus if the proper enzymatic properties are confirmed, and for that my blood becomes the most brilliant silencer. My test finds less than equivocal HVA – there is no acidic metabolization of dopamine, period. I make sure to document everything with precision, copying the total sum of my research onto four microchips, and holding onto them discreetly until I can place them in the usual spots: one with Jim, one inside the heart plaque in the cardiac ward, one in the Christmas decorations in the attic, and one somewhere no one would ever expect.

Jim comes over in the evening with a trough of "Tickle Chicken" that Mary made; some creamy casserole dish that is supposedly a staple "get well soon" dish in the south. Liz brings it to the kitchen and portions some out for Arthur and her, while Jim and I "go for a walk." Liz nags something about my needing to rest, but Jim assures her that I will be under doctoral supervision the entire time. She sarcastically sticks her tongue out at Jim, and all three of us laugh. Jim and I don't follow sidewalks, instead we cut through backyards and into the forest before we speak a single word to each other. The forest is beautiful this time of day, the sun shines down perfectly to turn yellow into gold, and amber into crimson. The birds sing, and all the beauty of the forest seems magnified.

"So, government pigs?" he begins.

"Yes."

"What'd they say?"

"That my questions about Obcasus end here, and that they'll kill me the next time they have to see me."

"And the jacket?" he probes.

"I stole a can of Obcasus. I tested with it this afternoon." I move my hand into the center of my pants and pull out the microchip for Jim.

"Ethan, did you just pull that out of your underwear?" He stares at it, but doesn't lift a hand to take it.

"I've recently learned it's a great place for hiding things," I say straightly.

"Ew, cowboy. That ain't right." He grabs it peculiarly with his two pinkies, and inserts it into his jean pocket. I restrain a compulsive laugh to spare my chest some pain.

"We need to talk about our plan for moving forward, Jim. We need to talk about how this ends for us." I look at him walking beside me, tall, thin, wearing a plaid button-up T-shirt. He looks innocent, his blue eyes, innocent, his greying hair, innocent –his whole person innocent. I should have left him uninvolved, I wish now that I had.

"Yes, we do," he agrees, and stares into the empty woods with contemplative gravity.

"I don't think they suspect you at all, I think that for the most part, you can continue on as normal. I'll be the one to pull the trigger on this. My family is going to go somewhere safe, and you're going to play dumb. Can you promise me that?"

"It doesn't seem right." He shakes his head.

"It's right. I promise. But I do need something from you. I need you to help me with something one more time. One last favor," I say, forcing a pause in our walking.

"What is it?" And then I tell him. I tell him exactly how we can cure Arthur, every detail of the procedure, all of the materials needed, a meeting time and even an operating room that we can appropriate. I don't withhold a single awful detail, I divulge every fact required for it to work, and when I finish his face falls with distress.

"You aren't serious, are you?" His voice nearly cracks under the weight of what I've suggested.

"I am," I state firmly.

"But Liz.... But Alice..." he hardly whispers, and their names hang in the air solemnly for a long time.

"I have to do it," I urge.

"Do you? I am your friend, and I am asking you, do you?"

CHAPTER 20

August 6th, 2047

When you're dreaming you don't ask questions about right or wrong, rational or irrational. The most untenable premises seem perfectly reasonable, and you adopt them as your worldview without equivocation. Can you fly? So you can, who couldn't? Does an affair seem like the perfect end to a long day, so it does, eat your heart out. In some ways this makes dreaming the only world of peace you can escape to, and in other ways it makes it tantamount to all of the chaos that the world contains.

After my father died I suffered from a recurring nightmare. Every few nights I would jolt awake with desperate gasps for air, drenched in my own sweat. The dream haunted me like it was something from outside myself that would slither into my thoughts, and not like something that originated in my own mind. I'm standing on the pinnacle of a mountain, it's frigidly cold and a howling rushes through the wind so loudly that I can hear nothing else. Right next to me, on this thinly spaced stone apex, stands a creature draped in black, hunched over, hiding its face from me. In his hand he holds a spear which he scrapes back and forth along the rock over and over, leaving trails of blood in its tracks. And then he turns to me, and if I look carefully I can see just his eyes through the black hood: white and bloodshot, but deformed so there are no pupils. Then he tells me that I have a choice: that I can jump off of the pinnacle to be impaled on the sharp rocks below, or that he can stab me through with his spear. Every single time in the dream I make it up in my mind to jump, thinking that if I jump there is certainly a chance for survival, but I can't. I can't jump, I freeze, unable to move as I watch his spear shove into me. The last thing I feel is the sensation of blood dripping down my back.

Psychologists will say that dreams like this are just the brain's attempt to synchronize what our bodies are physically experiencing with what our daily stresses are. Since I was sweating in my sleep, my brain explained that wet sensation with the dripping of blood, which I am sure they would say is somehow symbolic of my father's death. Tonight, I have that same dream, but at the pinnacle it isn't the deformed monster standing there with me, it's Liz. She's the one holding the spear, she's the one giving me the ultimatum. And just like every other time, I can't jump. I want to leave her, but I can't, I can't move at all. She takes the spear and slices it into me, the blood drips down slowly along my spine and I fall to my back where the blood begins pooling. She crouches above me and begins calling my name and shaking me, "Ethan, Ethan!" I try to hold on but I'm already slipping away. "Ethan, wake up!" She yells, and then I feel it. Actual wet. Not dream wet, real wet, and I'm in my bed. Liz is real, and she's shaking me.

"My water just broke. Are you awake?" She shakes me one more time in panic. I push through the fog of sleep almost instantly. "You should call Jim so that we can get to the hospital," she insists, rapidly nudging me.

"Let's evaluate labor progression for a second. Are you having contractions?" I ask, my throat dry from the night.

"Cramping *really* bad, here along the sides, and my back hurts, like aches, *really* bad!" she says while I turn on the bedside lamp, and crawl awkwardly off the wet sheets.

"Okay, what is *really* bad? On a scale of one to ten how severe is the abdominal cramping?" I gauge.

"Ten!" she asserts without hesitation, tears forming in her eyes.

"So, it probably isn't a ten, because you're moving around and able to communicate fine. With a ten I would expect something like a ruptured bladder and vaginal hemorrhaging or something," I explain slowly with as much warmth as I can.

"Love, I really need you to be my husband right now, not my doctor," she says. I begin rubbing around my eyes either in tiredness or confusion, or both. I'm unsure how she would expect me to agree with a "ten" on the basis of husbandly loyalty, when a ten is objectively a life and death pain level.

"What about the back pain?" I ask.

"Ten," she states again. Well that's helpful.

"Alright, let me just check your dilation and effacement before I call Jim, and if you have observable progression I will call," I tell her.

"Ethan, no. You're not an OB, you promised you wouldn't do this. Just call Jim so he can come over and we will go to the hospital as planned." Her voice sounds like she's on the verge of tears.

"I helped deliver babies before." I defend while slowly pulling off my amniotic-fluid drenched shirt.

"Two. Two babies. And that was, like, twenty years ago!" she yells, and then tears begin rolling down her cheeks. Should I hug her? Is it hormones? Is it pain?

"Baby, are you okay?" I try to sit beside her on the edge of the bed, but she curls up and holds her bare belly as if it were a stuffed animal. She struggles to fasten a pink nursing bra around her chest, so I come behind her and fasten the clip.

"No, I'm not. Alice is coming and something feels so wrong about it, Ethan. She's going to die or I'm going to die, or Arthur is going to hurt her, or I'm going to forget her in the car, or drop her. Don't you feel like that, like this isn't right?" As soon as she finished speaking she winces in pain and holds her breath for several seconds. I can see muscles physically contracting in her uncovered belly, and sweat begins to form on her forehead. I slowly pull a new shirt over my head, but then quickly fasten my back brace over it.

"Liz, everything is going to be okay. Alice is not going to die, you are not going to die, no one is going to die. But if you're asking if I feel some looming ominousness, yes, I feel that too.

Can I confess to you something and then I'll call Jim?" I ask her as softly as I can. She slowly moves off the bed, and throws yesterday's dress over her head. I take an intentionally slow breath while I organize my thoughts. I wipe tears off her cheek before taking her petite hands into mine.

"For so many years I thought that having a baby would be the most beautiful thing in the world. We had waited for so long with so much hope, and whatever little one entered our house would be the culmination of all that hope, they would be something so beautiful to us. But when years went by and when Arthur came, well, when I *brought* him in, it wasn't beautiful. It was the opposite of beautiful, something ugly, and I was okay with that, I thought. But when you told me you were pregnant, I had no category in my head for that. My hope category had been filled with this ugliness, and my child category had been filled with Arthur and there was no place left to put Alice at the end of the day. Even though I had no category for her, as you grew you became more and more beautiful to me, I felt more and more love for whoever this person is inside you. So I feel love, but it still feels wrong. It feels like she's not entering into a loving home but into a dysfunctional psych ward. It's not how you or I had ever planned our lives, and so yes, it feels wrong, but I think that's okay. I am beginning to think that maybe it's okay for things to feel wrong." As I speak she continues to cry, and her lips tremble as she breathes.

"That's exactly how I feel. I just needed to hear that I wasn't alone, that I wasn't just the worst mom in history, who feels as much nausea as I do excitement over the birth of my daughter." She pulls one of her hands from mine and wipes tears from her face.

"This year with Arthur, Liz, god. You're the most glorious thing to look at as a mother, so intuitive and capable, and kind in a way that I could never be. You are the queen of this castle, and I'm full of pride for you. Your crown can only be more splendid when our little girl is in your arms." She smiles, and not some consolation smile but one of those smiles that takes up her whole face and leaves a sparkle in her eyes.

I call Jim, issuing as many apologetic remarks as I can for the middle-of-the-night call. He insists that, on the contrary, it is the perfect time for him to come over because he won't need to watch the Barguest (his unaffectionate nickname for Arthur) as closely if he's still sleeping. In the interim, Liz and I clean ourselves up as best we can, double and triple check the hospital bag, and I fill a thermos full of coffee. When I see the headlights from Jim's truck flash beside our house, I open the front door for him and stand in the middle of the door frame, one leg in the house and one outside. I nervously tap my fingers along the wooden door, and begin feeling the waves of anxiousness crash over me. Jim approaches with sleep still in his eyes offset by a glowing smile plastered along his face. He shakes my hand firmly and pulls me in for hug, patting my back a few times with his spare hand.

"So today's the day we get to meet the King's progeny, ay?" He bellows a short laugh.

"I think so." I nod. Liz approaches behind me from the kitchen, but stops to lean on the staircase mantle as she winces through another contraction.

"So are you excited, Liz?" Jim asks, exposing all his teeth in a cheeky grin. She glares up to him from her crunched over position with a stare of vitriol.

"Alllllrighty, then. Well. Ahem. Make us proud out there, I'll just be, uh, here. Ya' know, watching the kid and uh, can't wait to see that cute little baby when ya'll get home." He moves toward the living room, inching past Liz cautiously as if she's a poisonous snake.

"Bye, Jim. I've got my phone on me. I'll keep you updated."

"Appreciate it, buddy." He winks at me before pulling a book from his back pocket and plopping to the couch.

***

You ask all of these questions over nine months of waiting, sometimes to yourself, sometimes to the other person, about what the child will be like. Will she look like Liz? Will she look like me? Will she have hair? What shade of blue would her eyes be? Will they end up brown like Liz's, or hazel like mine, or something else altogether? Will she be long, will she be heavy, will she be restless or calm? Thinking that today we will find the answers to all of these questions makes my heart begin racing with excitement.

Once at the hospital I push Liz in a wheelchair to the disenchanting maternity ward on the fourth floor which used its twelve-dollar decorating budget to paint putrid yellow and pink binkies on the walls. One nurse with dyed red hair and overgrown bangs checks us into the ward. The continual sound of spit sloshing around wears on me as she haphazardly moves her tongue around her mouth like a horse might with peanut butter while she types. If the hospital were to post superlatives the individuals working in the maternity ward would receive distinctions such as "Most likely to have dysfunctional home life," or "Most likely to actually be a serial killer." It isn't that they aren't friendly, it's just that they're totally insane. These are people who volunteer to eat cafeteria food, who have buggy eyes or twitches, and who compulsively talk about the most gruesome death stories involved in labor and delivery. I don't altogether blame them for their abnormalities. Their primary job is to deliver monsters, hand them to their mothers who typically chose to conceive as a selfish means of improved health for a few months, and then walk them through dark fact sheets about how to care for Inexorables. It's a thankless job, and instead of getting to come home with the feeling that they have contributed to society, they have to come home with the feeling that they've worsened it, and I pity that.

But they're kinder to us than to others. It helps that I work at the hospital, but one nurse corrects me that nepotism isn't the reason for their kindness: "It's not you! We only have a non-inexorable birth about once a week. It's what makes it worth it – the rest of it. We all hope that our shifts will fall on a healthy birth." They place us in a gynecological exam room and our physician, Dr. Roberts, checks Liz's dilation and effacement. The whole thing feels difficult to process, as my brain switches back and forth between doctor and husband. On the one hand it's very representative of my work life to see human bodies as objective materials made up of bigger and smaller parts. To the doctor's mind, there is no allure in a vaginal cavity – it is nothing more than bulbs, and glands, and membranes and tissue. On the other hand, I'm watching a man stick his hand inside of my wife, and for whatever reason, that feels intimate, and personal, and wrong, in instinctual ways that I can't quite shake. It could be that Dr. Roberts incessantly winks at people, or it could be some irrational ancestral instinct flaring inside of me.

"You're progressing very well, and fast! I'd say it's a good thing you came in when you did." He winks at Liz and removes her feet from the stirrups. He stands from his seat, pats me on the shoulder, and proceeds to stand directly beside me as if we were the closest of friends and not simply informal colleagues.

"See, I told you!" Liz snickers and sticks her tongue at me before wincing and groaning for another contraction. Now's a time when I'd like to be sarcastic, and tell her that if she can't be nice I won't hold her hand, but that doesn't seem wise given the situation.

"When would you expect actual delivery?" I ask, trying to inch away from his claustrophobically close stance.

"I would expect first pushing to begin within two hours. I know what we've talked about before but would you be reconsidering an epidural?" he addresses Liz again.

"No. I, don't.... Auuurgh." she groans, and crunches forward nearly clawing at the sides of her stomach.

"It's fine either way with me," he says at a rushed pace. "Our window for that is closing so if you do change your mind as labor continues to progress, please let one of the nurses know immediately." He winks at me with a smile, before exiting the room.

A nurse moves us from the exam room to a delivery room, which is nicer than I had remembered. Its layout is spacious with a blue suede recliner directly beside the hospital bed, dimming overhead lights which adjust not only for brightness but also for color temperature, an array of music stations which can be played from built in speakers, and full cable television which neither Liz nor I are disposed to. Liz suffers through the next several hours of labor with many yelps of pain, many laps around the room, many leanings of her weight on my still-healing ribs and spine. At times, she and I are both yelping in pain. When Dr. Roberts comes in for the fourth time to evaluate the labor progression, he tells Liz what she desperately wants to hear: it's time.

Nurses come in, the labor position is set, and we all prepare for the most painful part of the process. All Liz wants to do is push the entire time. Dr. Roberts and the nurses continually try to stop her so that she only pushes during contractions, expecting that her delivery will take hours on account of this being her first. She's gasping for breath, and sweating, and a nurse gives me a cold washcloth to pat along her forehead. I barrage her with supportive comments that go primarily unacknowledged, but I continue to tell her how amazing she is, and how well she's doing anyway. About twenty minutes in she gives up holding my hand and braces against the hospital bed with all her strength. She pushes with a fiercely red face, and cries off and on in discomfort.

At about an hour in, she begins to crown, and my heart picks up
another kick of adrenaline and pumps it through my body.
"You're doing great, Liz," Dr. Roberts says, both his hands
guiding the head of the baby. "Keep taking deep breaths. One
more push, you're doing great. Keep breathing. Okay, ready?
Push!" Liz grips the bed, her face scrunching in effort as she
pushes with one more shriek of exertion. And then a cry. A tiny,
most unique cry enters the world.

"Beautiful!" Dr. Roberts yells, and one of the nurses tells Liz
that she can rest now, but Liz can't hear her. She's just staring
enthralled at Alice, and I do too. I feel the same thing; the slowing
of time, the quieting of everything else. We just stare at her,
watching her squirm in his arms, and cry and live.

"Dad, do you want to cut the cord?" The short nurse asks me.
Whatever rational side is still in me double checks to make sure
they've clipped the cord first, and then I make my cut, severing
this sweet girl from her mother for the first time. The paternal
feelings that flood my heart are so intense that I feel primal, as if
somehow, just for this moment, I've stepped out of the 2040's
and into a time far simpler. This is my daughter, part of me, part
of Liz, and she seems in her tiny person to be something so
strong and magnificent, a queen, or a princess; something
perfect, and sweet, and majestic.

After they initially wipe Alice, clear out her lungs and ears,
and measure and weigh her, they wrap her up and place her in
Liz's arms. Liz gazes at me with joyful, tearful eyes, and I wipe
her sweaty hair back over her head.

"You were incredible," I tell her.

"She's incredible," she responds.

"Yes. She is."

We both stare down at Alice and begin pointing out her
features. Her tiny lips, though so small, are very full and pink like
Liz's. When she cries her bottom lip pouts so severely that it
shreds holes in my heart to look at, as if all of her joy has just

been destroyed by having to leave her loving mother to enter the real world full of light, and sound, and movement. I can relate to that disposition against overstimulation. Her nose is button-like, small, perfectly centered on her face. She has a short layer of dark hair, which could be either from me or Liz, but her skin tone is more olive like mine. She's unbelievably expressive, as if each thing she experiences, whether a yawn, or sneeze, or upset is the most dramatic thing in the world. And it is, for her. She's so small, and innocent, and sweet, and for a moment as Liz and I hold her in our arms, I forget that I have a son, I forget all about Arthur. It's just us three. It's just me, and Liz, and Alice Miriam King.

CHAPTER 21

Three days at home with my beautiful angel, and things have gone relatively smoothly. In some ways, Arthur acts as if he hasn't noticed the new addition at all; he still does all of the same activities, he still loves his show, he still loves spaghetti and cuddles in the mornings, and of course, he still tries to continuously stab me or Liz, but overall, the adjustment is going better than expected. I'm not as exhausted as Liz, but I'm a level of exhausted that I haven't felt since medical school. But just like the beginning of medical school, every single day I awaken to excitement. My three day-old Alice is scrunched in Liz's arms so closely, almost like she's forgotten that she was already born. It feels like I could live in this perfect place, just our family in this home, forever. I try to remember that I can't. I try to remember what I've worked so many hours on, devoted so much of my life to this past year. I try to remember that other people matter, and that the truth matters, but it all seems foreign and distant now. It seems as though the best thing for everyone would be to destroy my research, to cease all explorations in this front, to cozy up with my wife and Alice on the couch as we watch Arthur bounce incessantly on the floor while reciting to us things he has learned in his videos. The dream of it all, the serenity and even the chaos of it, seems right, and reality seems to be distorted. But I try. I force myself to detach from home, just enough that I can carry on in objectivity, just enough so that I can continue what I have started. And so I lie again, and I tell Liz that I have to go to the hospital today– but that isn't where I go. A sensible ache forms in my heart as I leave her, because I know I won't be back until the middle of the night, and I cannot explain why. Not to her. God, this would all be so much easier if I could have told her everything before Alice came, but now the secrets must stay secrets, and I carry them all alone. I hate every single step I make toward the door, but I leave anyway, and I don't answer her calls, I don't answer any calls at all. Until I get one that I don't expect, one that I knew was important.

When all of our friends first began having kids, long before Liz and I had considered infertility as a possibility for us, they often bemoaned that when the second child would come the first would suffer from behavioral changes, or night terrors. The stress of having a new person in the house, sucking up attention and time, was difficult for the first child to process. It should have seemed obvious that when you pair that stress with a psychopathic nature that something awful would come from it. I should have seen it coming, I should have been there. I slam on my horn as a driver cuts me off, and speed past him on the left shoulder, racing to Philadelphia East as fast as humanly possible. Jim's words on the phone keep replaying in my mind over and over: "It's Liz. It's bad." The car can't move fast enough and I beg the universe, God, whoever will listen, to help me get there faster. I need to save Liz, I need to see her again. None of this would have happened if I had just been home today. The thought makes me impossibly sick. If she dies I could kill myself over guilt, it was my job to protect her, I knew that this would be difficult, I knew that things would be bad with Alice in the picture, I just didn't expect this. I thought everything would be fine. I just thought I'd.... that doesn't matter now.

I whip into the parking garage and park unevenly in a space. I sprint to the emergency room, air from the sliding doors pushing my hair backward. I hardly stop at the check in desk, asking where Liz is, and they know off the top of their heads: 312. That's good, recovery patient room, it means she isn't in the ICU. I move in a haze through the emergency department and to the elevators against the back wall. They don't move fast enough, nothing is moving fast enough. As soon as the doors open on the third floor I see Jim, who rushes to me, blocking me with both of his hands against my chest to keep me from entering her room.

"Hey, Ethan, stop for just one second, please."

"Is she okay?" I exhale, and realize that I'm hyperventilating.

"She's going to be fine, Ethan. But, I have to warn you... this is going to be very difficult on you."

"What happened?!" I shout.

"Arthur attacked her with a knife," he answers slowly, eyes full of sadness. I shove past him and make a sharp right into Liz's room. She's laying on the bed holding Alice, but the entire upper portion of her head is covered in white bandaging so that I can't see her eyes.

"Liz." I rush to the side of her bed. A nurse standing in the room gives me a nasty look before exiting to give us privacy.

"Ethan?" Her voice sounds so tired and broken.

"I'm here, baby." I sit down in a chair propped perfectly against the bed. I stroke her arm gently.

"Can you take Alice?" she asks weakly, and I pull Alice's weight carefully into my arms. She's sleeping.

"Liz I'm so sorry." Hot tears flood my eyes, and I fight a sob.

"Where were you?" Her voice turns desperate.

"I can't tell you," I say in a whimper. I look through the window at the artificially lit city. It creates a blurry contrast with the black sky, and I consider how many hours she's been in the hospital alone.

"Ethan, what the hell?" She shakily raises her palms in front of her, demonstrating her frustration, her unbelief, and then she slams them down. "He tried to cut my eyes out, do you know that? He took a knife and cut into my face while I was sleeping. All I could see was black and red, there was blood everywhere, I thought I was blind!" She begins sobbing and so do I. Her long fingers dig into the white bedsheets.

"I'm so sorry," I say over and over. Then I remember, I remember the cat. I remember the blood, and the eyeballs, and his obsession with them. I remember never telling her, never warning her about it. The memory, Liz's condition now, makes me sick. It's all my fault. I rise from the chair move toward the patient bathroom, and while still holding Alice I vomit into the sink. It doesn't make me feel any better, I just feel sicker and sicker. Liz makes no comment. Not while I'm in the bathroom, not while I vomit, not while I clean up or return to her side.

"I love you so much," I tell her, my lips trembling as I say it.

"I love you too," she says straightly, as if it's out of mere obligation.

"How did he get a knife?"

"I cut a banana for Arthur, forgot about it, and fell asleep on the couch. Alice was upstairs, she was safe the whole time. It's because I'm not sleeping that I forgot, everything feels like a daze and I wasn't being safe." Her voice shakes as she retells it.

"It's not your fault. It's mine. If I had been there none of this would have happened!"

"Maybe so." She presses one of her hands against the bandage over her eyes. Her words cut into me like acid-drenched blades, so that it only hurts worse the longer I think about it. I tell Liz that I'll be right back and that I just need to talk to Jim. As I exit her room all of the doctors and nurses glare at me with contempt.

"Why are they staring at me like that?" I ask.

"Yeah, they think you sort of deserved this because ya adopted an Inex. Ignore the vultures," Jim yells the last part loudly for them to hear, and then pulls me in for a firm hug.

"Tell me about Liz's condition. Will she see again?"

"Oh sure, the knife actually didn't touch her eyes at all. The bones of her eye socket really did their job in protecting her, but she is going to be severely scarred for the rest of her life. When she came in bone was very visible. We put a combined forty stitches into her face, kinda like an X pattern over her eyes, extending from her forehead downward. She took it like a champ, that woman is tough as nails. At one point the police tried to take

Arthur away, and she screamed, threatening to sue until they finally agreed to do what she wanted," he says with relative calmness.

"And what did she want?"

"She wanted them to babysit Arthur in the waiting area until she could take him again." His face grows an amused grin.

"And they did that?" I stare skeptically at him.

"Well yeah, she was fairly persuasive. Actually, she was kind of a bully, it was hilarious. Or, ya know, it would have been, if things were different." He coughs on his words. I can't handle this, I can't handle my role in what's happened, the guilt is eating me alive. I would never want Liz to have to suffer like this, to have to blindly snatch a knife from Arthur's hands, restrain him and grab Alice from upstairs, call an ambulance, and all of this alone. She was alone. I should have been there. My head drops and tears fall uninhibitedly to the ground.

"It's a rite of passage for every good man to suffer for the truth," Jim utters, resting one of his hands on my shoulder.

"You think that's what this is? Truth?" I spit the response at him and gesture to the hospital room just feet away where Liz lies mangled. He pauses for a long time, taking slow steady breaths.

"I think that five years from now no one will ever have to go through this again." He sounds calm, strong.

"I have to start. I have to start right now. Arthur can't stay...." I look around at the staring eyes and choose not to finish my thought.

"I know," Jim says.

"I know you know."

The police make Arthur and I go home while Liz stays in the hospital overnight, an arrangement that pleases no one. The police want Arthur resolved in the Assistance Center, I want to be with my wife and newborn, Liz wants to be home, no one is satisfied. Coming home is more of a nightmare than I would have expected. As soon as we enter through the front door my stomach turns to stone. Trailing up the staircase, fingerprinted on the mantle, smeared across the floor in half footprints, spread along the wall in finger prints, is blood. It's on every corner of the house, not a drop here or there, but a lot of blood. I unapologetically tie Arthur to the banister, and compulsively replay the details in my mind as I walk through the house. Atop the wood table in the kitchen dried, brown banana slices of are now fused to a plate. To the left, a pale maple cutting board lies on the marble counter-top. I turn full circle and re-enter the living room, attempting to ignore the puddles of blood marking the wood floor. I stand behind the couch and look down. There's a cut in the leather by where Liz would have been laying her head, and only a few droplets of blood now dry as cement on the armrest. From where I stand I glance at Arthur, tethered tightly to the banister, and I fight the urge to choke him, or beat him, or throw him in the woods for wolves to eat. Boiling hot anger sears inside of me, and I want vengeance, I want someone to pay for what has happened. Take a deep breath. Keep your head. Take Arthur to the basement, and finish this once and for all.

Ignoring whether there's blood in my path or not, I single-mindedly rush over to Arthur, untie him, and carry him sideways tightly under my arm as if he's a log. He squirms and screams, and startles me when he says in his pathetic little voice "Red and red." I shiver at it, and it only fuels the fire of wrath that I'm restraining. I unlock the basement door, and sprint down the stairs with my shoes making pitter-patters sounds at my steps. I forcibly re-secure Arthur against one of the two chairs, and yank open a drawer in my desk. I snatch a sealed sedative injection and an alcohol swab, and push shut the drawer. Arthur begins talking incessantly: "Where are we? Are you mad?" "I made mommy bleed today. I had fun." My fingers shake as I pull back the corner of the wrapper and place the injection flat on the desk. Next I open the alcohol swab, its bitter pungent fume rising into my nostrils. I walk over to Arthur, who looks swallowed up by the size of the chair. I stare him straight in the eyes, and for the first time, the deadness rests in mine and not in his.

"You're never going to hurt anyone again." It's the last words I tell him before I insert the needle into his neck, and push in the sedative. He eyes glaze over, like he's staring out into space, his eyelids droop, and then his head falls against his chest, a few curls dangling in front of his face.

I open up the cabinets in the bottom of my desk and pull out a large blue surgical sheet. I lay it flat along the grey speckled flooring. I untie Arthur and lay his limp body carefully face down over the sheet. I move his head sideways, and listen carefully for his breathing. It's still there, steady and strong. I strip him of his clothes and from the cabinets I pull out an emergency medical kit which contains supplies that I've smuggled out of the hospital over the course of the year. Today, I will need most of it. I sanitize the surrounding area as best as possible, and perform a less than ideal surgical wash before sliding latex gloves over my hands. Placing my surgical mask over my face I carefully sanitize Arthur's body, applying povidone-iodine generously across his back, which leaves it discolored and dry looking. I try to steady my hands and remember why I'm doing this: Liz in the hospital, her blood splashed all over the house, his pride in what he has done, and then I begin.

Healing Arthur is more difficult than any treatment I've ever performed on a patient. In one sense it's just like treating any other systemic infection that attacks soft tissue: first you eradicate the infection, and then you work to restore the damaged material. That's always the order of operations, and it's no different here. But one thing is very different: extent of damage. Arthur's brain was injured in the development phase which means that it isn't enough to simply heal damaged tissue, as if cells can replicate and rebuild the same structures that they have in the past. No, in Arthur's brain, tissue must be generated which has never been there before, whole new segments of quadrants have to spontaneously begin forming. It isn't impossible, but it is experimental and the only method of completing the treatment requires some sacrifice, and maybe more than some.

The first part of the treatment is relatively easy, and it's something I can do from here in the basement. Part one begins tonight, an abrasive attack on the parasitic bacterial infection using a high dose antibiotic cocktail administered through IV. I've estimated that the regimen would take four weeks to complete, and while it helps for dosage that his body is so small, it doesn't help that he is impassably uncooperative. That's the purpose of this minor surgical operation, the insertion of the Mod-7. It's a relatively ubiquitous device used to treat long term bacterial infections, or used in treatment of people with chronic conditions. Mod-7 is similar to a port, in that once inserted under your skin, you can continually re-access it. However unlike a port, it holds a quantity of up to three medicines, and can be programed to release prescribed dosages. Since Arthur's body size is small enough it will only need be re-accessed and filled every other day. The goal in connecting it to a vein system in the back is that Arthur shouldn't be able to rip it out – which I believe he would do if it was in his chest. In order to draw out all of the bacteria, I programmed the Mod-7 to release a miniscule amount of Dopamine with the antibiotics in order to attract the bacteria to the release site.

With a medical marker I carefully draw out my incision lines, for which there are two, and then open the sterile packaging of the Mod-7 and set it beside myself on the floor. An operation to insert a Mod-7 typically runs twenty minutes by an experienced surgeon. For me, it takes hours. There is no suction for the blood which fills the open spaces after every minor cut, no additional hands to pass me tools or provide better lighting. It's just me on the basement floor with a bloody sedated Inexorable under my hands, and my fumbling as I insert a machine the size of a thick cucumber slice into his back while connecting its long piercing tube into a major blood source. When I finish, I successfully test the Mod-7, fill it with the first round of treatment by injection, and then stitch Arthur's skin over it. I smear his back with disinfectant again, place a bandage over him, and then pour myself the biggest glass of scotch I've ever had. My knees are bony, and bruised, and numb. My eyes are seeing light and blood where there is none, and my neck burns poignantly from strain. And so for a while I sink into a chair, look upon my makeshift surgical site, and enjoy a few sips of scotch – the only thing I've enjoyed all day.

CHAPTER 22

Even though Liz has been home for a week, nothing seems normal. She lays in bed all day long. Sometimes she nurses Alice, sometimes she changes a diaper, sometimes she tries to read a book, but for the most part she just sleeps. When her eyes are open she hardly talks, she mostly stares blankly at the wall. She's insisted four times now that she's not angry at me, and to stop asking. I think it's a mix of post-partum depression and PTSD, and I'm struggling to know how to handle it, or how to help her. The stitches over her face are very difficult to look at. A jagged X pattern of thin, black wire pieces warps down the lower portion of her forehead, through one of her eyebrows, slightly descending down her nose and then turning sharply under her eyes. The inflammation and bruising has finally reduced, but every time I look at her I well up with guilt. Underneath the stitches she still looks beautiful. Her pale eyelids contrast perfectly with her deep brown irises, her skin glows flawlessly otherwise, and her full lips are as kissable as ever. But that's an exerted effort to see trees through the forest. When I catch her out of the corner of my eye, she looks like an abused rag doll, or the creation of a horror movie. It will improve once her black stringy stitches are removed, but it's one of those injuries that as a doctor I know will impact her for the rest of her life. The scars will always be the first thing people see when they look at her. They will force themselves not to stare at her on the street, and they'll politely not mention it in conversation even though all they want is to know how such a dramatic marking could have been carved into her face. I wonder if she's worried about that, if she's thinking about what people will say. I wonder if she's thinking about anything at all, or just trying to make it through each miserable day with a remnant of dignity.

She hasn't seen Arthur close up since he attacked her. Jim suggested not letting them come into physical contact until her stitches are taken out two weeks from now. Arthur has been terribly lethargic since starting the treatment. He's unable to play, he's discontent with everything, he doesn't want to eat, he's sick of being held by me, and he thankfully doesn't have the energy to be violent. He keeps asking about "Mom," and why she isn't coming out anymore. Though I don't entirely understand how it works for him, I can tell that he misses her. Surely violent men, even psychopaths, experience longings for routine, right? Someone like Josef Mengele probably experienced missing someone at some point in his life, wicked as he was. Arthur can palpably sense the discontinuity around him, especially with people, even though it's people he's attacked. He wants the comfort but he hates the comforter. I try to rationalize it as the consequence of which brain structures of his were injured, but even that doesn't satisfy me. It is a challenge, because in his silent tears and audible requests for Liz I see something so vulnerable, so human. It's that desire for comfort that we all have, that even I have. He wants his mom back, and so do I. But he was also the one who "had fun" slicing her face open, and that's what makes it a challenge.

Balancing the load of home life feels impossible most moments of the day. Even a sick Arthur feels too difficult for me to handle on my own, and if Liz is not a cooker by nature, I am far worse. But I've learned in the last few days that rice is easy to cook in the microwave, and that I can stir a different vegetable in every day and add a different sauce to give it variety. On Monday we had rice with corn and peas and fajita mix, on Tuesday we had rice with spinach mixed in and tzatziki sauce, and on Wednesday I even ground a pound of turkey and mixed the rice with green beans and teriyaki sauce. It isn't really a sustainable diet, but in my mind it's fairly competitive with Liz's five meal rotation. Before we were married Liz used to pretend that she liked to cook, I guess she wanted to seem domestic and capable and as if she had something significant to contribute to our marriage. She does, but it isn't cooking, because she lied straight through her teeth every time she told me some recipe she had concocted or some dish she made "just because." It's impossible to think of her living in a society apart from fast food and delivery services. It flashes me to where I was the day Arthur attacked her, and I try to picture her there, the dirt, the heat, the desolation and unfriendly eyes always on me.

A ball of emotion forms in my throat thinking about it as I finish tonight's dinner, canned soup heated in a pot and accompanied unsurprisingly with rice. I serve Arthur first at the kitchen table, the sun setting through the front windows of the house. I sit in the chair beside him, repeatedly urging him to take another bite. His head hangs low and there are bags under his eyes like only sick children have. Adults have bags under their eyes constantly, but children only have bags like this when something is physically wrong. I finally lift Arthur out of his chair, take him into my arms, and hold him closely to my chest. He doesn't fight, he just sinks into me, nuzzling his head into my chest while he takes labored breaths. It's amazing how much he's changed since I first saw him. He's as tall as my hips, maybe fifty pounds, and on a normal day his skin is a deeply tan olive, but today it's more ashen and yellow from his health. His eyes are the same large bulbs they've always been, only now they're more defined by his thick eyelashes and larger eyebrows. His nose is still slightly too large for his face, but it seems more proportionate now than when I first saw him. Liz keeps his hair cut about the same length, black curls grow down to just below his ears giving him a loose hanging afro. All of it combined makes him seem so much older, but not as much as his vocabulary. I don't understand his obsession with words, but something there clicks inside of him with delight. Anytime Jim is alone with Arthur he teaches him an onslaught of peculiar words which get regurgitated back to me at unsuspecting moments. This week while injecting the Mod-7 with another round of drugs, Arthur, who was fully subdued on the floor under my weight, whispered out in melodic tone, as if it was a super-heroes mantra: "Injecting adjuvant!" I asked him, "Arthur, how do you know that word, 'adjuvant?'" And he recited a textbook definition to me, "Adjuvant is an agent that modifies other drug agents." But, when I asked "Can you tell me what an 'agent' is?" he responded unhesitatingly "A bad guy!" So he doesn't entirely understand, but the words fix in his mind like covalent bonds.

I put Arthur to bed early, and I sit on the floor next to him with an arm nestled around his chest for a while. It's unnerving to see him so sick, and it makes me concerned that I've misjudged the amount of antibiotics his body can handle. Intellectually I know that treatments this aggressive always make the patient sicker before they improve, I've seen it a thousand times. But it feels definably different when it's your own kid. I lock the metal cage surrounding his bed, and I make a quick turn-around to bring food from the kitchen upstairs for Liz. I'm thankful when I enter the bedroom to see her open eyes as she perches upward. Dim yellow light overlays her side of the bed from the lamp, while she gazes down affectionately at Alice, who's laying on top of her legs and cooing.

"It's nice to see you smile," I remark as I set the tray of food in the center of the bed. Alice is in a pink onesie with cartoonish owls on the feet. Her tiny cheeks look rosy and full, and her hands are both clenched in tight fists.

"It hurts to smile." Liz pushes her bottom lip out in a pouting fashion without breaking eye-contact with Alice, but a grin reforms instantly at the corners of her mouth.

"I put Arthur to bed and made dinner." I nudge the tray toward her another inch, finally her eye contact breaks with Alice and she looks at me stunned.

"Wow, he went to bed already? He must be having a growth spurt, because I can't believe how much he's sleeping lately!"

"I think he misses you," I suggest, in an attempt to keep her mood positive.

"I kind of miss him too. But, I'm also afraid of him again, a lot."

"I think that's understandable."

"I miss you as well." She lays her hand over my shoulder.

"I miss you so much." I see her more now than ever, but I miss *her*. I miss her liveliness, her sarcasm, her laugh.

"I know this isn't just hard on me, but sometimes it feels like it." She carefully moves the tray of food to her bedside table, then lifts Alice into her arms and cuddles closely against me.

"How old do you feel?" I ask her as I stroke Alice's alert face slowly with my thumb.

"Fourteen," Liz responds without much consideration.

"Why?" I glance down at her with strange curiosity.

"Everything felt hard and personal at fourteen. Fourteen sucked. How old do you feel?"

"Five," I say boldly, owning the true answer.

"Why five?" She laughs.

"I feel incapable. I'm so incapable without you. Like, what can a five year old do? What can Arthur do? Nothing. He can't brush his teeth, he hardly goes to the bathroom in the toilet, he needs to be cooked for and groomed. Forget about it. I need you." I make a cheeky grin.

"I think you're doing admirably," she responds softly, sweetly. I wish she hadn't said that, I wish she had said anything else. One thing I know for sure is that I am doing nothing admirably. But I let the words hang in the air for a while anyway. I soak in the warm cuddles of my two girls, adoring every single facial expression Alice makes, feeling the tender caresses of Liz's hand, and I treasure every minute, every second of it.

***

The next two weeks of separation between Liz and Arthur move painfully slow as cabin fever sets in. Liz wants desperately to be out in public, to see other faces, other scenery, but she can't bear it with her face in its current condition. Now that Arthur has his energy back I've been letting him play in the backyard, a large open space with nothing but grass until the woods edge. His energy is a very good sign that the infection is on its last leg, and that's it's almost time to proceed with the next step of the plan. I try not to think about it, I try to suppress it, but even when it isn't consciously in my thoughts I still carry it around with me like an apple lodged in my throat, making it impossible to breathe, to swallow. I have to put on an extra thick emotional guard because tonight, after I put Arthur to bed, I drive to the hospital to see Jim one last time before we commandeer an operating room for phase two of Arthur's treatment.

We meet outside the hospital on the west facing corner that is trafficked by prostitutes and drug-dealers at night. I see Jim from a distance, outside in the dark like a helpless dog pacing the sidewalk hoping to magically run into its owner. He stands out like a flashlight because of his white coat, which wisps upward every few seconds from wind.

"Lookin' for a good time?" I holler sarcastically at him while passing beside. He jolts for a second before recognizing me.

"I wouldn't lay a finger on something as hairy as you," he quips with a straight face.

"Just as well, you're not my type." We both smile. A gust of warm air carries with it the scent of sewage and exhaust.

"How long will you be gone for?" he asks, his eyes shifting to and fro with paranoia.

"As long as is necessary. I hold out some hope for a quick disposing of power, after all of the information is released, but not much."

"Me either. So let's run through operation day." He stops shifting his glance and looks straight at me. I nod in agreement.

"At three AM, Liz will drive the car to the safe house, I'll be picking the rest of ya'll up at the house in the truck," he says in a hushed tone. "I'll sneak ya'll into an OR, probably OR-2 it's small and smelly so no one likes to use it, and we'll perform the operation as quickly and safely as we can. Finally, I'll drive the rest of us to the safe house, and return to my life like nothing ever happened? Ethan, it sounds idiotic." He wiggles his lips left and right in a fast-paced motion like a rabbit.

"I know." I rub my knuckles against my thick layer of overgrown scruff.

"Is Liz still clueless?" He raises an eyebrow.

"Unfortunately," I admit. His face grows instantly angry and he shakes his head in disappointment.

"You don't have to do this, ya' know? The universe will not implode, its fabric will not disintegrate, if you do not heal Arthur." He pulls his hands from his pocket and shakes one in front of me for emphasis. It casts a precisely defined shadow on the sidewalk of his lanky fingers and baggy white coat sleeve.

"What sort of father would I be if it was in my power to save my son and I left him a monster? A monster who cuts open the face of my bride, for hell's sake!" He has to see how important it is, he has to see how right it is. If he doesn't, if he doesn't support me, then I can't do it. I can't go forward. I can't bear it all on my own.

"Well, I don't blame ya' there. I get it. I just don't want you to lose your marbles if it doesn't go just right. There is always some madness in love. But there is also always some reason in madness," he says the last part a little too smoothly.

"What dead guy said that?"

"Uh, nobody." He diverts eye contact.

"Who?" I press.

"What? Ya' don't think I'm sophisticated enough to say something meaningful at a time like this?" I don't respond, I just continue staring at him skeptically.

"Nietzsche," he finally admits, and scrapes his shoe along the ground.

"Charming. Have you ever thought about reading something a bit more modern and applicable to our current situation? Like, I don't know, insurgent strategy or something?"

"Ethan, I literally just applied what I've been reading to our situation. Half a second ago."

"And it was immensely helpful." I roll my eyes so dramatically that it takes my entire head back with them. He half-heartedly chuckles. It's been a long time since we've just been able to enjoy each other's company without things seeming unbearably heavy. It's one of the hardest things about leaving, about becoming a whistle-blower, is that I don't know when I'll see Jim next, or if we'll ever have an exclusively light-hearted moment again. He's been the only person who has known my secrets, the only person who has known the unspoken words screaming from my eyes. He's been the only one who could make me laugh at my circumstances, or who could bear the darkest parts of what needs to be done. I've had to hide a whole world away from every single person I know, except for Jim. In some ways he knows me deeper than anyone else could, but he also knows a side of me that shouldn't exist at all. It all started with Arthur, and it will all end with him. We talk through the operation one last time, quickly reassessing all of the surgical instruments we'll need along the way and realizing that we've forgotten more than one. Jim promises to gather the supplies slowly over the course of the next week and to alert me only when it's the right night for our move.

"I love ya', buddy," he says affectionately before returning to the hospital. And though I never would normally, I respond without hesitation, "I love you too, Jim."

The walk to the car is pitifully dark. I didn't want to park in the garage because I didn't want it to be insurmountably obvious that I was here for unofficial purposes. I pass by sketchy characters as I walk, but few look me in the eye. Even though it's so dark, the sky is devoid of moon and stars. Instead it seems filled with smog or clouds that reflect a grey haze of city lights back toward earth. As the car enters into view I hear the clapping of footsteps, maybe of a set of runners approaching from the sidewalk behind me. I quickly peer over my shoulder so I can know which side I ought to move toward to avoid them, but what I see startles me, instantly plummeting my heart deep inside my stomach with throbbing fear.

"Hey, Ethan, wait up!" a deep voice belts at me. The pattering steps of three black coats slows only feet away from my back. I turn around slowly and lift my hands in front of my chest gesturing for them to slow down and to stay back. Why the hell did I not bring a weapon? Why would I go out alone without something to protect me?

"So what are you doing out so late?" the one in the center says, and presses in so closely to me that I can smell the garlic on his breath. He's young, late twenties maybe, and he's exactly my height, his nose almost brushing against mine with his closeness. I don't recognize any of the men.

"Cabin fever. Just wanted to see a friend for a few minutes, get some air." My voice sounds confident. I stare the man directly in his eyes, but struggle not to flinch when he bumps his chest against mine before stepping backward.

"That's right, how is Liz?" He asks with a cocky smile while the other two black coats move to either side of me. "How's her face? Kind of a dick move to let her get sliced and diced like that, huh Ethan?"

One of them shoves me forcefully to the side, so that I begin falling over the curb, but the other catches me and pushes me from behind with his fingers, tense and straight so that they shove deeply into my muscles. I wince and groan, and am barely able to recover my breath as I stand up straight, now surrounded closely by them all. They're going to kill me, aren't they? That's what they said last time, that the next time they saw me they'd kill me. Should I begin fighting, or should I wait? If I moved suddenly I could puncture the throat of the one to my right with a pen. I twist it around in my pocket. But then what? Won't they just pull a gun, shoot me in the head, and blame the whole thing on street violence? I try to observe my surroundings, and I see multiple bypassers watching us from the other side of the street. I make eye contact with one, a young woman dressed inappropriately, probably a prostitute.

"Please, I don't want any trouble," I say with an anxious and gasping exhale, shifting my eyes back to the young one and lifting my hands above my shoulders to display resignation. He grabs me by my collar and yanks me toward him.

"Oh there's no trouble, no trouble, c'mon! We're just checking in on you, making sure you're recovering well." He releases his hold on my collar, giving me a few pats on my shoulder, and then all three of them walk away from the direction they came. I shake uncontrollably, my lungs feeling desperate for oxygen, but I force myself to move toward my car, locking the doors as soon as I'm inside. They're watching me, they've been watching me. I knew that, of course, but it's escalating. We can't stay, we can't stay another night. On the way home I call Jim and beg him to be ready tonight, not a week from now, but now. He adamantly protests, telling me that it'd be impossible to gather all of the supplies unnoticed if he only has tonight. But as he hears the panic in my voice, he promises that he will try.

I park in the driveway and with singlemindedness rush over the stone entranceway, push through the wooden door, and rush to the basement before I notice something out of the corner of my eye. It's someone on the couch, glaring at me. I jump when I see it, but it's only Liz, her disconsolate expression and stitches creating a terrifying pair. I'm too on edge.

"What the hell is in Arthur's back?" Her voice pierces the silence. My heart rate instantly increases. Did she find the Mod–7? Arthur was asleep, she wasn't supposed to be near him anyway.

"What?" Play dumb, maybe it's something else. Maybe she doesn't know.

"What freakish metal object did you sew into *our* son's back?" Her eyes are for a moment like Arthur's, little daggers trying to extend their deathly points into me. I stutter but am unable to get any words out. "As soon as you left today, I heard him crying from his bedroom 'Mommy, owwy, my back hurts.' When I turned on the light he was pointing to this hard round contraption sewn UNDER his skin!" she yells at me. Damnit, Arthur. He was obviously plotting for this.

"Come with me, now!" I walk over to the couch, grab her hand, and lead her quickly up the stairs. We enter our bedroom where Alice is sleeping soundly beside the bed, her chest making clear and comforting expansions and depressions. I pull Liz into the bathroom, turn on the shower, and pull her into it in the far back corner where you can stand without getting too wet. I wrap my fingers in her hair, and lean in so that my mouth almost forms to her ear, telling her everything in an inaudible whisper to any nearby listeners.

"When I went to the AC last year I discovered something in the Inexorables' brains. Every single one had a congenital infection given to them by their mother. I studied it, and discovered that the infection was responsible for the brain scarring that makes them Inexorables. I discovered that this infection is Obcasus, Obcasus is the infection, and that it's curable," as I whisper her hands begin to shake in mine more and more uncontrollably. "I found a cure for Arthur. I used the hospital laboratory in my research and some government military guys beat the crap out of me for it, that's what happened a few weeks ago. It wasn't homeless guys, Liz. They made the whole thing up, and told me I had to go along with it. Tonight some of them approached me again on the street, and seemed to threaten all of us. We need to go. We need to go somewhere else, immediately. I purchased us a safe house, that's where I was the day Arthur attacked you. I was finding us somewhere safe to go."

She doesn't ask any questions. Instead she works through shakes and sobs to pack up what she thinks we'll need. She puts everything from the safe in a suitcase, all of her jewelry, the personal documents, and then throws clothes on top. Afterward she stuffs the crevices full with baby clothes, and then begins another suitcase with clothes for me and Arthur. She runs up and down the stairs a few times, filling remaining space with formula, bottles, diapers, and first aid items. I go to the basement to grab a few necessities, including all of my medical supplies, research, and the half bottle of scotch which I seal securely using medical tape. By the time I return upstairs Liz has packed three additional bags. I stuff my arm full of items into one of the bags.

"Scotch, really?" Liz looks at me puzzled.

"You're going to want it come end of day." I'm tempted to promise, but I don't want to give her any hints of what is happening tonight. Not yet. When Jim shows up, she'll have to know at least part of it, but I can't tell her everything or she'd never let me go.

"Jim is going to drive over to help," I tell her. I wonder why she hasn't asked any questions.

"Good. I don't know how we're all going to fit with what we need." She nods to herself, but my throat tightens at the comment. While sitting on the floor surrounded by a pile of bags, she leans her upper body over Alice's bassinet, stokes her sleeping face, and begins weeping.

"Baby." My voice unintentionally cracks. I scoot behind her on the wooden floor, and wrap both my arms around her.

"I love you so much. All I want is to give you the peace and stability that you deserve. You deserve this home, and a happy life without secrets. All I want is to give that to you, you can't begin to understand how deeply I feel my failure to you as a husband." I squeeze her tighter, so that my face presses against her back, a few tears spilling over my eyes only to be absorbed by her shirt.

"You're not a failure," she whispers through her crying.

"A man is supposed to protect his family, and I can't protect anyone. I haven't even protected you." I gently move a finger over the edge of her stitches to remind her, but she pulls her head away from my touch. I glance at the clock, which beams a bright green 2:30 AM at my eyes. It's almost time. I help Liz lug the baggage down the stairs and then she wakes up Arthur while I carry Alice's bassinet downstairs. I carefully transfer her from the bassinet to the car seat, but not without making her cry. I needed to unswaddle her which jolted her awake, her thin newborn cry echoing through the house. I kiss both of her big cheeks before buckling the straps, and then I rock the car seat until she drifts back to sleep.

"Baby girl, you're my pride and joy, the closest thing to heaven I've ever been given in this hellish world. Please know that. Please, somehow, remember that," I whisper to her just before I hear Jim's knock on the front door. I stand and open it, and he and I exchange a similar pained expression. Jim begins loading bags into the car while Liz holds a half sleeping Arthur with his head sunk down over her shoulder. I walk to the kitchen and grab a post it note and pen. I write the address down: 67 West Camp, Richmond. When I rejoin Liz and Jim outside, I hear their hushed voices arguing in the unlit driveway. We all stand in complete darkness, while Liz snaps at Jim to stop placing bags inside the car "otherwise the children won't fit." When Jim sees me he pauses, and even through the darkness I can see the resignation in his face. It's time to tell her. I don't even know how to get the words out.

"Liz, this is the address." I hand her the post it note with a key. She holds the note against the window of the car so that it can catch an inch of interior light.

"West Camp, Ethan?" she asks under her breath. I nod to her affirmatively.

"But that's the Richmond slums." The words tremble out of her mouth, and her face caves in betrayal.

"I know," I say as apologetically as I can. She begins breathing heavier, I can tell that she's beginning to panic. She doesn't blink or shift her eye contact, but tears stream down her face. "It's the only place I knew that no one would look."

"Ethan, you have to tell her the rest," Jim urges me, carefully scanning the street for cars or onlookers as he picks up Alice's car seat and begins fastening it into the truck. Liz stares at me and seems to hold her breath for a minute.

"Baby, I need you to drive alone to Richmond with our stuff, and I will meet you there with the kids in several hours." I have to force each of the words out one by one, as if I'm pulling my own teeth out of my jaw.

"What? Why?!"

"I have to take the kids. I'll just be a few hours behind you. I can't tell you why."

"No, no, no," she just keeps repeating, and gasping for air as if the wind had been knocked out of her. I lean down to hug her, but she pushes me away.

"Why? What is happening?" Her volume increases.

"You have to trust me," I say, and it is those words which hurt me the most to say.

"How do you expect me to do that? Of all things? *Trust* you?" Her tone is venomous, and I can't blame her.

"After tonight, there will be no more secrets," I tell her, grabbing her hands to still their sporadic trembling.

"Ethan, you can't take Alice. She needs me. She hasn't even eaten tonight, how do you expect me to just let you take her without explanation?" Her voice pitches higher until it cracks and she begins sobbing. I suppress my urge to cry with her, feeling hot emotion welling up in my chest.

"I need you to know that I love you, that I love Alice with my whole heart, and that I will watch over our children and I will see you at the safe house just a few hours after you get there. I promise."

"Jim, tell me the truth. Is everything going to be okay?" Liz wipes her face carefully, trying to remove tears without scraping against her stitches.

"The only thing I can say for sure is that life is about to change. There is no way for me to tell whether what Ethan and I are doing tonight is going to make things easier on ya'll or harder. But I know that what we have to do is really important. We have to try." I vaguely see Jim like a shadow wrapping his arm around Liz while he speaks so quietly to her.

"No more secrets?" She looks at me desperately from under Jim's arm.

"Not even one. When I see you in the morning, I'll tell you everything. I promise." I pull her into me, holding her body tightly against mine. We share several long kisses, where I feel her wet tears along my cheeks and lips. It's so hard to keep it together, to hold my emotion back as if everything is okay, as if I could promise that I'll see her in a few hours. Before we depart on our separate paths, we set our phones on the bottom step of the staircase to ensure we are not tracked by GPS. As we shut the front door, Liz and I both stare at it for a minute, and then we say goodbye to a decade of our history.

CHAPTER 23

August 30th, 2047

" I hate that you didn't tell her," Jim says furiously as we drive toward the hospital. The roads are ghostly, empty, and the passing of dull street lamps is synchronized with the speed of my heart beat.

"What did you want me to do? If I had told her, she wouldn't have let us go!" My voice is loud enough that Alice makes stirring noises.

"Maybe she shouldn't have! She will remember my words, forever, as words of betrayal and that's on you, Ethan!" Jim says forcefully, though his volume is hushed.

"Join the freaking club! There's a lot on me right now."

We drive several miles in absolute silence, which allows both of the kids to fall back asleep, lulled by the bumping of his truck along the dips of the road.

"Were you able to test Arthur's bacterial level?" he breaks the silence, trying to keep his tone calm.

"No. But symptomatically his bacterial level seems to be low if not extinguished."

"Good," he remarks neutrally, but his knuckles are white from how tightly he's squeezing the steering wheel. His hair is disheveled, and he looks horrifically tired, as if he's aged around the eyes ten years since I saw him only a few hours ago. It's hard to imagine what the past several hours looked like for him, or how he's explained it to Mary. "It's easy to be pissed at you right now, but I wouldn't be here if I didn't think it was the right thing. It's just also so fucking backwards. How can this be the only way?" His words come out with a thicker drawl than normal.

"I don't know. Are you still in this with me?" I ask him as I see tears flooding his eyes.

"Of course."

I stare at the road ahead and pray that it goes on forever; that our destination would change or simply never arrive. For a moment I fantasize that maybe instead of taking us to a place where I must ruin my soul, the road would instead bring us somewhere free. But then the sound of his tires rolling across the garage sobers me.

We're here.

We sneak the unhappy children through an employee entrance on the first floor near the operating rooms. I systematically swing Alice's car seat to help keep her calm, and Jim carries Arthur on one side. He presses his ID against several electronic pads, allowing us access into the surgical wing which we run through so as not to be seen, and then we enter OR-2. The room is pitch black when we enter. There are no external windows, or even a peephole in the door. Jim flips on a few light switches and lays Arthur flat on the bed in the center of the tiny room, before making a beeline to a pile of supplies lying on the white ceramic floor against the back wall. More supplies lay haphazardly atop a steel rolling table next to him.

"Help me put this stuff together so we can introduce the sedative. The last thing we need is him making noise and drawing attention to us." Jim crouches down and inserts a breathing mask into a tube, and a tube into a single tank of anesthesia. I set down Alice's car seat and quickly roll the tank behind the surgical bed, inserting its tubing into the automated pump which is conveniently connected to the hospital's underground oxygen supply. I type in Arthur's weight, and press the perfectly obvious green "On" button before sealing the mask over his face. Every movement makes an echo in the room, making each clang, each click, and each pump of the machine sound infinitely louder than it is. My hands begin trembling, and I try to steady them.

Against the left wall of the room Jim constructs a makeshift bed for Alice, which is nothing more than a bed pad formed to make protective edges, draped in a white sheet. He places it on top of the rolling table, and I lay Alice on it without hesitation. Instantly her tiny face scrunches and gets bright red before she belts out one of the unhappiest and loudest cries I've heard. Her face becomes tightly pushed together, and her toothless gums are visibly exposed with each new belt of sound.

"Make her stop!" Jim says compulsively. I lay my hand over her mouth gently, while Jim anxiously inserts morphine into an infant syringe.

"Morphine?" I ask with skepticism.

"I didn't have time to research the safest infant sedative, Ethan. It's fine." He wipes down her hand with an alcohol swab, and then gently presses the syringe for about half a second cautiously monitoring the measurement markers on the side of the syringe, then he removes the morphine bottle but leaves the access point in. The crying worsens for a moment, and I feel heat rush to my face as the overwhelming sense that we're about to be caught sweeps over me. But then in an instant she sweetly falls asleep and the room returns to utter silence.

While Jim prepares supplies on another rolling table, I walk over to Arthur's bed and hold his small hand in mine for a moment, caressing it a few times. I am going to be a good father to him, that's what this is all for. Jim and I move to the recessed wash room attached to the OR, and begin our scrub in. The water splashing against the metallic sink fills the space with a serene sound, like a waterfall. I watch the soapy water spin in a grand circle before draining, and I wish that I could be sucked down with it. I picture myself small, smaller than Alice, smaller than her fingernail, and I feel myself getting sucked down by the force of the water, entering the drain, and floating away to somewhere else. I shake my head a few times to regather my thoughts. I feel like I'm quickly losing my sanity but I can't tell if it's only because it's three in the morning, or if it's a survival response, as if my body knows that I couldn't make it through the next several hours if I were sane. I dry my hands and put on my gloves, the thick unpleasant blue ones. Jim does too, before donning his surgical mask. All of the blues, his mask, the gloves, draw out the brightness of Jim's eyes, the baby blues that woo all of the injured women who come into the ER. I place my mask over my face, and we enter the operating room together. Our shoes make squeaking sounds along the tile floor, and we stand prepared over the patient.

"Are you ready?" I ask Jim. I look down with unsubdued affection, allowing myself just one more second to pretend that I'm at home and that I'm just watching the inhales and exhales of my sleeping child.

"I've been holdin' onto a quote I wanna share with you. It's the only thing that has kept me stable, kept me sure that I could do this after all. Ya mind?" Our eyes make contact from above our masks. I nod in approval, and then return my gaze downward. "Doesn't matter what the press says. Doesn't matter what the politicians or the mobs say. Doesn't matter if the whole country decides that something wrong is something right. This nation was founded on one principle above all else: the requirement that we stand up for what we believe, no matter the odds or the consequences. When the mob and the press and the whole world tell you to move, your job is to plant yourself like a tree beside the river of truth, and tell the whole world — 'No, you move,'" he says the quote as seamlessly as if he wrote it himself

"I appreciate that, Jim. Who said that?" I tug on the fingertips of my gloves gently.

"Captain America, in the Amazing Spider-Man issue 537," he says unabashedly. An impromptu laugh escapes from me, and Jim belts out a few chuckles too. "With that said, now, are *you* ready?" he poses the question to me, and I hesitate.

Step two of treatment is a Neural Stem Cell transplant. When you take stem cells from an embryo, you don't need to take brain specific cells because all of the cells are adaptable, they can turn into anything. But if you don't have an embryo, then the stem cells that you take must be brain-specific, they must be cells from a donor brain. The closest that you can get to an embryo, the closest that you can get to a brain that is still developing, the better the chance of success. A fetal human brain would have been ideal, but since there's no avenue for finding a healthy fetus the next best thing is the earliest developed healthy brain that I can find. In this case, I am presented with a three week-old brain, which still holds promise for the most adaptable neural stem cells. I gaze down at Alice, sedated and sterilized, tiny wires sticking to her chest and brain. She's so beautiful, so small, so dependent upon my protection and I fight the urge to weep. She's my baby.

"There is nothing I can compare it with. When she was born I asked questions I never asked before, like what was I born for, what was she?" Tears slip under my mask. Through blurriness I see Jim's eyes grow sorrowful.

"Ethan. You don't have to do this," he says for the hundredth time.

"It's the words I want to hear. All I want is to drop my instruments, to undo everything and walk out of this room as if we had never walked into it. I want it so badly that I would give my own life if I could! If I thought that we could walk out, I would not be tormented like this. If I thought that there was another way, you wouldn't see me hesitate. You have to do it. I can't." I pull back from the tiny table Alice is lying on, and begin stumbling steps backwards.

"If you won't do it neither will I, but if this is your path, my friend, I walk it with you. If we do everything right, both of them will be fine," he reminds me. I roll my eyes. We both know it's impossible that it will go exactly right. The operation is experimental, neither of us are brain surgeons yet alone accustomed to operating on newborns. My stomach begins turning and for a second I'm sure that I'm going to vomit, but I hold it back.

Jim picks up the thinnest scalpel in his hand, but he doesn't move with it. It will only be used for one incision inside the nostril and through the sinus cavity. Once it's made, one of us will use imaging tools to view inside the skull, while the other will insert a long needle into the brain to extract tissue. We need to hit with precision an area of the brain sixteen millimeters around, or we run the risk of destroying her ability to ever speak, or walk, and in several realistic scenarios, her heart would stop instantly on impact. I return to her bed, take a few deep breaths, and then tell Jim to begin.

I perform suction while he makes the initial incision. It makes the most sense for him to lead and for me to support because he has vastly more surgical experience than I do. I watch the blood fill the thin tube, and instantly my heart begins fluctuating. I feel lightheaded and air-hungry, but I push through it, gritting my teeth and counting my breaths.

"Making the posterior incision," Jim says evenly about ten minutes in, his hands perfectly steady. More blood fills the tube, but it sucks it away with ease, making wispy bubbling sounds.

"Making the interior incision," he says with more tension in his voice as he struggles to maneuver the blade.

"Shit!" he exclaims.

"What!?"

"Nothing, I thought, but no. It's fine." He takes a long slow inhale. Emotion splashes over me with as much intensity as a near death experience. I struggle to regain my focus, my steadiness. He pulls out the blade, but gestures for me to continue suction, while he reattaches and injects another marginal amount of morphine into Alice's hand.

"It's time for extraction, can you operate the endoscope or are you shaking?" He looks down at my hands skeptically, which tremble every few minutes, but overall are remarkably unwavering.

"I can do it," I assure him. I grab the tube, almost as thin as wire, and push it carefully through the incisions. Jim alternates between touching buttons on the monitor, and operating the suction in my place. When the screen turns toward us, we both stare at the image of the brain matter intently.

"It all looks the same," I tell him with a shake of fear.

"No, it doesn't. I can see where I'm supposed to be." His voice is perfectly confident, focused. He nods as if to assure himself that he really has discerned the minute differences in space, and he points to a region on the bottom right corner of the screen with more or less confidence. His breathing slows, and he picks up the thick-needled syringe, making eye contact with me for confirmation to continue.

"I'm ready."

He slowly inserts the needle through the nostril, following beside the wire-thin camera. Suddenly, a subdued alarm begins going off.

"Is that the hospital? Is that for us?" I ask Jim, but he stands perfectly rigid, and stares with unyielding concentration at something behind my shoulder.

"I don't know what's causing it," he says, and holds his arm as still as possible. When I look over my shoulder I see Alice's pulse and blood pressure rising rapidly, the alarm tone increasing to keep pace with her heart rate.

"Take it out!" I tell Jim.

"I can't. It could do more damage. Just wait," he tells me, and I stare at the monitor without blinking. It increases with uninterrupted speed, beep, beep, beep, filling the room faster and louder. When I know her heart is close to stopping, I switch my stare to her, trying to absorb every final second of her precious life. Then suddenly her pulse holds steady, and begins falling slowly over the course of several minutes, before returning to normal. Now my hands shake, but I am able to let go of the wire.

"I'm going to press on," Jim states, and suddenly the tip of the syringe enters into the view of the camera. With the slowest, steadiest movements, he maneuvers the tip of the syringe toward the lower right corner of the screen. I can't believe how quickly we've come to this, how fast the procedure has gone. But when I look at the clock, I realize it's only an illusion. We've been operating for more than an hour. I'm not sure I'm ready, I don't know if I'll ever be ready. Then suddenly I'm shocked by Jim speaking.

"Extraction of brain matter." He holds the base of the syringe steady, and with one hand pulls the prongs back slowly. I watch the tube fill with brain matter, and just as he finishes filling it, Alice begins uncontrollably shaking against the table. I force her skull and body to lie flatly on the table, restraining as much movement as I can with my hands, while Jim carefully extracts the needle and the wire from her.

"She's seizing," I say, and he moves with impossible speed, grabbing another vial and inserting it into the port on her hand. Her seizure stops almost instantly.

"Take care of her!" I yell at Jim, while grabbing the syringe of brain matter from him to disassociate the neural stem cells. I have to leave the operating room and go to the laboratory for this. I rip off my mask and gloves, and exit from the rear of the operating room. Everything is a haze. The hospital, the people passing by. I can't tell if people are staring, or if I'm just imagining everyone's eyes on me. Even the elevator takes me in and spits me out as if it were a dream, or even a nightmare.

I use Jim's ID to enter the laboratory, and quickly empty the syringe contents into two test tubes, rummaging through the refrigerated medical vials until I find the disassociation fluid. I quickly add the prescribed number of drops to both vials, but leave one in the farthest back corner of the cryo-freezer. I then push mindlessly out of the laboratory, and return as if I had never left to the operating room. As soon as I enter, Jim is standing next to Arthur and Arthur's neck is stained brown with povidone-iodine.

"Is Alice okay?"

"She's okay. Give me the stem cells. Quickly. We need to leave." His voice shakes. I hand him the test tube, and he carefully transfers it to an injection, and without hesitation inserts it into Arthur's carotid artery. Once inside however, he moves carefully, allowing the injection to take place over the course of several minutes. As he does that, I examine Alice, who is already stitched and detached from most of the machines.

"Put her in the car seat, Ethan. We need to move now!" Jim yells at me. As carefully as I can, I take her into my arms and place her, still mostly naked, into the seat – attempting to keep her as level as possible to prevent further bleeding. I force her eyes open and shine a flashlight into them. Her pupils are uneven.

"She'll need an MRI," I say quickly.

"Yes, but not now," he says, and as soon as he finishes the injection site care, he turns off the anesthesia, removes the mask from Arthur's face, and pulls him over his shoulder.

"Move Ethan, now." He virtually pushes me out the door we had entered through, and we run through the hallway, hearing voices and footsteps close behind us. We enter the garage and leave without any of the supplies we were supposed to take with us.

CHAPTER 24

The second to last time I saw Lapis, she and I bonded over our love of spring. I told her how Liz and I had taken Arthur to the park every chance we had, and occasionally we took longer trips to explore battlefields and gardens. She told me that even after all of my anecdotes, she still couldn't picture a happy family with an Inexorable in it.

"Do you think it's wrong for me to love my son? I mean, you kill Inexorables, but I feed them. Do you think that's wrong?" I asked, genuinely curious of her thoughts. She pursed her lips, tilting her head back and forth a couple times with a serious scowl between her eyebrows. Then she froze for a few seconds, a month in Lapis time, and smiled sweetly at me.

"The birds sing when the sun is shining, but the frogs sing when it's pouring rain. Who's to say which song is more beautiful?" She spoke slower than normal, but I stared at her confused.

"We're both trying to do well, you and I. If you look at it from the bird's perspective, the rain is bad, but the sun is dazzling enough to sing for. If you look at it from the frog's perspective, the sun is bad, but the storm's magnificence is worth songs of praise. The point is that they're both right." She explained with emphatic rises and falls in her tone.

"But which one are you?" I joked.

"A bird, obviously." She grinned.

"What does that make me?" I gave her my best skeptical expression.

"You're a bullfrog. I knew that from day one." She nodded assuredly while bouncing on her heels. I replay the scene in my mind, over and over, as if it's an escape from the hours of torturous silence echoing between me and Jim. I'm stuffed in the back cabin of the truck, carefully monitoring Alice and Arthur as the sun first peeks over the horizon. Alice struggles to breathe on her own, every ten minutes or so she'll stop for thirty seconds at a time before making a weak gasp in her sleep. Some residual blood has been leaking down her nostril and clogging it as it hardens. She looks pale and weak, and somewhere deep inside I'm afraid that she isn't going to make it.

"Jim, help me understand Alice's condition. Why is she struggling to breathe?" I ask, looking to Jim in the driver's seat.

"I think that her brain began swelling as a result of being penetrated. I think it caused a brain injury," he says matter-of-factly, no hint of emotion in any of his words.

"What kind of injury? Why is she struggling to breathe?"

"I don't know what kind of injury, I don't know what area of her brain was actually affected. From my line of sight, nothing seemed abnormal whatsoever. But I've been considering it for the past hour, and remember her pulse increase as soon as the needle was inserted? That's why I think it's an inflammation issue, the second that needle went in, the brain took issue with it." He gestures to the sign for Winchester, which reminds me that we're only an hour away from the slums.

"Do you think she'll recover fully then?"

"You know as well as me there's no way to know that."

"But you have emergency experience that I don't have. What would this type of injury most likely lead to?"

"Most likely? With an injury like this in an infant, I would have to guess, and this is book knowledge talkin' not experience, but... cerebral palsy maybe." He rolls down the window and lets the wind into the car for a moment. The air is that perfect morning temperature, not chilly, but not yet microwaved enough by the sun to feel warm either.

"Do you think that's why she isn't breathing properly?" I say more intensely.

"Ethan, I have no clue! She could fully recover for all I know." He makes an exaggerated shrug.

"She could die in her sleep," I whisper at a volume I doubt he can hear. He rolls up the windows and stares stiffly through the windshield.

"Sure, she could die in her sleep; from SIDS like any other baby. Or you could die in your sleep from a stroke, or any of us could. There's no use in speculating, you're just gonna run yourself mad. Besides, you're about to have to pitch to Liz why Alice is actually in perfect health or you'll be dyin' in your sleep for sure." I guess he could hear me.

My throat clenches at the thought of explaining this to Liz. The entire trip I've lived in such denial that I hadn't considered formulating a script, or rehearsing some explanation that's generous toward my side of things. She will have been awake all night, panicked, without any way to contact us, and I will have to deliver to her two unconscious children, one who is struggling to breathe. I don't know what to say. I don't even know if the treatment will have been effective. A newfound sense of panic works its way through my muscles and settles into my bones. I have no reasonable defense for what I've done, I don't have even a compelling emotional plea, unless they both recover and Arthur is healed. Unless it all works.

I had never been to the Richmond refugee camp before I purchased the safe house. The camp is exactly as Liz had described it, "slums," and it's difficult to know how long it's been in that condition. There hasn't been an active government or humanitarian presence in the camp for quite a while. After the D.C. attack, the government employed innumerable contractors to construct the five square mile town virtually overnight. Overly thin streets made of loose pavement pebbles are lined with miniature homes less than an arm's length apart from each other. The town is fairly abandoned at this point, with only a few radiation victims and peripheral homeless living there.

I purchased the keys to one of the houses from a disheveled man looking to move along and find somewhere better to live. The entire home cost me two hundred bucks, and I was able to change the locks then and there. The near-toothless man informed me that the tiny house had no electricity, and that cracks in the exterior cause significant bug issues. The outside of it is an eyesore. It's constructed entirely out of unstained wood and a rusting tin roof. The only color the home possesses is the military green paint flaking off the front door. As soon as you open it you see the ten square foot living space, complete with two rusted yellow lawn chairs, and a kitchenette behind it. The floor, the walls, are all the same wood as the outside, but inside the walls are painted an offensively bright blue and the floor is sealed with polyurethane. One thin bedroom runs along the length of the house, and it had two rusty cots pushed together against the back corner of the room, allowing for only a marginal space to walk beside the bed on the left side. That's where Liz has sat for all these hours, with no lights or air conditioning. I had intended to furnish the place, and clean it up, but that's when Jim called me with the news that Arthur had attacked Liz.

As we enter the town, the sound of Jim's tires rolling over the loosely stacked pebbles rumbles through the cabin. He rolls down his window and drives slowly as he gawks at crumbling homes, piles of abandoned garbage, and the stray, scarred souls that step out of their houses to stare back. His brow furrows as we pull behind the black car Liz drove here. My heart is drumming because even though I'm anxious about what to say, I want so desperately to wrap her up in my arms and kiss her, to have her so close again. I've missed her so much lately, I've missed her warmth, her comfort, her intimacy. Before I can fully exit the truck, she rushes through the green front door and over to me.

"Ethan!" she cries, and flinging her arms around me she kisses me, her stitches scraping along my cheeks.

"How are the kids?!" she asks, and peers behind me into the cabin.

"Tired," I remark, trying to buy myself time before having to go into detail. Jim pulls Arthur out of the truck, and I unlatch Alice's car seat and watch her chest for breathing motions as we carry them both inside. Liz watches Alice almost as closely as I do while we work single file through the front door. As soon as I set the carrier down, she unbuckles Alice and take her into her arms.

"Why is there blood in her nose? Did she get a nose bleed?" Liz carefully touches the blood clot, while pressing her body against mine just to be close. I freeze. I don't know what to say. Jim lays Arthur down on one of the cots in the bedroom, and then rejoins us to intercede.

"Liz, let me uh, get those stitches out for you while I'm here, and while I do that Ethan and I can tell ya' together what happened tonight. You can still hold Alice, but it'd be good if ya could sit down. I'll just grab the first aid kit from my car and I'll be right back." Jim gestures to one of the two lawn chairs, and as he turns to exit the house winks at me in support. Liz sits down in the chair slowly so as not to rock Alice awake, but she couldn't even if she tried.

"I thought you were all going to die tonight, Ethan. I really did." Liz begins crying, her cheeks growing bright red and her lip quivering.

"Oh baby, no. We're all here." I sit down beside her chair on the floor and caress her arm.

"Yeah." She sniffles and tries to compose herself.

"So did she get a nose bleed?"

Jim re-enters the tiny room, and pulls the second chair directly in front of Liz's, cracking open the brief case sized first aid kit and pulling out medical scissors.

"No, she didn't get a nose bleed," I tell her, and Jim and I make uncomfortable eye contact.

"This shouldn't hurt now, Liz. But I still need you to stay as still as possible," Jim says, before inching closely to her face and cutting through the first stitch.

"We performed a transplant on Arthur that required a donor, to heal him, so that the damaged areas of his brain would grow back..." I take a long pause. "Alice was the donor."

"Donor? What are you talking about?" She wrinkles her face, forcing Jim to adjust his scissors.

"Arthur needed stem cells, Liz. We extracted some neural stem cells from Alice," I say as steadily as I can, trying to keep the room calm.

"You what!? Neural? You mean like her brain?!" Her voice instantly picks up volume.

"Please try to stay still," Jim reminds her.

"Stop, Jim, stop! I need to look at her." Jim pulls his scissors away from her face, and she gazes down at Alice, touching her face and listening closely to her breaths.

"Why is she bleeding? Is she okay?" Liz gapes at me.

"I don't know." I fight a sob on my inhale, and tears instantly flood my eyes making them inflamed and blurry. Liz switches her glance to Alice for a second, then back to me, and paints the betrayal she's feeling all over her face with an intensely distraught expression. I can tell there is a lot she wants to say, but she grits her teeth and makes a large swallow before speaking again.

"What happened?" Her tone is controlled, but she looks at me above cheeks dripping with tears. I can't answer her. Emotion floods my lungs making it impossible to take in air, or spit it out again.

"We think her brain became inflamed during the procedure. She still might recover to perfect health Liz, but recovery time might be extended and difficult, especially in this setting," Jim responds softly, his face full of compassion. Liz turns her head toward him, and ignores me. I take a deep slow inhale trying to steady myself.

"And Arthur?" she asks, still refusing to look at me.

"He seems to be doing well, all things considered. But I just want you to be aware of this: if he is angry, even violent when he first wakes up, that is normal even for healthy people. It doesn't mean the operation failed. It will take several weeks before you see the true effects of the treatment, but you might see some preliminary improvement in his behavior before then. And even if it works perfectly, even if his brain fully heals and he has all of the emotions that you or I would have, he will still have to unlearn his life of violence. He will still have to learn what it means to be kind," Jim says cautiously, picking up the scissors again and returning to Liz's face.

"What about Alice's recovery? What do I need to do?" Her voice becomes calmer.

"Her recovery will be very difficult. I would expect the biggest issue will be her struggling to breathe, and to eat. You will have to find a more efficient way to feed her than breastfeeding right now." Jim completes the entire left side of the stitches, and pauses before beginning the right as Liz's face distorts to accompany her sobs. I stroke her back, but she yanks away from my touch and shakes her head in disapproval.

"Don't," she makes out through a slobbery, sorrowful, moan. It crushes me, my ears burn with heat, my chest shakes with every inhale and exhale, and I sit beside her, begging without words for her to look at me, to forgive me, to show me love. Jim finishes removing her stitches in silence, with no one speaking a word. When he's done, he tells me he'll leave us the first aid kit, but that he has to get back to Mary. I walk him out, and before he gets into his truck he hugs me painfully tight, and for a long time. When he releases me, he looks into my eyes with the gravest focus.

"You're a good man, Ethan. We did a good thing, just not in a good way, but there was no good way. So don't let guilt eat ya out here." He keeps his hands on my shoulders, and I nod.

"I'm going to miss you," I tell him.

"I'm gonna' miss ya too, buddy." He forces a full-toothed smile, but I can tell that he's seconds from crying, his eyes red and his voice breaking. But with that, he gets into the truck, waves one last time and drives away. I watch his truck until it leaves my line of sight, attempting not to think about what it means that he's leaving. I try not to think about this being our home for the near future, or the possibility that Alice might never wake up, or that Arthur could remain uncured. In my pocket I feel over one of the microchips with my fingers, and it helps me to stay focused. Evacuation was necessary, treating Arthur was key, but soon I need to actually propagate the information, I have to find a way to make it public – and for that, I know, I'll need to leave Liz again for some time. But not today, not now, not until we have peace. The sun grows too hot for pleasure, like I can feel the UV rays actually pummeling into my skin deeper and deeper. I look down our street, and see several faces staring at me through cracked doors, some pale, some burned, all of them skinny and elderly looking. Should I wave? They aren't waving. Instead I go back inside with that unnerving feeling of eyes stabbing into my back. When I come back inside Liz is in the bedroom sitting on the empty cot next to Arthur, holding Alice so closely.

"Can we talk?" I ask her with quiet desperation. She glares at me without an answer, but carefully crawls over Arthur, her long legs leading the way, still cradling Alice in her arms. She passes me without making eye contact and crosses the short barrier between the bedroom and living room and sits in one of the two folding chairs. I pull the other one in front of her, and I reach to touch her, but hesitate before making contact. Her face looks vastly better without the stitches, but the scar is remarkably noticeable; a shiny light pink with some darker shades outlining it. It will fade some with time. I try to think about this being the new Liz, and not some temporary injury, which is how I've been processing it until now. She looks beautiful underneath the scar, but I try to see her with it, I try to see her exactly as she is. Huge bags of exhaustion, sagging in her cheeks, a few grey hairs peeking out from her greasy dark roots, a tank top exposing her strong arms, and her long legs peering out from jean shorts. On her face is a distinctive look: hatred.

"I am a weak man, Elizabeth. I know that I have not done right by you in the past year. I know that my greatest failing was making decisions without consulting you, from the moment I brought Arthur home until now. I know that I might have to live with the grief of all that I've brought our family to for the rest of my life. But I need your love and forgiveness. I am begging you to try to understand, and to forgive me." The words flow easily because they have been a staple in my thought life for too long. "I will try to understand," is all she says.

I tell her about the experiments, about the research, even pulling out a memory chip and flashing it in front of her eyes. I tell her about Lapis and the Assistance Center, and the Obcasus testing, the black coats, everything. She nods along, with a quintessentially unimpressed look upon her face. Then I explain that this operation was the only way things could have happened, and *that* she doesn't want to hear.

"That's a damn lie. I don't want to talk about this anymore," and when she says it, I know that she means it. She just wants me to shut up and to leave her alone with Alice, who still lies too limp in her arms for comfort. But I want to hold Alice too, I want to take her in my arms and smother her in kisses, and tell her how sorry I am and how much I love her. But I can't. I would have to rip her from Liz's arms, and I would never do that. Instead I pretend that for a moment I'm not a husband or a father, but that I'm just a worker, that my purpose here is to better the house, to gather supplies, and to tend to the children with the best medical care I can offer. Maybe it's justice for everything I've done not to be able to hold my own child, or feel the loving touch of my wife. But is it? Did I commit evil, or did I commit good? I don't feel like I have any perspective anymore. I can't tell if this war is truly one worth fighting.

CHAPTER 25

I n two weeks I've been able to dramatically improve the house, build a functional fire-operated stove out of the fireplace, and stock up on imperishable foods. We've learned a lot in the past two weeks about our living scenario. The neighbors try to steal everything, and so I've installed steel bars and screens in our windows, which we keep open for the vast majority of the day. We're hot, we're smelly, we're too close together, and we're desperately missing our normal earthly comforts. But, ultimately, we're enduring. Liz and I have even improved our communication to including details about our daily food sources, but beside that she still doesn't want to speak to me. It's killing me because she's the only person here who I can have a real conversation with, and so every single day I try. Maybe it's a conversation about the weather, or about how she's feeling, or games we could play to entertain ourselves, but every single time she denies me. It hurts worse each time she gives me that blank stare and seals her lips together. At night, though, when she thinks I'm asleep, sometimes she whispers that she loves me, and it's what I hold onto to keep me sane.

Alice is very weak. She has many waking hours in the day, but she can hardly drink from her bottle and even when she does, she constantly chokes on it. Arthur, though still sleeping most of the day, is alert and talkative when he is awake. Today, he asked for me. I sat beside his cot as he lay on his side and looked at me, his big brown eyes crusted from sleeping.

"Owwy, ow, it hurts," he said with glossy red eyes.

"Where?" I asked anxiously. He tapped inside his chest a few times.

"Your heart?" I pressed my ear against his chest to listen to his breaths and heartbeats, all of which appeared normal.

"It's like being punished. When you hurt me, I feel something here." He rubbed over his chest again.

"I don't punish you there, Arthur. I never have."

"I hurt there when you punish me, like scared hurt," he said, barely leaning his head up from the pillow to tell me.

"Do you feel afraid?" I clarified.

"Yes." His thin voice cracked and he began crying. I held him there for a while, and eventually he fell back asleep. I truly believe that he's feeling, that he's experiencing a new range of human emotion for the first time. It isn't just the words he's saying, but it's in his eyes – that black plotting shell is melting off of them, and I can physically see from his expression that he's genuinely afraid, vulnerable in a way he hasn't been before. But Liz is ruthlessly skeptical. I think she just wants a reason to stay furious at me, almost as if she wants Arthur to stay an Inexorable simply to prove that what I've done is inarguably wrong.

I go out for new supplies every day, but I don't drive the car. I removed the plates so that it can't be traced to us, but a car without plates is still a target for police. I walk to the nearest town, Flemore about five miles away. Flemore is in some ways a magnificent improvement over West Camp, but in other ways it's a far sadder place to spend my time. It's better because the town of thirty or so people has electricity, but it's worse because it's as disregarded and abandoned as West Camp, except it's an actual town and not a refugee station. Nevertheless, Flemore has a gas station, and so it might as well be heaven to me.

"How's it going, Bobby?" the Indian clerk asks with a grin as I enter the thrillingly cool building for the eighth time this week. I told him my name was Bobby, but I still internally laugh every time he calls me that.

"I'm okay. Just out for a walk, as usual," I tell him with half a grin. It's nice to have an adult look me in the eyes and smile at me, even if it is just Neel from the gas station. Today I'm looking for a better way to light the house, so I want to purchase a mirror to make some refractory points for our lanterns. The gas station store is only four rows of rickety shelves which I've essentially memorized by now, but I search each shelf meticulously anyway. A television which hangs behind Neel's head projects local news by a typical Ken doll-style anchorman. Not one of the rows has a mirror, but the row closest to the back wall has aluminum foil which I could mold around a cardboard box and set the lantern inside of – or something else. I might have to experiment, but at least it's reflective. As I am checking out with my remaining quarters and dimes from yesterday, I am startled by the newscaster.

"Police continue their search for terrorist suspect, Ethan King, who previously served as a doctor on staff of Philadelphia East Hospital. He escaped police custody, and is considered armed and dangerous. If you see this man, please do not engage him, but call the police immediately. Again, do not approach Ethan King if you see him," the newscaster says as mindlessly as anything else, but I see right above Neel's head a picture of my face. I look Neel in the eyes and smile as he counts my change, attempting to distract his attention as best as I can until my photograph leaves the screen.

"So do you have a wife, Neel?" I ask. He nods and belts out a hearty chuckle.

"Oh yes! Would I have this belly if I had no wife?" He points to his protruding stomach and laughs some more. My picture vanishes from the screen as they switch to a news story about recalled cabbage.

"You look fine!" I insist, grasping my aluminum foil and leaning on the exit door.

"You're too kind! See you soon, Bobby." He waves me out. I run home, hiding my face from each passing car and all of the creepy neighbors. By the time I enter the house I'm panting, and Liz rushes toward me.

"What happened?" She mirrors my panic.

"I was on the news. They're calling me a terrorist!" I tell her between gasps for air.

"Do we have to leave?" she asks me impatiently. I shake my head.

"I doubt it. No one has a television here. But I can't go to Flemore again. You'll have to go the next time we need something." I walk over to the kitchen and grab a water bottle from inside the warm refrigerator we use for storage space. I feel a drop of sweat slowly sliding down the back of my skull, like a bug, and I instinctually smack it.

"I'm glad you're okay," she says, and for a second it looks like she might smile at me, but then she doesn't. We're so close, not to normal, but to a palpable sense of peace. That's all I need. She sits down on the floor, leaning against one of the walls, and I sit beside her quietly, slowly inching my hand toward hers but not quite touching it. She fights another smile, so I sit contentedly right there, wondering what she's thinking about but not having the nerve to ask.

Instead, I think about my new status as "terrorist" and the fallout of that. The purpose of this "terrorist" ploy is clearly to discredit me before I blow the whistle, but more than that, it's a significant deterrent to me going out in public, which I need to do. I need to amend my research to include the procedure results on Arthur, and to do that I need access to a computer. As if that isn't complicated enough, in the hospital laboratory a vial of disassociated neural stem cells sits in cryo, and with it the hope for innumerable other children. If I could successfully retrieve that vial, assuming it hasn't already been confiscated, then I could culture the contents and conceivably heal an indefinite number of Inexes. I have no way to do that here, but there is one person I could send the contents of the vial to and they could culture it until I come. Maybe a year. Maybe more. How many parents will it take, after learning that their dead children could have been saved but their government said otherwise? How many sick individuals will it take, after learning that Dopimazipal only masks the disease they've been given and that an actual treatment exists but was suppressed by Powell? How many women who voluntarily sterilized themselves will it take, once they've learned that they could have had healthy children all along? I suspect not many. But it depends entirely on the message being propagated, and I expect no reservation of power will be exerted in eliminating my message. I have to be wise about the medium of the message, the people I can trust, and the timing of delivery. But before I can even consider releasing the information I need to get into the hospital, get that vial, and get it into someone else's hands – and for that, I need a careful plan.

September 8th, 2047

Alice is a month old as of two days ago, and though she is eating more steadily, she hardly makes any noises, neither crying nor cooing. She doesn't smile for us, and she seems weaker and less responsive than she did even at birth. I know that recovery is supposed to take time, I'm the doctor in this house for goodness' sake, but it's unfathomably discouraging to see her struggling this much. It makes me nauseated to think that she might never be normal, that she might never remember a healthy day, and that on account of her father; on account of me. She lies on blanket on the living room floor, and I sit beside her. I watch her with unsurpassed attention, sunbeams dancing across her white onesie from the kitchenette window. Her startling blue eyes have thick dark rings around them, and I think that she's beginning to look more like me. Her nose seems rounder like mine, Liz's is long and straight. Alice's cheeks are still so full, fuller than mine, certainly, but she seems to lack the high cheek bones so iconic on

Liz. Maybe it's her eyes, maybe it's her ears, maybe it's that she doesn't smile, I'm not sure. She just looks like me.

"Can I have spaghetti, mommy?" Arthur pops out of the bedroom with energy in his step. He's sporting a red t-shirt with yellow accents which creates a trippy eyesore when contrasted with the bright blue wall behind him. He looks healthy, a warm tone coloring his face, and it isn't just the reflection of the sun on his skin. Something about him looks marvelously different, maybe he even looks happy. Sometimes I can't tell if I'm just reading too much into it, like I'm hypnotizing myself into seeing moral and experiential change in Arthur when it isn't there. But he hasn't tried to attack me or Liz since the operation. That could be attributed to his overall malaise, but even now as he seems spry and talkative, he holds no weapons in his hands. I know I'm going to leave today, and so I try not to over analyze it. I try to just enjoy every detail of what I'm seeing: my sweet baby girl being skipped over by the sun, and a completely normal boy asking his mother for spaghetti.

"Sure, Arthur. I think that's a great idea!" Liz responds enthusiastically, pulling out the one cast iron pot we own and setting it on the tiny counter space with a clang.

"Could you put Alice in the bedroom while you start the fire, Ethan?" Liz asks with half a grin, and I move instantly upon her request, simply thankful to have her eye contact. I swoop Alice from the ground, and kiss along her sweet tiny head before setting her in her bassinet. Everyone seems to be in a better mood today, including me. It's either that we've mildly adjusted to the miseries of West Camp, or because there are chillier breezes sweeping through the windows for the first time. I suspect it to be the latter.

As I start the fire I consider how to broach the subject of me leaving today. Liz knows I have to go, she understands how important it is, but she doesn't know that I plan to leave this evening. It's Sunday. Sunday is the least likely day of the week for hospital management staff to be in, for black coats to be perusing the city on duty, or for the labs to be busy; especially at night. I've run through my plan a hundred and a half times, and there is nothing which could improve it. I will walk into the hospital at the 9:30 PM shift change, surgical mask on. During the night shift change not one employee could care less who you are or what you're there for. The exiting shift members want to leave, and the incoming shift members want to ease into the night with their typical routines, and since no night shift workers are familiar with me it makes the likelihood of being caught minimal. It also helps that during shift changes the employee doors are frequently opened, allowing easy access inside without having to use my ID. Once inside I will travel straight to the cardiac unit, which will have an unoccupied waiting area, and I will retrieve the microchip from the heart plaque Liz gave me. I will go directly to the laboratory, put the specimen in a cryobox for transport and exit the building as quickly as I entered it. If all goes according to plan, it will be done within a five minute window. On the way back to West Camp I will stop off to mail the cryobox, then I will drive out of the way to Harrisburg to update my research and send it to as many individuals as I can at one of those crappy computer rental stores, and finally, I will return home.

The water bubbles in the pot as Liz and I sit together instinctually guarding Arthur from the fire, but he plays contentedly on the floor with a book.

"He's different." I nudge her as we both watch him, our backs to the fire.

"I see it too." She nods while chewing on the inside of her cheek.

"I'm leaving today," I say with more boldness than I intended to.

"What is your damn problem, Ethan? Today has been nice. Couldn't you let me have just one nice day?"

"Today is the right day. Please don't be mad," I beg her. She shifts to face me, knees crossed and face plastered with anger.

"I have an awful feeling about you going to the hospital. You can't go."

"I have to."

"Oh, just like you 'had' to cut into our daughter's brain?" Pain floods her face.

"Liz, I...." I try to stroke her cheek.

"Don't." She yanks her head away and inches herself out of my reach.

"I might not make it back here, please, baby. I am so sorry, I love you and Alice so much."

"Then don't go."

"I have to, or all of this will have been for nothing."

"You healed Arthur, you did what you intended to do. Now you have a sick daughter and a strained marriage. You don't get to leave now." She fights the tears forming in her eyes.

"I have to." *I have to save the others, I have to show the world the truth.* She sits in silence. Arthur stares at us now, completely distracted from his toys.

"Tell me you still love me. I can't leave, I can't do it... I need to know you still love me," I beg her. The first tear lands on her cheek and she wipes it away instantly before stirring the noodles and returning to face me. She masks her emotion with a stoic expression and a stiff tone of voice.

"You traded. You traded her for him, something a father would never do. Ethan, I love you. But to forgive you I need you to come back here. I need you to come back. It isn't fair for me alone to live with what you've done, you have to live. You have to live with it too. You think I didn't know? How would I not have known that every Thursday afternoon you weren't at work, or that our garbage was filled with strange disposal bags for the past six months, or that your desk was full of bizarre research? I knew since the day you came home from the Assistance Center that something was wrong, but I buried my head because that's what I thought I should do, that's what I thought a good wife would do. Your mess was not my mess, your obsession was not my obsession, your consequences were not my consequences. But now they are, and you can't make me carry them alone. I am telling you, that the awful feeling I had when you came home from the Assistance Center, I have it again. I have it about this." Her head shakes in disapproval over and over, until she finally drops it to her chest and lets tears fall unabatedly onto her legs.

"I love you with my entire heart," I whisper and wrap her up in my arms, running my hand over her hair and kissing along her cheek. Out of the corner of my eye I see Arthur continuing to stare, not with sorrow, not with joy, but with a face of curiosity – as if he doesn't understand.

"I love you," she says with raw pain, before pulling me even closer to her, not letting me go until she's satisfied. Arthur and I eat Spaghetti, but Liz can't stomach the food. A new piece of my heart shatters every time I look at her, her whole bearing broken while she continually fights the urge to cry.

"You need to talk to your son before you leave," she barely makes out as she grabs our empty dishes from us and walks over to the kitchenette. I know what she means when she says it. She wants me to speak to him about something important, in case I get caught, in case I don't come home.

What would I say if it were my last conversation with my son? A year ago I never thought I'd have a son, I hadn't even been fully persuaded that I could die. But I think about it now, the images race through my mind: getting caught, being tortured, interrogated, beaten. What do you say to someone who might not feel anything, but who might feel everything soon? What do you say to a cured Inexorable, the first of his kind? What do you say to your son, the one you rescued, the starving one you held in your arms, the one you brought into your warm home, the one you taught to speak, and to clap, and to call you "Daddy?" I hold his hands tightly in mine, tears dripping down my face.

"You are a testimony, you are my child, and I love you. I will always love you, and no matter what happens Arthur, you need to listen to your mother. She needs you to be strong, but more than that, she needs you to be kind. Can you be kind for me?" I ask him, begging him with my eyes as if my soul could be communicated through them.

"I know to be kind. But where are you going?" His voice is so quiet, his questions so childish, even innocent. I try to respond in a way that he will understand.

"On a trip, I will be gone for a while. I hope to come back in just a day, but in case I don't, I want you to be prepared. You might start to hurt soon, it's going to be painful, in here..." I point to my chest several times, just like he did. "You're going to be afraid, and one day you might even feel alone. But I want you to know, I need you to know, that just because you're one of a kind doesn't mean you're alone. You belong with us." My voice cracks as I say it.

"I'm a King's King!" he says sassily.

"Who taught you that?" I smile through my tears.

"Mommy."

"You're so smart, little man." I run my fingers through his hair, scratching along his skull, but I shift my eyes to Liz in the kitchen, who forces a smile at me through her own teary face. I can see so clearly now how much she loves me, and I look at this life we've built together, not the shambles of the house but this family, these people, and my heart aches with how much I love them. When it's time to leave, I take Alice into my arms one more time, and even though she's sleeping, I speak to her.

"Baby girl, I'm so sorry. Daddy loves you. He loves you more than you could ever understand." Liz takes her from me and looks up to me with bloodshot eyes. I fight crying by clenching my jaw. I take Liz in. That unique smell that is just hers, her skin, and her lips, and her eyes, and her scar. Her love, her unshakeable love, for her children... for me. I hug her so closely, so tightly, never wanting to let her go. And then I kiss her, just a few brief, but immensely sweet, kisses.

"You are the most beautiful woman I have ever laid my eyes on. In here." I press my hand flat against her chest. "And here." I stroke her face once. Her bottom lip quivers but she tries to stay strong, for me, I think. As I exit the house she grabs my hand, and pulls me in for one last kiss.

"I love you," she tells me, just so I know it. Just so I have the comfort of knowing it.

"I couldn't love you more," I tell her, and this time it's the utter truth.

I replace the car's plates before making the long drive to Philadelphia. It's risky having the plates on, but it's far riskier to drive without them. I try to pass the time with music, with radio, with fantasies about the life I will provide Liz and the kids once this deceptive regime falls to the truth, but not one thing calms my stirring mind. I'm constantly brought back to my last moments with Liz and the kids. I try to fight sentimentality, and stay focused, like a warrior. But I'm realizing quickly that I am not a warrior. It is exactly as I told Liz, I am a weak man. So weak.

***

When I finally arrive, I street park just outside of the parking garage, only a few minutes before shift change. I pull my white coat over my shirt, and place a surgical mask over my face, before entering the parking garage by foot and walking up to the third story. I wait outside one of the doors, and when some grossly thin nurse finally shoves her way out of the hospital entrance, I catch the door and sneak inside behind her. I forgot what daily life sounded like, even at night shift it seems so loud and bright. The white lights burn my eyes, causing me to repeatedly wince to make it through the first hallway, and the voices of people bustling to and from their work stations rumbles in my ears. I follow my plan with focused accuracy, entering the first elevator I see, and standing uncomfortably close to a few nurses and doctors.

"Sunday night, always a surgery night huh," one man remarks sarcastically from behind me, while tapping me on the shoulder.

"Invariably," I respond with too much stiffness in my voice and posture, struggling to keep my breathing at a normal pace. I exit into the cardiac ward, and wait for the elevator door to shut fully before walking over to the receptionist's desk. I search behind it frantically, moving fake plants and monitors before finally finding the plaque stuffed in the corner of the desk. I pick it up, and as I feel it in my hands I am reminded of the first time Liz gave it to me, the same day she told me she was pregnant with Alice, agony slicing through me to remember. I wipe my eyes, hoping the memory gets wiped away with it, and smoothly pull the microchip from the plaque. I race toward the elevator again, but this time when it opens, it's empty. It shouldn't be empty, it should be full. It should have a lot of people in it for shift change. It's coincidence, I tell myself, and force my breathing to steady. Then I exit for the laboratory, as I have so many times before, my shoes making the familiar pattering sound as I turn the corner. I snarl at the ugly walls as I always do, and I approach the laboratory door with conspicuous speed, but as I pull the handle, it's unsurprisingly locked. Shit.

I stand beside the door, trying to look inconspicuous, which is impossible while wearing a surgical mask on this floor. Suddenly a male nurse runs into my shoulder as he walks beside me in the hallway, dropping a bedpan and a few pieces of garbage.

"I'm so sorry!" I tell him, as I help him pick the items off the floor.

"They know you're here. Take my ID. Jim told me to help you," he says under his breath, his ID laying face up on the floor. Jeremy Michaels, it says. I stuff it into my pocket, and look to see his face, but before I can catch it he's rushing toward the elevator. I've never heard his voice before. My pulse skyrockets, and I enter the empty laboratory, making a scene out of every fridge and freezer, consistently throwing items out in case I'm seen. My heart gorges with relief when in the cryo freezer I feel my vial still there, in the exact same spot it was before. I throw several items out of the cryo freezer, and seamlessly stuff the vial into my coat simultaneously, doing everything within my power to hide it from any security cameras which might be on me now. Bottles crash along the floor as I fake frustration, and I storm out of the laboratory, turning left toward the elevator. But already I hear it. Outside, sirens. Not ambulance sirens, police. I make a quick decision to turn toward the windows, and as I peer down, the hospital becomes surrounded with cops and a few black SUV's. *What do I do!? Think!*

I rush to the mailing room, only a few steps away from the laboratory, and break open one of the cryoboxes to make it active. I quickly stuff the vial inside, and write in capital letters on the tube: "ALICE." I push my microchip into the box, before shoving the entire thing inside of an envelope. I write an address on it, and squish it in the center of a huge stack of outgoing blood samples. I pull my microchip from my wallet and quickly insert it into the mailroom computer, opening several files on it as a distraction, before exiting the room and rushing toward the stair case.

As I descend the staircase I begin hearing my name being spoken through a police megaphone: "Ethan King, surrender yourself with your hands on top of your head!" Tears flood my eyes as I think of Liz sitting there without me, waiting for me to come home. I push as fast as I can down the steps and through the same hallway I entered without any altercations. I exit into the parking garage, and suddenly become aware of how many police cars are surrounding me. I ignore it, and run as fast as I can down to the second floor, but stop and jolt back when I hear the screeching of tires in front of me rising from the first floor. My lungs are already aching from exhaustion and burning with each strained inhale of the heavy air. I hear every gasping breath like the whirling of tornado gusts. My thunderous steps jolt up my legs and into my spine, but I run faster and harder, pushing my way into the garage stairwell.

The door slams with a loud clang, and I begin descending as quickly as I can, stumbling every few steps, but not falling. The bottom of the staircase leads to the outer west side of the parking garage, but it is already surrounded by vehicles. The faint sound of a helicopter approaching does not give me much hope for the rooftop, and the arduous sound of my heartbeat in my ears makes me skeptical that I could ascend before they enter the stairwell anyway. I accomplished my purpose, so why am I running? I run because I do not believe that what I have done is enough to affect change. I run because they will find Arthur and they will kill him. I run because I have to come home to Liz. I reach the bottom of the staircase and I know that I must exit. What faces me is death. They will not arrest me, they will not grant me a trial, they will kill me. I am a good man. I do not deserve for my blood to be splattered against the wall of this garage. I deserve to live. But what I deserve doesn't matter in this world. What is justice, and who carries its torch? I hear a slam above me, and patters of footsteps descending the staircase. I tell myself that my life is not what matters in this circumstance, but that isn't what I feel. I lived a good life but I am not ready to die. I lived a good life but I want to die a good death, and this is not a good death. I am afraid, and my whole body trembles. The footsteps grow louder, closer. It is my move or theirs. I choose mine.

I open the door. Time is slow. Bright lights shine at my face, creating an unsurpassable contrast between the natural night and what I am able to see. Vague figures move behind the wall of light and the helicopter hovers above me, but I hear nothing except silence. The silence of chaos. I take one step over the curb and into the street, feeling its gritty texture under my shoe. I lift my hands up in surrender, but instantly a defined twinge of intense pressure enters the center of my chest. It confuses me. It does not sting, it does not ache, but wet heat begins pouring out over my chest and stomach. I look down but my vision fails, I think it was red, was it red? I fall suddenly to the ground like an anchor hitting the sea floor. I blink, but I cannot see or hear anything, and terrible pain begins to form in my chest.

I see only flashes. Liz on our wedding day, pulling me close to her by my suspenders, kissing me deeply with those gorgeous pink lips and telling me "You're mine, forever." Arthur, the day he was named, held so tightly in Liz's arms; sensing her safety, even when he could not understand it. The moment we first held Alice, her sweet tiny nose, her tender face when she cried, informing my heart of the depths of love it was capable of holding. Arthur weeping in my arms because he could feel.

My hands stop trembling. It feels cold, like winter, like I'm camping in the mountains and it's snowing at night and it's time to sleep. It's time to sleep. I'm home, Liz has her legs wrapped over me, and I hold her so close. Our blankets swallow us up together. It's time to sleep. I take a weak breath and then I fade into, what almost feels like... rest.

EPILOGUE

[Associated Press Transcript – 10:45pm, 09-08-47]

At 9:52 PM police shot and killed terrorist suspect, Dr. Ethan King, outside of Philadelphia East Hospital. King had been under police surveillance since the beginning of 2047, and had recently obtained Obcasus nerve gas responsible for over four thousand deaths and incalculable American suffering caused on the Day of Destruction. It is believed that King intended to launch a Day of Destruction-type attack on the general population. Micah Fischer, Director of the FBI, stated in an interview: "We are very thankful to have caught him as soon as we did, before any of his plans could be brought to fruition. It's always a scary situation when a terrorist possesses the mental instability that King did." Earlier this week it was discovered that King had kidnapped his healthy son and newborn daughter, and performed intrusive and unnecessary surgical operations on them with the assistance of a co-worker Dr. Jim Wilson. Wilson has been arrested and charged with the illegal practice of medicine, two counts of aggravated assault against a minor, and fleeing police custody. Dr. Wilson is currently being investigated for his role in King's premeditated acts of terrorism; however, he is not the subject of any current terrorist activity. King's activities have sparked an FBI investigation into his correspondence and connection with a Mujahadeen sympathizer, believed to be located in Salem, Massachusetts.

COMING SOON

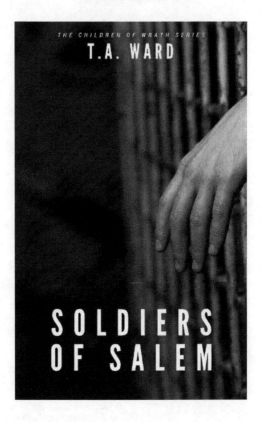

Soldiers of Salem, the second book in the Children of Wrath Trilogy, follows a seventeen year old A.K. (Arthur King) as he becomes the key figure in a subversive underground cohort against the militarized dictatorship of Bryan Powell. A.K. struggles with his responsibilities when he becomes involved with a particular girl, Skiv, and a group of Inexorables whose murderous night club in Salem, Massachusetts threatens the entire cohort. This book leaves the reader questioning the validity of self-determination, the power of love, and the breaking point of the human soul.

Cover art: *Canva* Stock Media

Made in the USA
Lexington, KY
29 January 2019